In the Clutches of the Wicked

In the Clutches of the Wicked

A Christopher Worthy/Father Fortis Mystery

DAVID CARLSON

coffeetownpress
Seattle, WA

Epicenter Press
6524 NE 181st St.
Suite 2
Kenmore, WA 98028

www.epicenterpress.com
www.camelpress.com
www.coffeetownpress.com

For more information go to: www.davidccarlson.org

Cover design by Dawn Anderson
Cover art by Kathy Carlson

ISBN: 9781941890714 (Trade Paper)
ISBN: 9781941890899 (eBook)

Library of Congress Control Number: 0002019945119

Produced in the United States of America

To libraries and all who work in them
—you are the keepers of the magic.

"God delivers me to the ungodly, and casts me into the hands of the wicked."

Job 16:11 RSV

Acknowledgments

The first person to read these mysteries is my wife, Kathy. I am grateful for both her expertise as an editor and her good humor in untangling the knots I'm sometimes prone to forming in my writing.

I am also blessed to be surrounded by creative family members—Kathy, Leif, Marten, and Mandy. Among them is a painter, several writers, a screenwriter and filmmaker, and a photographer. And I'm grateful to Felix and Freya, my grandchildren, who live the creative life every moment.

Thanks also to my literary agent, Sara Camilli, and to Jennifer McCord of Coffeetown Press. I count on, but do not take for granted, their shared belief in this series and their wise counsel.

For this fourth mystery in the Christopher Worthy and Father Fortis series, I want to thank Lt. Col. Peter Schnurr, who, while serving in Afghanistan, advised me on proper military terminology and procedures.

Finally, I want to thank all the readers who love the series and its two main characters, Christopher Worthy and Father Nicholas (Nick) Fortis. I love Worthy and Father Nick as well and am so grateful that they showed up one day twenty-four years ago.

Chapter One

March 24

Sera Lacey sat on the end of her bed, her hands gripped in her lap as she stared at the photo on the wall. The three images—one of her husband, Freddie; one of her son, Felipe; and the other of herself—shimmered through her tears, and she sensed she could float away in her grief.

The photo was from the past Christmas and yet a lifetime ago. Since the photo, the smile on Freddie's face as well as at least thirty pounds of muscle had evaporated. His hand on Felipe's shoulder had also disappeared, leaving Felipe, an inch taller now, on his own as a young man.

And her face? The happy woman squeezing next to her son in the photo was hardly whom she saw in the mirror now. Her hair was just as dark, but it was now thinner. And in the photo, she had no worry lines around her mouth.

The bomb that would destroy her family was already ticking in the photo; that was what terrified her. She just didn't realize it at the time, but then who did? Freddie had returned from his second tour of duty in Afghanistan before Christmas and didn't know that, just two months later, he would be redeployed.

She could almost hear her son's laughter in the photo, proof of his relief and joy at having Freddie back in his life again, even if Freddie was technically his step-father. In those halcyon months, the three were almost inseparable—camping and fishing on weekends, playing endless games of Sorry and Crazy Eights after Felipe completed his homework on weeknights.

Should she have known that their life together was too good to last? As a homicide detective, should she have recognized the clues of the disintegration about to happen?

Wiping her eyes broke her concentration on the photo. That was the past, and looking at the smiling faces over and over again wouldn't bring those days back. She checked her watch. Two-thirty. Enough time to drive to the Army base prison in Albuquerque for afternoon visiting hours with Freddie. Was it still considered "visiting" if Freddie was unable to speak?

Then she'd return to the precinct for her latest meeting with Captain Cortini. After that, she would try to eat something—she had no appetite, though—before driving to Santa Fe's juvenile detention center to receive more abuse from Felipe.

This was reality. This was her present life, a daily bout of being pulled by two men, a husband and a son, who both needed more than she could give. As the department's therapist kept telling her, she had to be strong for others, but she also had to take care of herself.

She turned away from the photo, her eye locking on the crucifix over her bed. And how do I take care of myself? she muttered.

✝

SO YOU SEE, NICK, I AM someone begging for your help.

In his room at St. Simeon's Orthodox Monastery outside Tiffin, Ohio, Father Fortis reread the line in the letter and sighed audibly. Sera Lacey saved his life four years before, even as she would say he saved hers. He closed his eyes to offer a prayer, and, as he did so, he recalled the photo that Sera Lacey sent just three months ago, a picture of the three in front of a Christmas tree. Freddie, Sera's husband looked buff, his smile matching Sera's and Felipe's. There was nothing in the photo to hint of what Sera described as her nightmare.

Father Fortis heard a great number of confessions over the years, in the monastery, in various parishes, and even in prison, but he never read as sad an account as Sera Lacey's story of a family's decline over a three-month period.

My husband, Freddie, was captured on his third tour of duty in Afghanistan and held captive by the Taliban. After two weeks of torture, he was traded (not admitted by the Army) and sent home with severe PTSD. Father Fortis knew such a diagnosis was a strain that proved too much for many military families to bear.

But my story gets worse, Nick. Freddie was charged with the murder of a fellow soldier here in Santa Fe. I know he's innocent, but—and this is the worst part—he's confessed. I have to accept that he confessed, but I don't think he even knows what he's doing.

Father Fortis slumped in his desk chair, his right hand making the sign of the cross slowly as if he were carrying Sera Lacey's burden. He turned the letter over and realized that the saga, unbelievably, continued. *Our son, Felipe, has been affected by all that has happened even more than I am. Ten days ago, he was picked up—his second time since Freddie returned—and charged with beating up a homeless man. He's now in juvenile detention. If I haven't already lost him, I'm close to that.*

A tree can only bend so far in the face of a storm before it breaks, Father Fortis thought. He sat back, pulled at his beard, and stared at the icon of the crucifixion on his wall. He was convinced that the suffering of God continued in the pain of the world, and while he prayed for the glory of Christ's resurrection to descend on Sera's family, he feared that he was reading more an obituary than a request for prayer. The cost of the war on terror was being paid by families such as Sera Lacey's, and the only "shock and awe" felt now, sixteen years after the advent of the war, was the shock and awe experienced by shattered vets and their shattered families.

Father Fortis sighed heavily as he focused on the letter's plea for help. It wouldn't be up to him, but his abbot, to decide if he could accede to her request. And he was none too confident that Abbot Lucas would agree. Father Fortis had returned from Venice a little less than a year before, having helped his friend Christopher Worthy solve a case of missing relics and murder. On his return, his abbot greeted him with one question: "Are you a monk or a detective?"

Monks and nuns through the centuries were permitted creative outlets—beekeeping, throwing pots, weaving, writing poetry, photography, or gardening, but these pursuits fit nicely within the early afternoon of the monastic day between noonday and late afternoon prayers.

Despite his girth, Father Fortis was not the sedentary type, interested neither in bees nor sitting at a loom. And while his abbot had no objection to Father Fortis' academic interest in early Christian chant, as that could promote spiritual reflection, he was increasingly frustrated with Father Fortis' talent for detection. Teaming up with Christopher Worthy to solve grisly murders seemed to the abbot and fellow monks at St. Simeon's to bend a tree beyond its breaking point.

The real rub with his detection activities, however, lay elsewhere. When Father Fortis returned to St. Simeon's after the last three ventures with Worthy, his fellow monks in chapter complained of his "chattering."Father Fortis doubted the sincerity of the complaint. He returned no more talkative than before his time away. Beneath the complaint was the displeasure of his brother monks and the abbot with his long absences.

One of the ancient monastic vows is stability, meaning a monk is to remain in the same place where God has placed him, and Father Fortis' adventures created a sense of instability for the entire community. There is no such thing as a part-time monk.

A second monastic vow he took fifteen years before was obedience to the voice of Christ as that voice came through the abbot, and Father Fortis imagined Abbot Lucas hearing his request to help Sera Lacey to be one request too many.

To all of this, Father Fortis would point out that what made him effective in detection was a skill he'd honed as confessor to the novices at St. Simeon: understanding the mind and heart of those burdened with problems. That was his advantage in probing the inner lives of both victims and killers.

If Sera Lacey's litany of sorrow was somehow insufficient to touch Father Fortis' heart, her mention in the final paragraph that she was also appealing for Christopher Worthy's help settled the issue for him. It was nearly a year since he'd seen his closest friend, though the two maintained contact via e-mail. He wondered if Worthy would have a difficult time securing release from his duties in the homicide division of the Detroit P. D. , given that Sera wasn't in a position to ask for his official assistance. No, she was asking a personal favor, yet Father Fortis knew nothing would keep Worthy from responding to Sera Lacey's pain.

Chapter Two

March 25

Christopher Worthy held Sera Lacey's letter in his hand long after he'd finished rereading it. He closed his eyes and recalled the last time he saw her. He'd stopped by her new office in Santa Fe's homicide division to say goodbye as she was unpacking a photo of her son, Felipe, to place front and center on her desk. He stopped by not only to congratulate her on her promotion but to ask a favor of her.

She accepted his request and never told another person, as far as he knew, what he asked of her. And now Sera was asking him for a favor. He hadn't seen Sera Lacey for four years, but he'd not forgotten her stunning looks—the sheen of her black hair, her olive skin, and her riveting eyes. He blushed as he recalled his hope at the time that the two of them might be more than partners on a murder case. But before he found the courage to confide his feelings in her, he learned that she was engaged to be married to Freddie, the man whose predicament was now the reason for her letter.

In hindsight, Worthy could see that any relationship that might have developed between Sera and him was doomed to fail. They came from different worlds, her world still making room for a God whom he hadn't believed in at the time and still couldn't. How odd, he thought, that his greatest wish for Sera after reading her letter was that her faith would be strong and give her what she needed.

Worthy was less worried about his own ability to return to New Mexico than his friend, Father Fortis, receiving permission to assist in the investigation. After their last case together in Venice, Father Fortis wrote to share that his abbot's resistance to his detective "vacations" had hardened. His own situation was quite different. He wasn't working an active case at present. In fact, his last three months had been spent sitting at his desk reviewing cold cases from the years before DNA was available. Because of his complaining, his captain was well aware that he needed an active case, and Sera Lacey's traumatic story certainly qualified.

†

MARCH 26

KNOWING THAT ABBOT LUCAS DIDN'T LIKE surprises and hated being cornered, Father Fortis sent a copy of Sera's request, along with his formal request to be granted permission to return to New Mexico, to the abbot the day before their meeting. Had this only given Abbot Lucas time to marshal his arguments for denying the request?

In the chapel, Father Fortis struggled to lift his heavy body from his knees, his prayers for guidance and patience finished, his meeting with the abbot upon him. As he paused to venerate an icon of the Theotokos, the Blessed Virgin Mary, he thought of a fellow monk, Thomas Merton, who had presented similar requests for leaves to his own abbot at the Trappist monastery of the Abbey of Gethsemani in Kentucky. All of Merton's requests, except for the last one, had been denied, with Merton's abbot giving many of the same reasons for refusal as Father Fortis was likely to hear from his own abbot in the next half hour.

Not for the first time, Father Fortis compared his situation with that of a convict appearing before a parole board. The monk was the convict, the abbot was the warden, and the power of God in the hands of the abbot was comparable to the power of the state behind the parole board.

Even as a convict was expected to show good behavior for parole consideration, as well as offer pledges of law-abiding behavior upon release, so the monk had to prove his trustworthiness and pledge that he wouldn't be tempted, while away, to forsake his vows.

And that's what frustrates me, Father Fortis thought. His previous absences from the monastery were never "vacations," to use his abbot's term, or occasions when he shirked his prayers and devotions. In fact, in every case he worked with Christopher Worthy, he stayed in another monastery or was somehow connected with an Orthodox parish. Even when he was literally tied up and facing death, he didn't forget his vocation.

Yet, the trump card that Abbot Lucas played before and would likely play again would be that nagging either-or question: "Father Fortis, are you a monk or a detective?" How was he to answer that? How was he to explain that he could be both?

But I do have a bit of leverage, Father Fortis thought, as he knocked on the abbot's door. Even though Abbot Lucas routinely expressed his frustration with him in the past, focusing on both his talkative nature and his failure at dieting, the abbot was also prone to seek his advice on ticklish personnel concerns, and from that Father Fortis always believed that his abbot wanted him to remain not just a monk, but a monk at St. Simeon's.

From the other side of the door, the abbot called out, "Come in, Father Fortis."

I should know his verdict by the expression on his face, he thought, as he opened the door. He entered the abbot's office and saw the abbot sitting behind his desk, his eyes down on a stack of paper. The shiny crown of his balding head resembled a halo, but Father Fortis held no illusions that abbots were chosen for their angelic nature. No, abbots were more frequently chosen much as CEOs of companies were chosen—to run a business.

The room's silence grew into several awkward moments, leaving Father Fortis to wonder if he was expected to initiate the meeting. If the silence was the abbot's way of letting him know the meeting would be none too pleasant, the tactic was working. But given that his talkative nature was one of the issues Abbot Lucas had with him, he chose to say nothing and waited with what for him amounted to patience.

The abbot finally spoke though without looking up. "Sit, Father." Father Fortis did so, and again the room returned to silence.

Are we waiting for God to speak? he wondered. He could hear his own heavy breathing and fished beneath his robe for a spearmint to calm himself. If the abbot's answer to his request was no, then he wished this silly game to end quickly.

Abbot Lucas finally looked up and met Father Fortis' eye. The abbot's lengthy beard was half grey, half white, and Father Fortis felt a pang of guilt for how little he tried to understand the demands on an abbot.

But any sympathy he felt in that moment disappeared as the abbot said, "And here we are again; you asking for a leave despite our being in Lent, me trying to determine what is God's will."

"I'm sure, Father Lucas, you could sense from her letter how desperate this woman is."

"Undoubtedly so, but does that mean you have to be the one to respond? Surely, there are others who are better placed and better trained to offer assistance."

"I think from the letter it's clear Lt. Lacey has exhausted all the predictable avenues." Father Fortis sensed the abbot was extending the conversation for some reason. *Maybe he's seriously considering letting me go, or maybe he's toying with me,* he thought.

"A police officer in so much trouble. Is she one of those...easily troubled women?"

A wave of anger gripped Father Fortis' throat. The "maybe the woman is to blame for her own troubles" was none too subtle. But he tried once again to see the request from the abbot's viewpoint. Women were allowed to come on retreat to St. Simeon's one weekend a month. A small but noticeable number of those who came were what the abbot would call "easily troubled women." Indeed, over the years a few developed an unhealthy attachment to one monk or the other and had to be told they could not return. A woman with many troubles was considered dangerous to the monastery, with the result being a series of restrictions on such encounters.

And that was the issue lurking below the "troubled woman" comment. Father Fortis recognized that the abbot needed some assurance that he was not being drawn into something dangerous to his vocation.

"Lt. Lacey is a wonderful police officer and a very caring mother. She is also a very caring wife who's been given incredible burdens to bear. Perhaps I should also say that she once saved my life."

"Incredible burdens, indeed," the abbot replied, and Father Fortis noted that Abbot Lucas hadn't backed down from his implicit distrust of Sera Lacey.

Say nothing, he told himself. *The only person in the room with real power is Abbot Lucas, so let him make the next move.*

The abbot continued to stare at Father Fortis, and Father Fortis noted red splotches appearing on both sides of the abbot's neck. *I'm wrong,* he thought. *He's not playing with me but hating to say what he's going to say.*

"If I had my wish, I'd repeat what I asked you when you came back from Italy last year: are you a detective or a monk?"

Does that mean he won't get his wish? Father Fortis wondered. He knew that an abbot, according to canon law, answered only to Christ. So why was the abbot hesitating?

"Metropolitan Iakovos from Detroit has requested that you be granted this leave. It seems you're becoming somewhat famous in the media, and not just in the newspapers of Detroit and Columbus. The Metropolitan has informed me that parishes all over the country have experienced an upsurge in visitors."

Father Fortis fought the urge to comment that what the metropolitan, the Orthodox equivalent of a bishop, had written should be taken as good news.

"When asked how these visitors first became aware of Orthodoxy, several replied that they read about your detecting work in various magazines. And apparently, there is a YouTube video of an interview you gave when you returned from Italy last year."

The red splotches now advanced from the abbot's neck to his ears. In addition, Father Fortis noticed the abbot's hands gripped the edge of the desk as if the abbot were holding it down.

"As I am sure you are aware, Metropolitan Iakovos has no authority over me as an abbot," Abbot Lucas said with more force.

"Yes, of course, Reverend Father."

The abbot raised the index finger on his right hand and pointed at the ceiling. "But there is brotherly affection between all the hierarchs and the abbots of our country."

Father Fortis let that dubious claim pass without comment. What existed between the metropolitans and abbots of the country was often politics.

The abbot's raised finger dropped as if it were a bird shot down by a hunter. "So I have agreed to let you help this Lacey woman."

"Most kind of you, Reverend Father. I appreciate your graciousness with this request, and I ask for your prayers."

He noticed that those last words brought a scowl to the abbot's face, and for a moment Father Fortis thought the abbot was going to reach for something on his desk—the stapler or the paperweight—to throw at him. A tense silence returned to the room, but, like the inmate who'd been granted parole, Father Fortis waited to be dismissed.

"You may leave, Father Fortis. How you finance this is strictly your affair. St. Simeon's budget has no line item for such...such ventures. Oh, can we hope to see you back by Holy Week Pascha—Easter?"

"God willing, I hope for the same."

He rose and walked toward the door. As he reached for the knob, he heard the abbot's voice. "By the way, Father Fortis, try your best not to fail. The Metropolitan wouldn't like that."

But you would, Father Fortis thought as he closed the door behind him.

Chapter Three

March 28

Sera Lacey tried unsuccessfully to quiet her jiggling left leg. She used her police I. D. to come through airport security so she could sit at the gate where the flight from Detroit would arrive. The flight was delayed because of a late winter snowstorm that gripped most of the Middle West, and the extra two hours waiting hadn't helped her nerves. She wouldn't be surprised if someone waiting for the next flight out reported this jumpy woman as a potential terrorist. *No, you're looking at a victim of terrorism,* she thought.

She felt relief for the first time in over a month when Worthy and Father Nick each e-mailed her that he would be coming to Santa Fe. Their communications couldn't have come at a better time, as the day before she felt as low as she thought humanly possible. In the last weeks, it seemed as if she were falling through a floor to a lower level, only to fall through that lower level to yet an even lower one. She was no longer able to tell herself that there could be no lower level beyond that, as life had convinced her otherwise. And yesterday, she sank to a new depth, when Captain Cortini reassigned her to her old division in the precinct, that of missing persons "for your own good and the good of the department."

What Cortini meant was that her colleagues were complaining about the awkwardness of her presence in the department's homicide division. In the case against her husband, her own division was busy putting together all the evidence necessary for the prosecutor. Her sitting at her desk and trying to look busy, she could admit, curtailed the back-and-forth banter common on such cases. And being exiled in missing persons was better than being placed on leave, which would mean sitting at home and worrying about Freddie and Felipe.

So, as grateful as she was that Worthy and Father Fortis were coming to assist in her own investigation into the innocence of her husband, she also felt both guilty and defeated as she sat in the airport. The guilt stemmed from her neediness, the sense of defeat she felt from all those around her who believed Freddy guilty of murder. Even Captain Cortini, whom she worked under for most of her career, dropped his professional mask two days before when he stopped by her house and advised her to divorce Freddie before he pulled her and Felipe down with him. Her captain was out of uniform, in a polo shirt, jeans, and scuffed cowboy boots, trying to give the impression, Sera thought, that this was just a casual conversation.

But what he had to say was hardly casual. "Sera, I'm telling you this for your own good. I've read the file on Freddie. He confessed. Not just once, but over and over again," Cortini reminded her from the chair across the room.

"He's confused, captain," she tried to explain. "When he got back, he roamed the house sometimes all night long, most of the time talking to himself. Always about Afghanistan."

Cortini leaned forward. "And now he's confessed to killing a fellow soldier from his unit, Sera."

"He's got PTSD and, from what I've been told, he's headed into a catatonic state, which apparently isn't common with PTSD."

Cortini stood and walked to the door. "Sera, you're not just a good investigator. You're one of the best. So, please, for your sake and for Felipe's, try to be objective about the evidence. We've got his blood at the scene, remember?"

Sera could do nothing more than lower her head. "But I know Freddie."

"Do you? Do you know the Freddie who came back from Afghanistan this last time? Look, Sera, we all know he's a sick man. That will be a big part of his defense. But we've talked to others who were on his plane coming back. They heard him mutter about you needing to forget him, letting him rot. That sounds pretty right-on to me, not confused at all."

She hadn't the energy to say anything at that point. Cortini was right about what Freddie had been heard to say, but that wasn't what she believed in her heart. *If I don't stay with him, he'll curl up and die. Plus, I know he didn't do this. Yes, he knew the victim, someone he served with in Afghanistan, but he didn't kill him. I just know it.*

And that was the problem with being a homicide detective. She'd heard so many women vouch for the innocence of their husbands, their certainty, in the end, being only a form of denial. That was how Cortini saw her. *Is he right?*

Four years before, she sat in this same airport, waiting for Christopher Worthy. It was at that same time that she'd first met Father Fortis. Then, the men had simply been two names, the one a tall, trim, fair-haired homicide detective from Detroit who'd been sent out to find a missing college girl and the other a massive monk with beard and ponytail who was staying at a monastery where a young nun was recently murdered. Laurel and Hardy, she thought at the time.

In the weeks that followed, the three of them became close, although Worthy and she fought as much as they agreed. She had never worked with a smarter investigator than Worthy, but his stubbornness and arrogance initially clouded their working relationship. Over their time together, however, she got to know the wounded man beneath that arrogance. And she knew that Worthy, unlike Captain Cortini, wouldn't glibly recommend divorce as her best option. He survived his divorce, but barely.

Her relationship with Father Nick was less complicated. Was that only because the two of them almost died together at the hands of a serial killer? No, those moments would always link the two of them, but she'd already found in Father Nick someone who understood both her and Worthy. That was quite a feat, she admitted, and she wasn't ashamed to credit his mediating presence, more than anything else, as what had salvaged her relationship with Worthy.

A buzzer sounded and Sera realized that the jet way door was about to open. She stood, her heart racing as she looked for the two men. What would she see on their faces? *Oh, God, please don't let me see pity.*

WORTHY ALWAYS MARVELED AT THE EASE he felt with Father Fortis. The two e-mailed over the past year but, out of respect for monastic rules, hadn't seen each other. Yet, within minutes of greeting one another at the Detroit airport, Worthy began to relax.

How does Nick do it? he thought, as the two sat together on the flight. He saw Father Fortis create the same calming effect three years before—on parishioners at St. Cosmas in Detroit, on monks four years ago at St. Mary of the Snows in Truchas, New Mexico, and more recently on his daughter Allyson. In fact, the only persons to whom Father Fortis didn't immediately relate were those who lived their religion by the book. *Nick is too human for them.*

Worthy let the pleasurable feeling sink in as he opened the file before him, the one Sera Lacey had sent as an attachment to both of them the day before. In it were the standard documents of any arrest connected with homicide, except that these were the documents of Freddie Contreras, Sera's husband.

The official report of the murder scene was familiar to him. The setting was new, the parking lot of a bar in Santa Fe, but the details were those he'd seen on other cases. The disturbed gravel was evidence of a confrontation that covered about five yards in haphazard directions. One photo showed the victim *in situ*, a twenty-six-year-old man according to the file, who was dressed in white t-shirt and jeans, flip flops and sporting a military buzz cut, his face in profile covered with blood. Another photo showed the crime scene after the body was removed. There were splotches of blood in various places in the disturbed circle, but the main blood trace left a crazy Rorschach in the dirt, not unlike a map of Alaska, with a trail of blood flowing down to the left like the Aleutian Archipelago.

He turned to the photos of the corpse, laid out naked on the mortuary table. There was bruising on both sides of the face as well as a trail of blood from the right ear. The elbows and knees were abraded, which supported the notion of bodies grappling on the stony ground. But the wounds that ended the fight and this man's life were three knife wounds in his back.

Worthy leafed through the pages to find the identification of the weapon. "A serrated blade five inches long, one-inch wide, of possible military issue." The "of possible" told him that the weapon hadn't been found.

He returned to the mug shots of the accused, and tried to imagine this disheveled man, with uneven stubble on his chin and a bloody right cheek and ear, with Sera for the past four years. But a mug shot was always hard to evaluate. *How is it that I've never seen a mug shot that made the person look innocent?* In some way that Worthy couldn't explain, the assumed guilt of the person was caught in the photos.

Beyond looking disheveled and guilty, Freddie looked haunted. Worthy had seen such dark circles around the eyes only on the faces of hardcore drug addicts, those within days if not hours of dying. Yet, the tox screen of Freddie Contreras in the file was negative, and the examining officer found no needle marks in the usual or the unusual places on his body. The only needle mark noted was made by the one used to draw blood at the V. A. hospital.

He pulled out Freddie Contreras' written confession. He'd read through it before, but this time he focused on the fact that the interrogation, from beginning to end, lasted less than an hour, a time so brief that police often referred to such interrogations as "slam dunks."

Worthy winced, never impressed with such confessions. The real question wasn't how long it took before Freddie broke down, but if the details he offered in the interrogation were proof of guilt. What seemed a thread of hope was that Freddie couldn't tell what happened to the knife.

"You've been looking at that page for quite a while, my friend. Do you see something, something helpful?" Father Fortis asked from the adjoining seat.

"Helpful, Nick? I'm not sure, but I don't like how quickly they got a confession. Look here."

Father Fortis looked down to where Worthy was pointing. "I see what you mean. That seems much too quick. Do you think there was coercion?"

Worthy shook his head. "Nothing in Sera's e-mail suggests that. I think Freddie wanted the interrogation over as quickly as possible. Which means that he might have confessed to almost anything."

"Why would he do that?"

"Looking at his photos, I'd say this guy is a walking bundle of nerves. We know he was soon exhibiting signs of catatonia. But in this photo, I see pure free-floating anxiety, Nick. What if he confessed so he could get the hell out of that room?"

"Even if it made him look guilty? Isn't that more the behavior of an addict? Unless I missed something in the file, I didn't see that he's that at all, Christopher."

"I agree. Sera would have told us if she thought that was Freddie's problem, and the tox screen is clear. On the other hand, we have to keep in mind that Sera may not be able to see the whole picture."

Father Fortis sighed. "I thought the same, but didn't want to say it, especially until we meet with her. She may be too close..."

"...and given that she's dealing with the problems with her son as well as her husband, how objective can she be?" Worthy asked.

"So we have to be sure to stay objective. Is that it, Christopher?"

Worthy nodded as he closed the file. "We'll start with Freddie's psychiatric records from the V. A. hospital. Better yet, we'll interview his psychiatrist."

"Without Sera knowing that we're going behind her back?" Father Fortis asked. "That won't be easy. If my memory serves me correctly, she doesn't miss much."

"Look, Nick. We have to be on the same page about this. Sera Lacey is a terrific detective. If all this was happening to someone else in New Mexico, I'd want her to lead the investigation. But Sera wants us to prove Freddie is innocent, despite his confession, and that's not why we're going to Santa Fe. Do you follow?"

Father Fortis pulled on his beard and then nodded slowly. "Yes, I see what you're saying. We've come to find the truth, whatever the truth is. And that means Sera might ultimately wish we hadn't come. What we uncover could just as easily destroy Sera and her family as save it."

✝

"Ah, Sera, Sera," Father Fortis said as he hugged and held onto her. He could feel her shaking and said, "No, don't try to say anything. There's nothing that needs to be said right now."

When he felt her gain control, Father Fortis released her and let Worthy step in to hug her. He heard her say, "Don't look at me. I'm such a mess."

"No, you're not," Worthy assured her. "You're just exhausted."

"You're such a liar," she said, in a sound that was a mix of a sob and an attempt at a laugh.

Sera wiped the tears from her face. "I wish I knew where to start. Nothing happens, at least nothing good happens, and then too much happens."

Worthy smiled. "We start where we always do—with what we know and with what we know we need to know."

The three walked together to the baggage claim carousels. Sera accepted Father Fortis' arm and said, "I asked my cousins, aunts, and uncles, if you could stay with them, but...well, I didn't hear back, so I don't even know where you're going to stay."

"Not to worry, not to worry. We're staying at St. Mary's, where we did last time. The new abbot, Abbot Peter, was very generous with my request, saying he is aware of the monastery's debt to the three of us from four years ago."

"Four years," Sera repeated. "Seems like a lifetime ago."Tears again fell on her cheeks as she said, "Maybe it is just that—something from another lifetime. I look in the mirror and think, 'who is that sad old woman?'"

"Hardly old, my dear. And you have every right to be sad," Father Fortis said.

"Who's staying with you, Sera?" Worthy asked.

"Lourdes stops by almost every day. She's been my best friend for as long as I can remember. And she's really been a lifeline since this all happened."

"And Felipe is still in juvenile detention?" Father Fortis asked.

"Yes."She paused and looked away. "I'm at a loss, I really am. I don't know what to do anymore."

"Look," Father Fortis said. "We'll grab our bags and then find someplace to sit down together."

"There's a Starbucks out there," Sera said, pointing to a walkway leading to one of the airport's exits.

Five minutes later, their bags retrieved, the three found the coffee shop and sat down together around a table. Father Fortis looked from Sera to Worthy, not knowing where to begin. "Christopher, why don't you start?"

Worthy opened the folder to a blank page. "Okay. Sera, I'm sure you can guess the questions I have to start with. So, this may sound a bit cut and dried, but that's probably for the best."

Both of Sera's hands cupped the coffee in front of her. *She isn't drinking as much as warming herself,* Father Fortis noticed.

"Go ahead," she said.

Father Fortis watched as Worthy drew a line down the middle of the sheet of paper.

"We have two cases, Freddie's and Felipe's. From what I can tell, Felipe's problems began soon after Freddie returned home from Afghanistan this last time. So let's go back to that point. What was the date?"

"Freddie came home the first of March," Sera said.

"It's pretty clear that Freddie was in bad shape."

Sera shivered. "As I wrote to you, this wasn't just another tour of duty for Freddie. He was captured and held by the Taliban for almost two weeks before the government traded for him. The official story is different, that Freddie escaped and was picked up by a patrol."

"Because we don't officially negotiate with terrorists, right?" Worthy asked.

"But thank God we do," Sera replied.

"Does Felipe know the truth?" Father Fortis asked.

"I was told...no, I was ordered not to tell him. The Army doesn't think he could keep the secret. So he doesn't even know Freddie was captured."

"So, if I'm Felipe, what do I think when I see my stepdad come off the plane?" Father Fortis asked.

Sera teared up again at the question. "Freddie came back twice before. No problem, and no one could have been happier than Felipe. They are...they *were* so close. Freddie immediately became Felipe's dad. We never thought of him as his stepdad."

The three said nothing until Worthy asked, "How much time was there between Freddie coming back and Felipe first getting into trouble?"

Sera shivered again. "I'm cold all of a sudden."

"Drink some coffee, my dear," Father Fortis advised.

Sera did so before saying, "Between Freddie coming back and Felipe getting into trouble was eight days, I think."

"And Freddie was at your house?"

"He spent the first five days being debriefed at a hospital for active duty troops, but after that they sent him home."

Worthy jotted a note down before asking, "How long was Freddie in the house before Felipe got into trouble the first time, the vandalism at his high school?"

"Three days."

Worthy cleared his throat. "This is going to be a tough question, so I'm warning you in advance."

Father Fortis saw Sera flinch, but nod that she understood.

"What was Freddie like during those five days? What I mean is, what did Felipe see?"

Sera used her handkerchief to dab at her eyes. "At first, Freddie watched

TV or just slept. When Felipe got home from school, Felipe would sit with him in front of the TV, but then Freddie began pacing."

"Did they talk?" Father Fortis asked.

"No, not really. Felipe asked some questions, simple ones, about the TV show, but I don't think Freddie said more than 'yes' or 'no.' I don't know how to explain this, but Freddie seemed more agitated with Felipe around."

"And then what, my dear?" Father Fortis asked.

"The pacing got worse. Freddie would just pace, even in the middle of the night."

"And Felipe saw and heard this?" Father Fortis asked.

Sera nodded. "Felipe told me he'd heard Freddie at his bedroom door. Freddie whispered, 'Is that you, Felipe?' two or three times. That's when I took Freddie back to the V.A., hoping they'd up his meds, but the pacing only got worse."

The three sat in silence for a moment before Worthy asked, "What was Freddie's reaction when Felipe was picked up for vandalism that first time?"

Sera's lower lip began to tremble. "He didn't say anything. It was like he didn't notice. I've told myself I'm wrong, but I wondered if Freddie wasn't somehow relieved," she finally managed to say, looking from Worthy to Father Fortis.

"So, if I'm Felipe...?" Father Fortis asked the question again as tenderly as he could manage.

Sera broke down and sobbed into a napkin.

"So, if I'm Felipe, I'd think my dad doesn't care about me anymore," Worthy answered for her.

Chapter Four

March 28

Worthy drove the rental four-wheel drive and let the GPS determine their route to St. Mary of the Snows. When the overly cheery voice on the GPS ordered a turn one way or another, they both described feeling familiar with the route and the sites they were seeing. The sun was setting behind the mountains to the west of I-25, yet there was still enough light in the sky for them to appreciate the long vistas.

Worthy yawned noisily as he drove. "Now I'm tired."

"Yes, first the plane trip, and then seeing and hearing Sera. It's been a long day."

"It's hard to believe we're back in New Mexico. Everything—the mountains, the desert, the view—seems even bigger than I remembered," Worthy said.

"I feel the same," Father Fortis added. "It's impossible to confuse it with Ohio."

"Or Detroit."

"As long as I'm a monk, I know I'll always return to St. Simeon's in Ohio. Not to be morbid, but I'll be buried there. But four years ago, I wondered if you might decide to stay out here."

Worthy nodded. "There wasn't much calling me back to Detroit at the time. My marriage was gone, Allyson hated me, and things at the precinct were tough. My captain, a guy named Spicer at the time, was none too happy when I returned without the missing girl, and there are a bunch of guys at the precinct I'll never be close with."

"Back then, I wondered if you thought of staying because of Sera," Father Fortis said.

Worthy adjusted himself in the driver's seat. "You do wonder a lot, don't you, Nick? But yes, that possibility crossed my mind a couple of times. She was so beautiful and so full of life. But then I found out she was engaged to Freddie, and we disagreed about so much, especially the Penitentes."

"Ah, the Penitentes," Father Fortis said. "She didn't say anything in her letter, but I wonder if Sera has stayed in contact with them."

"I hope so, for Felipe's sake as well as hers. This is just too much for anyone, even Sera, a good a cop as she is, to handle on her own."

They turned off I-25 to head east in the direction of Truchas. The car pinged a bit as it ascended the foothills leading to the snow-capped mountains ahead of them. Five miles on the other side of Truchas, Worthy turned onto the dirt road leading to St. Mary of the Snows.

"Did we learn anything important from what Sera told us?" Worthy asked.

Father Fortis popped a mint into his mouth before replying. "I'm not sure about Freddie, but I think I understand Felipe better. I think Felipe got himself into trouble on purpose, to get Freddie's attention."

And that is what Nick does better than anyone else I know, certainly better than me, Worthy thought. In their brief conversation with Sera, Father Fortis was the one who'd put himself in Felipe's place, asking Sera to think about how Freddie's descent had affected her son.

"I suspect you're right. And for all we know, Felipe's second run-in was motivated by the same wish—to shake Freddie up."

The two sat in silence for a few moments while Worthy did his best to steer around the potholes.

"Then again," Father Fortis said, "maybe by the second time Felipe got into trouble, he'd already given up on his dad. Imagine being sixteen, no longer a boy, not yet a man, and you lose your dad and then your mom, as she becomes increasingly preoccupied with Freddie. If that happened to me, I'd certainly be depressed."

Worthy ran his fingers through his hair. "What puzzles me is why Freddie was worse when Felipe was around. And what was going through his mind when he looked in on Felipe sleeping and asked if he really was Felipe? Was he delusional? Was he hallucinating then, or later when he might have killed his buddy?"

"There's a lot to figure out," Father Fortis said. "I sense you're more focused on Freddie, while I'm thinking more about Felipe. Should each of us follow things up that way, at least at the beginning?"

"Sounds like a good idea. Where will you start?" Worthy asked.

"I'm hoping Sera will take me with her on her next visit with her son. I want to see Felipe for myself."

"Okay. I'll start with Freddie's psychiatrist at the VA, a Lt. Col. Bratton, according to the file. Then, we'll compare notes. If Felipe's acting-out is linked to Freddie's PTSD, we help Felipe by helping Freddie."

"And maybe we help Freddie by helping Felipe. And most importantly, we help Sera."

"*If* we can," Worthy said.

"If we can," Father Fortis repeated. "I don't think anyone has graded this road since we were here four years ago. I'm almost certain we hit those same potholes last time. But if I'm going to see Felipe, let me ask you this, Christopher. Was it a good or bad idea that no one let Felipe know what happened to Freddie in Afghanistan?"

Worthy concentrated on the road and didn't say anything for a moment. "I bet that decision was made to protect the Army, maybe the Pentagon, or even higher. I don't think they considered how that cover-up would affect Felipe."

"Should I tell Felipe if I have the chance?"

"Nick, if either of us says anything about that and it gets back to the authorities, our asses will both be in a sling. And we'll be on the next flight home."

"Granted, but should we encourage Sera to tell Felipe?"

"Same problem, Nick. We don't know, given Felipe's problems, if his knowing the truth now would help him or make matters worse. What I do know is if it gets out that she told Felipe, she's out of a job."

Father Fortis sighed. "Perhaps the right time to tell Felipe was when Freddie came home. Now it might be too late."

"Do what you said: go with Sera to see Felipe the next time. For now, let's not upset the Army."

"I hope you don't get stonewalled at the hospital, my friend."

"Why do you say that, Nick?"

"His psychiatrist will be a government employee, right?"

"Of course. Most likely Army. So?"

"Then it seems we're going to have to trust the government, the same government that wants to control the story."

Worthy slowed to a halt and let the engine idle. On a hill about two miles down the road, he could see the lights of the monastery, shining like a lighthouse onto a sea of sand and rock. A hawk screamed as it dove across the road in front of them and pounced on something in the sagebrush. At the same moment, Worthy felt the weight of the task before them. Solving homicides always involved breaking through the walls of secrecy created by killers. But how could a visiting homicide detective and a monk breach walls constructed and manned by the U. S. government?

Putting the car in gear, Worthy edged back onto the dirt track and headed toward the lights ahead. As they rounded a slight curve, they came upon a cross on the left side of the road.

Father Fortis made the sign of the cross, before saying, "Christopher, I know I'm usually the optimist, but I have a bad feeling about this whole case."

The next morning, Worthy returned from a morning run to open the file on the victim. Ashton (Ash) Burgess was a Private First Class, US Army Intelligence Division, who was stabbed to death March 13, twenty-one days after his unit returned from Afghanistan. This had been his first tour in Afghanistan, where he was assigned to an interrogation unit led by Sgt. Frederick Contreras.

From the two noticeably small newspaper accounts, the first of Burgess' murder, the second of the arrest of Freddie, Worthy learned that Private Burgess was born in Golden, Colorado, but grew up in Santa Fe, the only son of an insurance agent father and an attorney mother. He graduated from one of the local high schools, before taking five years to complete a Bachelor's degree in Middle Eastern history at The University of New Mexico. *That explained his assignment in the Army,* Worthy thought. Burgess was divorced in 2016, no children, and worked in various fitness centers in Albuquerque and Santa Fe before enlisting in the Army.

Worthy could tell little about Ash Burgess from his Army ID photo. Like so many other soldiers trying to look the part, Burgess sported a shaved head, a frown, and a chin pulled in for the photo, accentuating the girth of his neck. Worthy remembered tattoos on Burgess' forearms from the coroner's photos.

Burgess' record was blemish-free since basic training, when he was sanctioned for fighting in his barracks. He'd broken a fellow soldier's arm by twisting it until a bone snapped. Since that incident, Burgess's record looked clean even if unspectacular. He received no commendations, but then again, Worthy realized, he had only the one tour of duty.

While the file contributed little insight into the victim, Worthy understood that he knew enough to begin to interview other members of the unit. Given that all were from New Mexico or southern Colorado, he hoped to conduct those interviews within the next week to ten days.

Worthy considered these interviews to be a rare piece of good fortune in the case. The other members of the interrogation unit would be invaluable in describing Ash Burgess in Afghanistan. The same witnesses would be able to describe Sgt. Freddie Contreras as the company's leader in Afghanistan. How was he viewed by those under his command? What was the quality of Burgess' and Freddie's interaction in the field—had there been friction between them and, if so, what was the cause of it?

But beyond those questions, Worthy knew that members of the company were at the Milky Way Bar south of Santa Fe on Cerrillos Rd. on March 13, all present at a reunion of the group upon returning stateside. They all observed Freddie in the minutes before Burgess and Freddie left the bar and ended up in the parking lot. More than anyone, the other members of the unit would be able to shed light on the second question that troubled Worthy: how was it that Sgt. Contreras, a heavily-medicated soldier with advanced PTSD, got into a fight that ended in murder and then managed to dispose of the murder weapon so cleverly that it was never found?

Worthy suspected that he'd have to gain permission from Freddie's defense attorney, a Captain Warren Mills, to conduct those interviews. *What I don't understand is the outcome the Army wants for this case,* he thought. He knew that Capt. Mills would have the answer to that, but would the Army's goal be the same outcome Sera was hoping for?

SERA HAD VISITED ENOUGH JAILS AND detention centers to know that the visiting area was the nicest room in the building. That made her previous visits to see Felipe all the more depressing, as the visiting room in the county's juvenile detention facility seemed to create a type of vacuum, this one with its cracking linoleum and chipped table tops sucking out any vestige of hope.

What had terrified Sera on her previous visits was how Felipe resembled every other offender in the room. All sat either slumped in one of the plastic chairs or resting their identically shaved heads on their arms. Many boys' arms and necks already sported tattoos, some obviously drawn by amateurish hands of other offenders. She hadn't noticed any on Felipe to this point, but he might have some on parts of his body covered by the orange jumpsuit.

The worst part of the visitors' room was the dead looks on the faces of the boys. Of course, she knew that looking dead was a self-protection mechanism, but it tore at her heart to see that same blankness on her son's face. *Oh, God,* she thought, *he's starting to look the part.*

As Father Fortis and she walked into the room together, she wondered how the place would look to her friend. He'd discarded his usual monastic robe, the *rasa*, but kept his clerical collar with a black short-sleeved shirt. She wasn't sure that she'd ever seen a man with forearms as beefy as those of Father Nick.

As the two of them approached the table where Felipe was already seated, Sera watched her son look up briefly to check out the new visitor. The thought crossing her mind, that her son looked older and dumber, disturbed her before Felipe had said even a word.

"Felipe, do you remember Father Nick?" Sera asked.

Without looking up, Felipe shrugged.

"Last time I saw you, you were in Little League," Father Fortis said.

Felipe shook his head slowly as if Father Fortis were remembering someone else. But Sera remembered the photo of Felipe that she still had in her office. That was the summer before she married Freddie. Freddie hadn't served overseas yet, and, in his new role as stepfather, he'd spent a lot of time with Felipe, either playing catch or fishing. Part of her agreed with Felipe's shake of the head. That happy boy seemed a different person from the teenager slumped on the other side of the table.

"You doing okay in here?" Sera asked, scanning what she could see of any evidence of fights.

Felipe looked past his two visitors in the direction of another table. "Great, mom. Everyone's so friendly."

Sera ignored the sarcasm. "Freddie wanted me to tell you 'hi,'" she lied. Freddie had descended into a semi-catatonic state and hadn't spoken in over a week. Two days before, the jail staff had begun to feed him intravenously.

"Wow, the killer speaks."

He's angrier than he was two days ago, Sera thought. *Had something happened to her son in detention, or was he showing off for Father Nick?*

"I was in a place like this," Father Fortis said in a steady voice. "I hated it."

For a second, Felipe looked over at the priest before looking again at his hands. "In for what?"

"One of my buddies decided to steal beer from liquor stores. I thought he shoplifted, but the police said he pretended to have a gun in his pocket. So they charged him with robbery, and all of us out in the car were booked as accessories. I suppose somewhere out in Maryland that's still on my record."

Felipe sneered. "Heard it all before. We're all innocent in here. You just thought your buddy was stealing cigarettes, right?"

"No, he'd done it before, and I'd been waiting in the car before. So I knew he was after some beer. What I didn't know was that he had a screwdriver in his jacket pocket, so it looked like he might have a gun."

Suddenly, Felipe sat forward and reached his hand across the table. "Well, sir, let me be the first to congratulate you as a bad kid who turned good, became a priest. Let me guess. You're working with young offenders; that's your mission, right? What an inspiration."

Sera felt like reaching across the table to slap Felipe, but saw that Father Fortis didn't look fazed. "No, I'm a monk. I haven't been in one of these rooms since back then. I hate places like this, and so do you. It can't be easy being the son of a cop in here."

Felipe closed his eyes but didn't say anything for a moment. "Why are you here?" Felipe finally asked.

"I'm here to see if I can help your mother and your dad. And maybe you."

Sera felt the burning tears but managed to turn them off. She knew how much Felipe hated it when she cried.

"Ah, Freddie. What a father figure, don't you think?" Felipe asked in that same flat voice. "Comes back from wherever but can't sleep and can hardly feed himself. But he finds a way to kill a buddy. Some hero, huh, Mom?"

Sera couldn't look at Felipe anymore. She couldn't bear the anger.

If Felipe was irritating Father Fortis, she couldn't tell. He continued to look directly at Felipe. Maybe he remembers what I told him on the drive, that just six months ago Felipe was starting on the baseball team and was still in scouting. She wondered if Felipe remembered that version of himself.

"Some people think your stepdad is innocent," Father Fortis said.

"Then they've been talking to Mom too long."Felipe sat forward and stabbed the table with his index finger. "If you want to help me, never mention that man's name again. I'm in here because of him, but she," here Felipe looked directly at Sera, "she can't see that."

"Okay, Felipe, I get the picture, and that's enough for your mother," Father Fortis said, touching Sera's arm. "We'll come back. Both of us. In the meantime, stay safe."

Chapter Five

Father Fortis sat silently in the passenger seat as Sera drove away from the detention center. He could hear Sera sniffling as she drove, and he knew she was replaying the wounding things Felipe had said. But he was thinking about something else, something that struck him while he sat in a visiting room awash with hopelessness and fear. He couldn't save everyone, but he was thinking there might still be a way to save this one boy.

"I have a thought," he said.

With her free hand, Sera swept some errant hair back behind her ear and sat up straighter in the driver's seat. She cleared her throat before saying, "Oh? What's that, Nick?"

"We have to get Felipe out of there," he said.

He heard Sera start to reply and then catch herself. She cleared her throat again and looked intently in the rear-view mirror, as if something or someone behind them needed her full attention.

"I don't mean to say the obvious," he continued. "I know the judge can't just magically let him come home."

"Even if that could happen, I don't think I can…."Sera left the sentence unfinished.

"Yes, yes, I know you're all done in, Sera."He turned so that he was facing her profile, not just looking out the car's front window. He could see she made an effort, had used makeup around her eyes and on her lips.

"Here's what I'm thinking," he continued. "Felipe should stay with the monks at St. Mary of the Snows."

Sera spun her face toward him and stared at him. "Wha—?" She stopped, her mouth agape.

She thinks I've lost my mind, he thought. "If we leave Felipe in that place, he's going to get the wrong kind of education."

"Everyone knows that, Nick!" Sera yelled as she banged her fist on the steering wheel. "Everyone knows that. I know it, you know it, Worthy knows it, his case worker knows it, but Felipe can't go to a monastery."

"Why?" he asked, then plowed on. "Look, I know you think I'm crazy or that I'm grasping at straws, but what I'm suggesting has been done before." Father Fortis chose to omit that sending felons to monasteries was rarely an option in recent centuries. "Felipe needs discipline, he needs mentors who'll direct him toward the good. And most of all, he needs someone to listen to him, even to listen to his silence. Sera, St. Mary's has all of that. You've been there. You know what I'm saying is true."

Sera gripped both hands on the steering wheel and screamed, "Nick, he won't go to a monastery! He won't. I can't get him to even go to Mass with me." She turned and stared at Father Fortis. "And what the hell would you, a monk, know about what's best for my child?"

Sera pulled the car over to the side of the road, turned off the ignition, and sobbed. Father Fortis sat in silence. Sera didn't need him to try to sell her further on his bizarre notion. From his listening to confessions, he knew that Sera was someone who needed him to listen to her screams, her anger, her sobs, and now her silence. He understood that Sera had been crying a great deal and needed to do so, but he doubted if anyone had listened to her grief. Why, he wondered, did people assume, when they met someone in deep distress, that they needed to talk that person out of that feeling?

After a few moments, Sera sighed. "I'm sorry, Nick. Sorry about what I said. You've been nothing but kind to me, flying out here, trying to make sense of Freddie, and now coming with me to see Felipe. And what do I do? I try to hurt you."

"All very natural, my dear. And I didn't pay attention to what you said, but what's behind those words. The loneliness."

Sera leaned back against the headrest and groaned. "That's the worst of it. Bad enough that I can't fix one iota of the mess that my family's in. What makes it worse is that all my friends think I ought to leave Freddie."

She looked over at Father Fortis again, but he saw no anger this time. "One of my cousins said the same thing as Captain Cortini, that I have to choose between Freddie and Felipe. That I can't save both. I hated him for saying it, but now I wonder if he's right. What if Freddie can't be helped?"

Father Fortis said nothing. If the psychiatrist didn't know if Freddie was too far gone, then he certainly didn't.

"And what if I've already lost Felipe because of spending or maybe wasting all my energy on Freddie? That's what Felipe is accusing me of, isn't it?"

"I heard what Felipe said, but this is what I believe, Sera. I believe that the last person who wants you to cut and run from Freddie is your son. His pain, his angry words mean that he loves Freddie, more than he's willing to admit."After a moment's pause, he added. "We have a saying in the Orthodox church, Sera, and my guess is that it's in the Catholic church as well. 'We won't be saved individually. We'll be saved together or not at all.'"

Sera held his gaze. "So you think...?"

"Yes, I don't think you're supposed to choose between helping Freddie or Felipe. Despite what everyone is saying, even what Felipe said to hurt you, the truth is that we save Felipe by saving Freddie. And we save Freddie by saving Felipe."

Unbuckling her seat belt, Sera leaned across the seat and buried her head in Father Fortis' shoulder. "You said 'we,' not 'you,'" she managed to say between her sobs. "That's the kindest thing anyone has said to me in God knows how long."

Chapter Six

March 30

The next morning, Worthy bristled as the young private manning the desk at the Veteran's Administration hospital raised a finger and turned away to relay Worthy's request to the person on the other end of the line. Eventually, the young man turned and glanced briefly up at Worthy.

"Lt. Col. Bratton has a full schedule today, but she wants to know why Detroit police are interested in Sgt. Contreras."

She? Worthy thought. He chastised himself for assuming the Army psychiatrist would be a male. "You can tell her that I'm a friend of Sgt. Contreras' wife. Sera Lacey asked me to assist in his defense."

The young soldier scowled and turned away again to relay the message. Lt. Col. Bratton apparently had enough free time to talk on the phone.

After a few moments of "yes, ma'am," "no, ma'am," the private put the phone down and faced Worthy and said, "Lt. Col. Bratton reminded me of protocols and procedures. You'll have to be authorized to talk with her by Sgt. Contreras' defense attorney."

Worthy couldn't tell if he were being played or if protocols were this strict at the VA. Even though he knew Sera could give him the answer to his next question, he wanted to see if he could expect more obstacles from the military. "I don't suppose you can give me the name of his appointed counsel."

The private, no more than a kid still in his teens, didn't bother to consult higher authorities on this question. "Indeed, I can't," he said with what seemed to Worthy a slight smile of satisfaction. "Is there anything else I can help you with?"

Help me with? Worthy thought. *That's rich.* Without bothering to reply, Worthy turned and went outside where he opted for a walk around the city's central plaza as he tried to decide if he was deliberately stonewalled, and, if so, what that portended for the case. The young private was an ass, but his behavior could be caused by any number of factors. Maybe he'd never served in combat and was in love with the uniform. Or maybe he'd been forced by his low rank to seek the authority of those with higher rank so often that he loved being able to throw his own weight around a bit.

The truth, Worthy knew, was that Freddie Contreras was giving the military a big headache. Yes, the Army could court martial him and even seek the death penalty, but in the courtroom, the Army wouldn't be able to hide how psychologically destroyed Freddie had been by his last tour in Afghanistan. His condition, even if he had killed Pvt. Burgess, would raise serious questions about his sanity and how devastating PTSD could be. The Army would want a quick trial to avoid undue media attention. The last thing the Army wanted was Sgt. Frederick Contreras, veteran of three tours of combat duty, as the poster child of all that goes wrong in war.

Sera saw her hand shake a bit as she raised the coffee to her mouth. *I wonder if they make tranquilizers for failing mothers,* she thought. She gazed around her in the missing person's office of the police department. Captain Cortini had reassigned her to the previous unit she served in before she was promoted to homicide four years before, but she recognized only two of the other officers sitting at desks.

Cortini was obviously worried about her and suggested that the last thing she needed at that moment was a leave of absence. He was right. After the past days of worrying alternately about Freddie and Felipe, she felt she was teetering along the edge of some cliff. But in such a state, how was she expected to concentrate on a missing person's case?

Cortini had argued otherwise, citing the soft spot Sera had for kids. She didn't know whether to laugh or scream when he said that. *My own son, in his own way, is a missing person, and look what good I am for him.*

She reread the name on the file that she'd found on her desk when she arrived that morning. Noah Frost. Why did that name seem familiar? An Anglo, she thought, before realizing her own last name, kept from her first marriage, Lacey, looked Anglo to anyone who didn't know her.

She opened the file and started at the top. Noah Samuel Frost, fifteen, in his senior year of high school. *The boy must have skipped a couple grades, which means he's bright,* she thought. Middle child of Reverend Daniel and Naomi Frost. *Ah, now I remember.* Frost was the name she'd heard in commercials on the radio and TV advertising a Protestant mega-church on the outskirts of Santa Fe.

For the next quarter of an hour, she focused on the case and felt, for the first time in weeks, a sliver of distance from her troubles. A prominent minister's son had run away. She read down through the report. The boy had been missing three days before her unit was notified by the father. Why the delay?

Reading further, she saw that Noah never ran away before. Yet, he left a brief note in his room, writing he needed some time away on his own. The family had no clue where he might have gone or whom he might be staying with. The boy was described in the file as quiet, but not having noticeable emotional difficulties. Sera wondered as she looked over the rest of the file if the family sensed something amiss in the days and weeks before he ran away. That would be one of the first questions she'd ask the family in her initial interview.

Sera turned back to the photo supplied by the family of a short, thin boy with brown hair and glasses standing beside a tree, his hand shielding his eyes from the sun. To Sera, the boy looked shy, even a bit frightened, so unlike the mask Felipe had adopted over the past two weeks. She felt a lump in her throat. How she wished the expressions on the two boys could be reversed, that Felipe would be a frightened boy whom she could lovingly comfort.

Loving comfort—that was what most troubled Sera: that love was, in the end, not the answer to everything. Decades before, the love of the Penitentes had saved her grandfather and, through him, the family. The love of the Penitente family had saved the little boy Felipe and her when her first husband was killed in a work-related accident. She had banked again on the power of love when she married Freddie Contreras and he became Felipe's new father.

But in the last weeks, Sera felt that love deserted them all and, if God is love, then she felt that God was simply another name for the weakness she felt. Perhaps, she thought, this is what Worthy felt when his wife left him and his own daughter ran away. She shook her head, determined to return her attention to Noah Frost. She remembered the mantra from her years before in the missing persons unit. Some individuals run *away* from something horrible; others run *toward* what they hope is a better future, and yet others flee for both reasons. What about Noah Frost?

As much as she was worrying about Felipe and Freddie, she found herself concerned, the more she read the file, about Noah Frost. While there was nothing in the Frost file to suggest suicide, her worry that Freddie, in his near-catatonic state, was considering this step made it easy for her to believe that the shy boy from the photo, the son of a prominent minister, had a secret life that he too kept hidden.

Chapter Seven

March 31

From the file that Sera had faxed to Father Fortis and him, Worthy knew that the Army had assigned a captain from the Office of Staff Judge Advocate as Freddie's defense attorney. Worthy himself would have preferred a civilian attorney to join the team as a check on any possible bias by the military, but he also knew Sera couldn't afford that.

After a wait of about forty-five minutes at the Army base, Captain Phillip Mills ushered him into his office. A lifer, Worthy thought, judging the attorney to be in his late forties and a bit overweight. In an age of corrective laser surgery, Worthy was surprised to see someone still wearing glasses with thick lenses, lenses so thick that the eyes behind them looked comically oversized. Worthy thought the man's brown hair was dyed, perhaps an indication of vanity.

"I understand you're interested in the Frederick Contreras case," Mills said. "In what capacity?"

Worthy pulled out his ID and handed it across the desk. Captain Mills raised it close to his nose to study it before passing it back. "Does Sgt. Contreras have priors back in Detroit that I should know about?"

"No," Worthy replied. "I worked with Lt. Lacey on a previous case, and she's asked me to offer whatever help I can."

"So you flew out from Detroit for this case?"

"Along with some other business," Worthy replied, not wanting to bring up Felipe's situation.

"What kind of help are you offering, Lieutenant? Sgt. Contreras' wife hasn't been the most cooperative."

"Can you blame her? Her husband comes back from Afghanistan a basket case, and he gets charged with murder. Remember, she's a cop, so she knows how some investigations are crippled by biases."

As he thought, his last comment had got the lawyer's attention. His bug eyes glared at Worthy; his lips pursed. "Are you suggesting the Army won't give Sgt. Contreras a fair trial?"

"I'm not suggesting anything, but we both know that the quality of an accused's defense often determines the outcome. For example, how many attorneys and investigators does the prosecution have, and how many do you have?"

"All you need to know is that my client will receive the best defense I can provide."

Worthy noted that Mills hadn't answered the question.

"Just so Freddie is innocent until proven otherwise," Worthy said.

Mills leaned back in his chair and exhaled. "Let's get one thing straight, Lt. Worthy. Freddie's only hope is my ability to sell the court on an insanity plea."

"Which means he'll be locked up with the key thrown away," Worthy said.

Captain Mills sat forward in his chair. "Do you have any idea how difficult it will be to keep Freddie from being convicted of first-degree murder? I'm going to have to prove that Freddie's PTSD is so severe that he didn't know what he was doing, all that against an Army bureaucracy that doesn't want to admit that soldiers returning from war zones might have been driven insane. That doesn't fit the noble image of fighting for your country."

"Lt. Lacey doesn't want the insanity plea. She's convinced Freddie is innocent."

"Look, Lieutenant. If you work homicide, you know that the prosecution in this case has what it needs to convict on the murder charge. There's his blood at the scene and there's the confession, for God's sake. A confession. Freddie says he did it; the blood says he did it. There is no way he's innocent."

Worthy leaned forward as well. "If you're going to argue for insanity, how do you know he was in his right mind when he confessed?"

That made the defense attorney stop. Finally, Mills said, "We have the video of his confession. Freddie looks agitated, but they ask him the basic questions of orientation—who's president, what month we're in, his rank and serial number. He gets them all correct. And after he confesses, they repeat the charge several times."

"Did he offer details?"

Mills nodded. "Each time, he admits to the killing. 'I did it,' he keeps saying. So now you see the mountain that I have to get over. I have to establish that he was lucid enough when he confessed but wasn't in his right mind when he committed the crime."

Worthy could see the problem Mills faced. "You must be relying heavily on the psychiatrist's diagnosis."

"And the other team will have a second and maybe a third opinion from their psychiatrists. Look, Lieutenant, I'm no rookie Staff Judge Advocate. The Army could have dumped Freddie on a raw Second Lieutenant, but they brought me in. Freddie will get his fair hearing."

Worthy thought it time to pose the question that had brought him to Mills' office. "Would you give me permission to talk with Freddie's psychiatrist at the VA?"

Captain Mills gazed out the window at the oversized American flag in the center of a courtyard. *Does Mills have blurry vision in more than one respect?* he asked himself. For a moment, Worthy thought he was going to deny the request, but then Mills took a pen off his desk and scribbled something on a pad of paper.

"Okay, Lieutenant. I'll trade you. You can meet with his doctor, but I want to tell you something they won't tell you, and that is that Sgt. Contreras tried to hang himself two days ago in his cell. His wife hasn't been told, but the point is this. If you truly want to help her, do me, her, and most of all Freddie, a favor. Make her see that her husband's best chance is the insanity plea."

FRESH BACK FROM ANOTHER THIRTY MINUTES with Freddie, who now had gone more than a week without saying a word, Sera closed the Noah Frost file and looked out her own window at the snow-capped peaks of the Sangre de Christo range. *It's all melting away,* she thought as she glanced down at the photo of Freddie, Felipe, and her on her desk. *Maybe it's already gone.*

As had happened so many times to her over the last weeks, she couldn't stop her mind from searching for what she did wrong. The worst part was that her search had come to a door behind which lay the answer. She sensed, rather than knew, that the answer to that question was so terrible that a part of her was working hard, and exhausting her all the more, to keep the door closed.

But as she left the Army's prison hospital, she knew her ability to resist was gone. What seemed more certain over the past week was that Freddie would likely never return to her. And now it also seemed that Felipe would have the same fate, living his life in and out of trouble or behind bars. She hadn't wanted to believe Captain Cortini when he repeated his advice to let Freddie go.

Closing her eyes, she felt empty and spent, unable to prevent the door in her mind from swinging open on its own. There it was, the truth that she hadn't wanted to admit. *If Freddie had died in Afghanistan, Felipe would be better off. He would have grieved the father he loved and who loved him, but he'd still be my Felipe.*

†

Rising from his knees, Father Fortis made the sign of the cross and bowed one last time toward the altar and the reserved sacrament before leaving the monastery's chapel for his meeting with the abbot. Four years ago, he'd brought another request to the same office. But then it was Abbot Timothy, who in the years since had slipped into dementia. The old abbot was in hospice care in Albuquerque, not expected to live more than three months.

The new abbot, Abbot Peter, was young and, according to some of the monks Father Fortis remembered from four years before, a progressive. Two of the monks referred to him as both clear-headed and deeply spiritual, high praise indeed and praise that Father Fortis prayed was justified. Certainly, the community of St. Mary of the Snows had grown in numbers over the past four years, which bucked the trend of fewer vocations in most monasteries in the world.

But Father Fortis knew that Abbot Peter, even with a progressive temperament, could still balk at the request he was going to present. His plea this time was nothing so minor as asking permission for Worthy to stay at the monastery. No, this request had the potential of upsetting the entire community, and abbots were tasked by their office with ensuring peace and harmony.

Father Fortis took a deep breath and knocked on the abbot's door. Hearing an invitation to enter, he opened the door even as Abbot Peter was rising from behind his desk to greet him. The new abbot was not as young as Father Fortis had been led to believe, but he could see how the monks of St. Mary, comparing Abbot Peter to Abbot Timothy, would see him as young.

What Father Fortis first noticed was not the height of the abbot, easily six feet, nor his trim build, nor his piercing eyes, but rather the austerity of his office. There was one crucifix of modest size on the wall behind the uncluttered desk, a calendar on a side wall showing the façade of the Vatican in Rome, two chairs on the visitors' side of the desk and a similar straight-backed chair on the other side, a couple of bookcases, and two filing cabinets. Father Fortis thought it looked more like the office of a car salesman who just happened to be religious: no frills, all business.

I'm guessing German or Swiss, Father Fortis thought, as he shook the hand offered to him before sitting down.

"Welcome to St. Mary's, Father," the abbot said.

"It's good to be back, Reverend Father."

The abbot held Father Fortis' gaze, in contrast to the way Abbot Timothy never seemed to focus. "Although, as I understand it, your errand is quite sad. Some time you must visit us when there is no tragedy to unravel."

"I'd welcome that," Father Fortis replied, although he knew his own abbot agreed to his return visit to St. Mary's only because of Sera Lacey's tragedy.

"Do you find St. Mary's much changed?" the abbot asked.

"I was sorry to hear that Father Linus died. But we can't stop the river of time, can we?"

"Nor the need for change as we now try to navigate that same river. As is no doubt true of your monastery, St. Simeon's, we must hold fast to what is eternal and yet not assume everything falls into that category."

The abbot's smart, Father Fortis thought. *No, he's savvy. But the next few minutes will reveal if he's flexible.*

"How can St. Mary's help you, Father?" the abbot asked.

"St. Mary's is once again more than hospitable, your grace. I can sense God's Spirit in the house, and I don't say such things lightly. But, yes, I do have a request, and I know it's quite unusual."

The abbot offered a wry smile. "My interest is truly piqued, Father. If we can oblige, St. Mary's will be happy to do so."

Father Fortis shifted in his chair and uttered a silent prayer for what would come next.

"Abbot Peter, are you aware that some monasteries have taken in individuals recently released from incarceration?" Father Fortis was relieved that he didn't have to ask Abbot Timothy that question. Even explaining the question would have taken half an hour with the old abbot.

"Yes," Abbot Peter replied very slowly as if he suspected what might be coming next. "The practice is not very common in recent times and certainly not in this country."

Father Fortis took a deep breath before continuing. "I have a special case that I pray St. Mary's will consider."He quickly outlined how the tragedy of Freddie Contreras affected his adopted son, Felipe, how Felipe was in danger of falling deeper into hopelessness and crime, and the role St. Mary's could play in rescuing the boy.

As Abbot Peter sat quietly, Father Fortis could tell that the abbot was giving the thought his full attention.

"Has the boy been asked about this?"

"No, your grace, but I did suggest the possibility, as hypothetical, to his mother, Lt. Sera Lacey."

"Am I right to assume she is in favor of it?"

Father Fortis had to shake his head. "I can't in all honesty say that. Yes, she does want him away from the influences of juvenile detention, but...she isn't convinced her son won't try to run away."

"So what is your thought—that our being fifteen miles off the main highway would keep this boy here?"

"That, as well as the positive influence of the community. I met with the boy, and I can attest that his spirit is broken."

"What exactly did he do to be detained, Father?"

"After his father came back from Afghanistan, clearly disturbed, Felipe joined a group of boys who vandalized at first."After a pause, Father Fortis added, "Then the boy assaulted a homeless man."

"Oh," the abbot replied and let that word hang in the air for a moment. "You realize what you're asking, Father? To bring to St. Mary's a young man who seems intent on violence and, as far as I can tell, is someone who has no desire to change."

"That about sums it up, your grace. But this isn't the same Felipe from three months ago. We're talking about a boy who was on his high school baseball team and who was in scouting. The Felipe I sat with this week is totally confused. I think the boy, in one sense, can't believe what he's become. This is someone who is literally not in his right mind."

"And you're thinking...you're hoping that his being here will bring him back to his senses."

Father Fortis nodded.

The abbot looked down at his hands. "We sometimes hire workers from Truchas, for the gardening mainly as well as general maintenance. But they drive back to town each day after work. Your young man would have to live in a dormitory room, eat with us in the refectory, and live within a schedule that doesn't intrude on ours. We couldn't have him wandering around the grounds or in any of the buildings after Compline."

"Of course. Lt. Worthy or I would do our best to keep an eye on that."

"And I suspect we'd have to dispense with any requirement that he attend the daily offices, the prayers."After a moment's silence, the abbot said, "Life at St. Mary's is a tough life for anyone, Father, as you know, even for those who want to be here."

"I believe this kind of life is exactly what he needs. Felipe's world fell apart when his father came back from Afghanistan. He needs structure, your grace, and even more than structure, he needs mercy."

"Well, Father, you've given me a lot to think about...a lot to pray about, actually. But unless the young man is open to coming here and accepting what life would be like, what we're talking about is, as you said before, hypothetical. But I give you permission to tell his mother that I haven't said no, at least not yet."

Chapter Eight

March 31

Worthy didn't even bother to respond when the same young private at the VA told him that Lt. Col. Bratton's office was down the corridor, third door on the left.

The tiles on the walls, the faded linoleum on the floor, and the fluorescent lights humming above reminded Worthy of the sixties. In that era, returning soldiers shattered by the war in Vietnam were the patients locked up in wards like these. Now, vets like Freddie sat in the cells, often with the same readjustment issues. The technology of war was constantly upgraded because of frequent hikes in defense spending. Worthy doubted, however, that treatment options offered in these offices had changed very much.

As he knocked on the door, Worthy thought, *Face it, war can be made to look sexy, like an adventure. War can also be good business for a wide range of corporations. But those human bodies and minds broken by war? There's nothing sexy about amputees and prosthetics, and there's nothing sexy about the Freddies of the world.*

Hearing a female voice invite him to enter, Worthy was reminded of his sexist assumption about Army doctors. As he entered the room, a tall African-American woman with hair pulled back tightly into a bun, rose from behind the desk.

"Lieutenant Worthy, please have a seat. I appreciate your persistence, and I apologize if we frustrated you."

Tell the private out there, Worthy thought.

"Please know before anything else is said that I understand that you'd undoubtedly like more information than I'm allowed by law to share with you."

Worthy nodded that he understood, but he also knew from past experience that mental health officials divulged as little or as much as they wanted to share. Sometimes the "That's confidential" tagline was spoken in a way or with a look that encouraged Worthy to rephrase his question. At other times, the expression was a solid brick wall. Worthy wondered what it would be in this case.

Worthy, however, had interviewed enough physicians and clergy to have a game plan. He would begin with something shocking, and he thought he knew what that was. Behind where Lt. Col. Bratton was seated, he noted the name "Contreras" along with two other names with blue stars beside them on a notice board. Was it possible, he thought, that all psychiatric facilities used the same blue star as code for patients on suicide watch?

"How long ago was it that Freddie Contreras tried to kill himself?" he asked.

The question had the effect he hoped, and he knew he guessed right.

Lt. Col. Bratton turned around to see the names on the board. "You've worked in psychiatric facilities?"

"Many years ago, when I was in college, but yes," Worthy said. "How did he manage it?"

The psychiatrist paused for a moment before answering. "He tore up a bedsheet and threaded two strips of material through the ceiling's sprinkler system. He failed because his weight pulled out the entire system. A real mess—not just water everywhere, but chemically-treated water."

The doctor paused, seemingly seeking a way to regain control of the conversation. "Let me get something straight. Unless I'm been misinformed, you're a friend, a volunteer, if you will."

"That's right. I'm here as a friend," he said pausing, before adding, "a friend who happens to be a homicide detective."

"Fair enough. I'll treat you as a specialist, then, who happens to have a background in psychiatric work. Why don't you ask me your questions as a homicide detective, and I'll determine if I can answer them?"

"Okay. I assume you've met Sera Lacey, Freddie's wife."

"And I assume, as you are her friend, that you already know I have and that we haven't told her about Freddie's suicide attempt."

"Does it surprise you that she, as a police officer herself, thinks Freddie is innocent?"

Lt. Col. Bratton shrugged, looked down at her neat desk, and said, "I'm not surprised, because that's what most spouses believe. Or, should I say, 'want to believe?'"

"Should I also assume that you know what's been going on with Freddie's son, Felipe?"

"I don't really consider that relevant, Lieutenant."

"Well, isn't it true that Felipe's problems began after Freddie returned from Afghanistan, where he was a Taliban hostage for what, two weeks?"

"I'm not allowed to comment on that, as you're not an officer of the court."

Worthy looked around the office and focused on the diplomas on the wall. He thought her road, as an African-American psychiatrist, couldn't have been an easy one.

"Was Freddie in your care before the Burgess murder?" he asked.

"Why do you ask?" she said.

She's stalling, he thought.

"I assume the answer to that is yes. I know that as soon as Freddie returned from Afghanistan, he was hospitalized for a few days."

After a moment, Bratton said, "Let's assume he was my patient." At that, her jaw closed firmly.

Knowing she was unlikely to say much more about Freddie specifically, Worthy changed his tactics. "Let me ask a hypothetical question, one not about Freddie. I just want to understand more about how PTSD works. In your experience, do veterans with serious PTSD ever confess to crimes they didn't commit?"

The psychiatrist said nothing for a moment, but her eyes narrowed.

"Yes, they can, but almost any aberrant behavior can accompany PTSD. Now, whether or not PTSD is present in this case, I'm not allowed to say." The way she said that, however, gave Worthy the impression that she already considered the possibility.

"Again hypothetically, I assume that some soldiers return from war zones with a heavy sense of guilt," Worthy said.

"No doubt. War is rarely clean and neat. I'm sure in police work you've done some things that troubled you later."

Nice reversal, Worthy thought. *But you're not going to derail me that easily.* "Are delusions common in cases like this?"

"If you're talking about flashbacks, then all I can assume is that you took an introduction to psychology in college."

Worthy looked up to see if she meant that to sting. She had. *She's not enjoying this one bit.* "No, not flashbacks," Worthy said, "but something longer lasting."

"We call that dissociative ideation, Lieutenant. Yes, that *can* happen, but once again I'm not saying that was present in this case."

Worthy noted that she'd switched back to referring to him by rank. "Of course. I'm pretty sure I remember from intro to psych what can cause flashbacks, like fireworks, or a gun going off, or a car backfiring, but what might bring on this dissociative ideation?"

Lt. Col. Bratton checked the time on her wristwatch. Was she tiring of his questions, or was he getting close to something?

"A word, a face, an expression, or even something unconscious could bring on dissociative ideation. Take your pick, Lieutenant."Her weight in the chair shifted forward, and Worthy knew she was about to stand up.

"One more question, Colonel. Do my colleague, Nicholas Fortis, and I have your permission to talk with Sgt. Contreras?"

The psychiatrist hesitated before standing, and Worthy waited for her to refuse his request.

Instead, the psychiatrist nodded. "Yes, by all means, see Sgt. Contraras for yourself. I think with your background, you might then understand what we're up against in this case."

That night, Father Fortis knocked on Worthy's room after the last service of compline. "Do you have a minute, Christopher?"

Worthy looked up from his notes. "Of course. The basketball game isn't on for another half-hour. Oh, I forgot, I don't have a TV. Just kidding, Nick. St. Mary's is a very quiet place to work, but I wouldn't mind a distraction or two."

"Point taken. Maybe we should stay in a motel in Santa Fe."

"Really, Nick, I'm just kidding. If I need a distraction, I can go for miles on a walk, or do what I'm doing now—write a letter to Allyson."

Father Fortis noted the look of joy that appeared on his friend's face when he said his older daughter's name.

"She's doing well in her FBI internship?"

"As far as I can tell. She's not allowed to share much, but I can tell she's taken to the challenge," Worthy replied.

Father Fortis thought back on their time at St. Mary's four years before. Worthy's face then, especially his eyes, bore a heaviness, as if life itself were a series of losses. So much had changed since his relationship with Allyson had been rescued.

His reminiscences were interrupted by Worthy's voice. "Sorry, my friend, my thoughts were elsewhere. What did you say?"

"I want to update you on where things stand with Freddie."

Father Fortis sighed heavily as he took the chair by the window. "And I need to tell you about my time with Sera and Felipe."

"Why, what happened?"

Father Fortis relayed the painful conversation with Felipe in detention.

"Earlier today, I let Abbot Peter know that Sera is open to the idea of bringing Felipe here. Now, all we have to do is get Felipe and the judge to agree."

"That won't be easy, Nick. The courts aren't usually in favor of deals that remove felons from custody."

Father Fortis closed his eyes and offered a brief prayer of thanksgiving.

Looking up, Father Fortis said, "Thank you, my friend, what you said helps."

"What? I don't think I said anything particularly hopeful."

"You said the word 'custody.' That's how we'll explain the offer to the judge. Felipe will still be in custody. He'll be isolated out here, fifteen miles from any highway, and he'll be supervised. But the main difference is that he'll be safe, safe from attacks in juvenile detention."

"Okay, but explain to me how you're going to get Felipe to agree. Won't the offer look like we're saying he's weak?" Worthy said. "And won't his being here seem a bit like solitary confinement?"

Father Fortis was quiet again for a moment. "Sera has similar worries, but we won't know until we ask, Christopher. And I believe this: Felipe will be listening not just to our words, but to what's behind them."

"I'm not sure I follow."

"If when we're explaining the option to Felipe we're certain that he'll refuse, then he will. That's why I'll ask Sera to let the two of us, not her, be the ones to make the offer. But if the two of us believe with our whole hearts and minds that St. Mary's is where Felipe belongs, that this is where he will begin to heal, then he might sense this as well. You see, Christopher, I don't think Felipe wants to continue down the road he's on. I think he's like the rest of us—he wants to find his way back home."

DEAR ALLYSON,

I trust you're well. I try not to worry about where they'll assign you after graduation from training, but given your facility with languages, I can imagine the FBI will want to take advantage of that. Let me know what you're allowed to share.

I'm back in New Mexico. It's four years since Nick and I were here the last time. There are moments when I look out at the desert and the mountains beyond or when, as I am now, sitting in an almost identical room to the one I stayed in at the monastery four years before, and think that little has changed. Once again, I find myself embroiled in a case with Sera Lacey and Nick, and it seems that the past four years are no more than six months.

But I know that so much has changed. To work with Sera Lacey again, but see the despair and fatigue that have left her only a poor version of the person I once knew, has reminded me that a life can fall apart in weeks if not days.

Of course, knowing me as you do, warts and all, you can imagine how much I want to fix things here, to find some way to help Sera Lacey recover her life, to recover her husband, and to recover her son. But I'm beginning to doubt this is possible. It's foolish to expect healing when even stopping the bleeding would be a major achievement. Unless matters change quickly, her husband will escape life in a military prison only by being sent to a psychiatric ward in that same prison. And with that outcome, time will become for Sera one long grey ordeal with no relief.

And her son? He seems determined to throw his life away. Thankfully, Nick is here, and I count on Nick's faith in what he calls redemption. Because of this, I know that Nick, who is more worried than I've ever seen him, is still a far greater help to Sera than I can be right now.

As you know, I'm usually the pessimist, although I might prefer the word realist. This case will end for me when we determine if Sera's husband did the killing. The best that can come out of all of this is that we might be able to rescue her son, Felipe, who's sitting in juvenile detention. But even if we do that, he'll have a series of felonies on his record that will make his life harder from now on. Time won't erase that.

You've had enough experience already, Allyson, to know that all we in law enforcement can hope for is that we uncover the truth. In a sense, I'm out here to conduct an autopsy on Sera's family. But as a priest, Nick believes that Sera, her husband, and her son can be a whole family again. Where I see death, he still manages to see the possibility of life. As I said, Nick is better for Sera than I can be.

Sorry to burden you with this, but I needed to put it down on paper.

Love, Dad

Chapter nine

April 1

The next day, after Father Fortis presented his research on Roman chant to the monks of St. Mary's, he was looking out from his room to the snow-capped mountains to the north when he saw Sera Lacey's car pull into the monastery's parking lot. He glanced at his watch—3:30 pm. *That's odd,* he thought. He waited, expecting to see Sera exit her car, but he could see her remain in her front seat. After a moment, he saw her head fall forward and rest on the steering wheel.

Something's happened, and it's not good, he thought. His first fear was that Freddie managed to end his life, despite his being on suicide watch in the military prison. Worthy had told him not only about Freddie's suicide attempt but also not to say anything to Sera. But with every minute that Sera remained slumped over the steering wheel in her car, Father Fortis was becoming convinced the news was dire.

At the very moment Father Fortis decided to walk out to the parking lot, Sera emerged from her car. With her hands in her pockets, she walked slowly, as if bearing a great weight, toward the entrance of St. Mary's. Yet, after five minutes, Sera hadn't knocked on his door nor on Worthy's door across the hall.

I can't wait any longer, Father Fortis thought, aware that his abbot at St. Simeon's would cite this as yet another example of his impatience. He walked down the central flight of stairs only to find the entry way empty. Confused, he looked down both corridors and saw no one. *Where is she?*

He noticed the door to the chapel slightly ajar and approached it. Gently easing the door open another few inches, he peeked in to see Sera kneeling in the front row. He paused and heard her sobs.

This is why I'm a priest, he thought. *There were all kinds of sensible reasons to let a person grieve in private. But I can't do that if I'm to be true to my vocation.*

As he walked down the central aisle, he was relieved to hear his rubber soles squeak. He slowed his pace to give Sera a moment to collect herself. She dabbed her eyes with a balled-up handkerchief, smearing her mascara even more in the process.

Father Fortis eased into her pew and sat down next to her. Though he was frequently chastised by his abbot for his talkativeness, he knew that there are times when silence is the greatest gift we can give another. And though he wanted to, he didn't coax Sera into speaking by putting his arm on her shoulder. If the time wasn't right, that arm would feel like just one more weight pressing down on his friend.

Instead, he gazed out of the chapel's huge wall of windows at the cliff face and to the wooden cross atop it. He remembered sitting in this chapel four years before, praying for the soul of Sister Anna. He prayed now again, this time for Sera and her family as well as for guidance for Worthy and himself.

Sera blew her nose and cleared her throat several times without looking at Father Fortis. Father Fortis could see that she was gazing at the huge bleeding Christ on the cross suspended over the altar, and he did the same.

Whatever has happened, dear Lord, give her peace through your loving death. May she experience the hope of your resurrection, he prayed.

After a moment, Sera lowered her head on his shoulder and with spasmodic mini-sobs, sighed deeply. He felt her grief enter his body as a heavy ache. Yet he remained silent and waited.

"It's Felipe, Nick," she managed to say.

"Felipe?"

"He's in the hospital. He was beaten up in the shower. They think he sustained a ruptured spleen and maybe a detached retina."

Father Fortis let the news sink into him before he asked, "Because he's from another gang?"

There were only quiet sobs for a few moments. "They think someone recognized me when we visited last week. He was beaten because of me, because I'm a cop."

All the more reason to get him out of there, Father Fortis thought, but did not vocalize the thought. "How long will they keep him in the hospital?"

"Three days, they said. I wish it were three months. At least there he's safe."

Father Fortis felt the urge to tell her she couldn't blame herself for this, but that would be like telling a drowning person to lie back and enjoy looking up at the sky. Instead he said, "You must feel that this is all your fault. I know I would."

Sera did not say anything, but Father Fortis heard her breathe more easily.

"The other day, Nick, you said we had to get Felipe out of there, and I said your idea about bringing him here to St. Mary's was crazy. If I'm learning anything from all of this, it's that something crazy might be the only thing that makes sense."

Father Fortis waited a moment before saying, "I've talked to the abbot. He hasn't said yes, but he hasn't said no. I think a lot depends on Felipe's reaction."

After a moment, Sera said, "Would you go with me when I see him tomorrow?"

Father Fortis paused. "Sera, I'm going to ask you to agree to something you may not like."

"What?"

"Let Christopher and me visit Felipe alone and make the suggestion."

Sera drew back, obviously hurt by the suggestion. "Why?"

"I don't have to tell you that Felipe has been with you through a lot of ups and downs. First, your first husband, his father, was killed, then you were almost killed, and now Freddie is in bad shape."

Sera nodded.

"When you and I visited Felipe the other day, it was clear to me that the two of you are tuned into each other. He knows what you're thinking, what you're hoping for, and what you fear. That's why he can hurt you so deeply."

Sera looked down. "You think we're too close."

"Not in a bad way, Sera. But if you're there when we make the offer, Felipe could react to how much you want him to agree to the idea. And his pride could make him refuse just because of that. He has no any emotional history with Christopher or me. Do you see what I mean?"

Sera groaned. "I feel so worthless, Nick. Is there nothing I can do?"

"Of course there is, my dear. You can do the hard work. You can hope."

April 2

The following day, Sera, Father Fortis, and Worthy, having been searched, sat together in a waiting area of the prison for nearly forty-five minutes.

"Sometimes, I get the impression that the military needs to remind everyone that they have the power," Worthy said.

Sera gazed down at the floor. "I don't see it that way, Chris. As bad as Freddie looks when I come to visit, I know they've given him a shave and wet down his hair."

Nice one, Worthy thought to himself. *Seeing your husband in cuffs is bad enough without my adding to the pain.*

"Sorry I asked," Worthy said softly in apology.

Sera didn't look up, but Worthy understood that she might have different feelings about having to wait. Since his suicide attempt, which Sera wasn't told about, Freddie hadn't said a word. Why would she be in a hurry to see her husband in that kind of shape? For Sera's sake, he promised to stay silent and then, when Freddie was brought in in cuffs, not to react, no matter how bad he looked.

If he hadn't committed to that, he knew his face would have registered his shock when the three were led down a hallway to an interview room, where Freddie was already handcuffed to a ring on a metal table.

As far as he could remember, Worthy had only seen two photos of Freddie, one from the arrest file and the other, a family photo, from the past Christmas. The man seated before them bore almost no resemblance to the Christmas photos and looked even worse than in the mug shot. Freddie's black hair was indeed wet, but it looked like it hadn't been cut in months. A small nick on his chin showed where an orderly or guard slipped in shaving him.

Yet it was his gauntness that alarmed Worthy the most, and he could see that Father Fortis was also shocked. Maybe five feet nine or ten, Freddie looked to be no more than a hundred and twenty pounds.

Two guards stood inside the room by the only door. Everything that would pass between them would be heard and, no doubt, be written down for the prosecutor and defense attorney to evaluate.

Before sitting down, Sera stood over Freddie and bent down to kiss his cheek. Freddie gave no indication that he was aware of the affection, nor did he respond when Sera whispered, "I love you."

Recalling his college experience working in a psychiatric facility, Worthy needed only a moment to recognize that Freddie was in or nearly in a catatonic stage. Freddie's untrimmed nails offered Worthy a further clue of severe mental illness. That together with Freddie's blank expression and his unchanging pupils made Worthy wonder if Freddie even knew they were there.

Worthy reviewed the past weeks from Freddie's perspective. The man across the table wasn't this far gone when he gave his confession, and his suicide attempt proved, as recently as a week before, that he'd had the necessary fine-motor functioning.

"Freddie, these are my two friends, the ones I told you about. This is Father Nick," she said, placing her hand on Father Fortis' arm, "and this is Christopher Worthy, a police detective."

Freddie's reaction was to close his eyes and drop his head to his chest.

Sera continued with the introduction. "They're here to help prove your innocence, Freddie."

There was no response from Freddie, nor was there the slightest flicker of a gaze from the two guards.

Sera continued to talk to Freddie as if he were processing every word she was saying. She explained where Father Fortis and Worthy came from, how they were friends of hers back when she and Freddie were engaged and when Felipe was just a boy of twelve. She repeated what she'd told Freddie many times, that several years before, the three of them worked together on the murder case of the nun staying at St. Mary of the Snows.

When Freddie still didn't respond, Sera's voice began to quiver, and she stopped talking, looking helplessly from Worthy to Father Fortis. Worthy knew now why the psychiatrist was so willing for him to see Freddie. Whoever Freddie was, that man was gone. In his present state, Freddie would be unable to help with his defense and explain why he'd confessed.

His thoughts were interrupted by the sharp intake of air from Father Fortis. *Nick sees something I missed*, Worthy thought.

When Father Fortis spoke, his voice was low, the pace of the words slow. "Mr. Contreras, my name is Father Nick, as Sera said. I can see that you're suffering, and I suspect you feel you're at the bottom of a deep cave."

As far as Worthy could tell, Freddie offered no indication that he'd heard what Father Fortis said. *Nick must have imagined whatever he thought he saw. If this guy won't talk to his wife, he won't talk to a perfect stranger.*

At that moment, Father Fortis surprised Worthy and Sera, judging by her soft cry, by reaching across the table and placing his massive hand on top of Freddie's hands and manacles. Freddie didn't react, but Worthy realized it was possible that his not pulling his hands away could be considered a reaction.

The room was silent, no one moving. Finally, Father Fortis spoke. "I know much of your pain, Mr. Contreras, is wondering about Felipe."

Worthy could see that Freddie's shoulders twitched slightly.

Sera saw it too, judging by a second soft cry.

"You know Felipe is in detention, and I can only imagine how much you worry about that. I want you to know that we're doing our best to move Felipe to a safer place, a monastery where Lieutenant Worthy and I are staying. I want you to know this, because I can imagine that your concern for Felipe is too much to bear right now."

There was no movement of the shoulders this time, but Worthy could see that Freddie, even though his head was down, had opened his eyes slightly. He also heard Sera's sniffle and thought it likely that this small gesture was the most Freddie had communicated in days.

One of the guards coughed, and Worthy looked up at him sharply. *Don't even think about ending this,* he thought, hoping the guard picked up on his scowl.

But Father Fortis seemed satisfied. He removed his hand and thanked Freddie for allowing them to visit. "I promise to return, Mr. Contreras, and every time I do, I'll let you know how Felipe is doing. I'll always tell you the truth, but I trust that you'll feel better when you hear how Felipe is getting his life straightened out."

He looked up at the guards. "Can I leave this icon with Mr. Contreras?"

"Let me see it," the older of the guards said.

Father Fortis handed the icon of the Virgin Mary and the Christ child to him.

"It's just paper?" the guard asked.

Worthy saw Father Fortis nod, obviously understanding this wasn't the time or place to explain that an icon, even a paper one, was far more than paper.

Standing next to Freddie, the guard shoved the small icon into Freddie's pocket. Freddie didn't move, nor did he resist when the guards unshackled him, pulled him out the chair, and lifted, more than escorted, him from the room.

Out in the hallway, Sera gave in to her tears. For a few moments, she did nothing but hug both men and sob. "That isn't the man I married," she was finally able to say.

"The Freddie you married is still inside the man we saw. Don't forget that, my dear," Father Fortis said.

The three stood in silence until Worthy said, "Nick, I must have missed something you saw."

"I missed it too," Sera confessed. "Am I dreaming, or did you make some contact with Freddie?"

Father Fortis shrugged. "I felt some change in the room while we were talking. I don't even remember who said what, but I felt another person showed up in the room. I took that to be Freddie, but I could be wrong. Maybe Felipe showed up somehow. I don't know, really, but I felt Freddie began to hear us."

"Whatever happened, Nick," Worthy said, "what you said before seems right. If we can help Felipe, we're going to help Freddie."

"I hope the reverse is just as true," Sera said, wiping her eyes with a tissue. "That if we can help Freddie, we help Felipe somehow."

Worthy knew the thought was comforting to Sera, but he felt uneasy as he anticipated the upcoming trial. The Freddie with whom they'd spent the last twenty minutes would most likely be confined in a maximum-security facility, but it would be a locked unit in a hospital, not a prison. What troubled

Worthy was the realization that if Freddie was brought back to his right mind, the Army might decide to try him for first-degree murder.

Chapter Ten

April 3

While it would be inaccurate to say that Father Fortis didn't think about the case on the next day, Sunday, it was true that he spent the day attending all six services at St. Mary of the Snows. The time with Freddie Contreras tired him more than he knew until his restive night, when his mind felt like a pinball, jumping from one worry to another. He realized that this was how Sera must have felt every day for the past weeks, with Freddie being one seemingly unfixable problem and Felipe being a second.

During the Sunday services, the second Sunday before Easter in the Western Christian calendar, Father Fortis tried to focus his mind on the chanting, the bowing toward the altar, the hymns, and the readings from Scripture and books of monastic wisdom. *I need this,* he thought, *to be any good on this case. And I won't be good for anyone else, if I let myself be eaten up by worry.*

He thought of the three of them: Sera, overwhelmed by the Job-like trials she was facing; Worthy, still managing, thankfully, to remain somewhat objective as he probed the various elements of the case; and he, somewhere in between the two, yet more in danger of falling into Sera's abyss than sharing Worthy's more detached perspective.

Are the three of us a good team, he wondered? Four years before, each of the three solved a part of the case where the other two would have failed. This case, however, claimed not only Freddie and Felipe, but also Sera, who in some ways was as much a victim as the other two.

Perhaps, he thought, that was the reason he suggested to Sera that she let Worthy and him speak to Felipe alone. And that led him to wonder if Worthy and he might have better results with Freddie if Sera could be kept at a distance. He foresaw painful discussions and decisions, ones that could tax, if not destroy, their friendships.

Later that afternoon, the prospect of such a conversation loomed closer, as Sera e-mailed that Felipe could be sent back to juvenile detention from the hospital within the week. For Father Fortis, that meant that he had a matter of days to convince Felipe of the wisdom of the proposal, update Abbot Peter on the new threat to Felipe, gain from the abbot his formal permission to have Felipe stay at St. Mary's, and set up a conference with the juvenile judge to present the new option.

In a note to the abbot, Father Fortis explained the urgency of the situation. Father Fortis was aware the entire time of how making such a request to the previous abbot, Timothy, would have been pointless. But Abbot Peter was not only younger. He was clearly more open to ideas outside the routine rules of a monastic community. And, as Abbot Peter had admitted, there did exist an ancient, if not recent, precedent for welcoming troubled souls into the life of a monastery.

The following morning, on the way to the hospital to see Felipe, Worthy and Father Fortis discussed how best to broach the subject. From what Sera said about Felipe's injuries, Worthy surmised he was attacked by a gang. That, Worthy said, was not unusual in detention facilities and prisons. What Worthy found harder to understand was the absence of the guards during what must have been a noisy altercation.

"It's possible the gang members were given permission, maybe even encouragement, from someone higher up," Worthy said.

"That makes no sense to me," Father Fortis said. "Why would a guard do that?"

"Good question, Nick. I know that Sera thinks it was all because of her, but I can't see a guard having a beef with Sera, so we have to consider another possibility. What I'm saying is that the attack might have something to do with Freddie as much as with Sera. Just like a gang kicked Felipe around in the shower, someone wants to kick Freddie and Sera around, while both of them are already at the breaking point. Is that coincidence, Nick, or something more?"

LATER THAT MORNING, WHEN THE TWO men visited Felipe in the hospital, the patch over his left eye, the swollen lower lip, and the bruising on the face, neck, and arms showed the ferocity of the attack. Judging by Felipe's wiry but muscular build, Father Fortis agreed with Worthy that Felipe was attacked by more than one assailant.

Felipe's gaze followed the two men as they entered his room, but he said nothing for a moment. Both men moved to the left side of the bed, so Felipe could more easily see them.

"Where's my Mom?" The words came out thick, and Father Fortis guessed Felipe's tongue had been lacerated in the fight.

"It's just the two of us. Do you remember me, Felipe?" Father Fortis asked.

Felipe slowly nodded.

"This is Lieutenant Worthy from Detroit. We're here to help with your Dad's defense."

Felipe offered no wisecrack this time about that statement.

"Felipe, don't bother saying you fell down in the shower," Worthy said. "If I were you, I wouldn't tell who did this to me, either."

Felipe looked at Worthy but said nothing.

"We think you're not safe back in detention," Father Fortis said.

Felipe grimaced and looked away.

Worthy moved closer to the bed. "We're not saying that because we think you're weak. I'm sure you gave as well as you got. But we think those assigned to protect you chose not to do that."

Felipe looked at Worthy as if the thought was a new one for him to ponder.

"We think you were beaten up to rattle your mom and your dad," Worthy added, to the surprise of Father Fortis. *Chris has chosen to lay all the cards on the table.*

"I screamed," Felipe managed to say.

"And no one came, right?" Worthy asked.

Felipe shook his head slowly.

"Lieutenant Worthy and I are trying to make other arrangements for you. But the court can't even hear us as long as you insist what happened to you was an accident."

"I can't snitch."

"The judge will probably accept that those who attacked you covered their identity," Worthy said.

"Why would I be any safer someplace else?" Felipe asked.

At least he seems interested, Father Fortis thought.

"You'd be safer because the place we're thinking of is fifteen miles from the nearest highway, and instead of guards there are monks," Worthy explained.

Felipe was silent for a moment before saying, "I don't get it."

"It's a Trappist monastery up past Truchas. That's what we want to present to the judge," Father Fortis said.

Felipe shook his head slightly. "God and me, we don't get along."

Father Fortis shook his head. "Until your trial, you'd be there as a worker.

Grounds-keeping, dishwashing, floor mopping, that sort of thing. You wouldn't be expected to do anything too strenuous, given your injuries, or anything religious. And, you'd be supervised."

"Who'd do that?"

"One of the monks, but Lieutenant Worthy and I would be receiving daily reports."

Felipe shook his head again. "I deserve what I got. I got beat up because I beat up a homeless guy. Seems fair to me."

"A lot that's happened to you hasn't been fair, Felipe. Your father died when you were six. Freddie was sent back repeatedly to Afghanistan. And then he came home in the shape he's in. No one is excusing what you did to that homeless man, but nothing was achieved by your getting beat up," Father Fortis said.

Felipe frowned and remained silent.

Father Fortis offered a silent prayer, asking for guidance. Without clear evidence of Felipe's willingness, he thought his chances of getting the judge's approval would be slim. What came to mind was Worthy and Sera's last exchange yesterday after seeing Freddie in jail: Worthy's "If we can help Felipe, we're going to help Freddie," and Sera's "I pray to God the reverse is just as true, that if we can help Freddie, we help Felipe somehow." *Freddie seemed to recognize the connection of Felipe's crimes with his own shattered life. Did Felipe see the connection?* Father Fortis wondered.

He took a deep breath before saying almost exactly what he'd said to Freddie the day before. "Felipe, I know you're worried about your Dad. We met with Freddie yesterday, and he let us know as clearly as he could that he's concerned about you."

Felipe stared at Father Fortis. "Did he say that?"

It only took Father Fortis a fraction of a second to decide that stretching the truth was both the greater good and the greater truth. "Yes, that's exactly what he communicated."

His lips trembling, Felipe closed his one good eye.

"We explained to your Dad about moving you to the monastery," Worthy said. "He wants you to accept the offer. So, what do you say?"

Even with his one eye closed, Felipe teared up, and for a moment Father Fortis didn't know if that was a good or a bad sign. *Does Felipe hate Freddie or still need him?*

Finally, as if to answer that question, Freddie nodded his assent.

BEFORE WORTHY DROPPED FATHER FORTIS OFF at the jail to see Freddie, he said, "We need to find out what Freddie's precise role was in the interrogations in Afghanistan."

"You think that's important, Christopher?"

"I think it might be. Why did the Army kept sending Freddie back, instead of somebody else?"

"And they'll tell us?" Father Fortis asked.

"Maybe Sera knows. She told me she's off work today, so I'm going to drop by her house, maybe take her out for lunch."

Worthy had to pound on Sera's door to be heard over the vacuum cleaner. As he was ushered in, Worthy evaluated the floor as spotless, as neat as the stack of magazines on the coffee table.

Worthy's own response when his marriage fell apart was the opposite. The apartment he rented, with his accumulating dirty dishes and laundry, reflected the creeping sense that his life was over. For Sera, the cleanliness of the room screamed of her anxiety.

Sitting on the edge of her couch, she cried as Worthy shared Felipe's willingness to being transferred to the monastery. Looking up, she said, "I don't know how to thank you, Chris."

"I'd save that for Nick. He's the one who broke through to Felipe."

Sera tried to laugh, but the sound that came out still seemed like a sob. "Nick's really something, isn't he?"

Worthy nodded. "I dropped him off at the prison hospital so he could tell Freddie the news."

Sera looked down at her hands, hands that seemed chapped to Worthy. "Better than the two of us, I suppose. We're just cops, Chris. Some in my own family tell me they feel grilled when I talk to them." Sera looked up, "I'm sorry, Chris. I shouldn't have implied that you..."

"Don't apologize, Sera. My daughter Allyson said that very thing to me a couple of years ago. If I was working a case—and when wasn't I? —she said the man who came home at night was not a dad, but a cop."

"But Nick is just Nick. Or maybe Nick is always a priest—I don't know, but he doesn't scare people away like some priests I know."

"You were right the first time. Nick is always just Nick. I was wondering, do you have time for me to take you for a coffee, or better yet, take you to lunch?"

Sera rose from the couch. "God knows I really need to get out of this house. It feels like a prison with ghosts."

Worthy stood as well and nodded toward the vacuum cleaner. "Your floors could also use a break, don't you think?"

Sera managed the beginning of a smile. "I need to control something."

The two found a table without delay at La Choza. Four years before, Sera and Worthy ate at the same place after an unexpected turn in the case. Then,

Worthy entertained the hope that Sera could be the answer to his loneliness, a way he could try again with a relationship, maybe even marriage. He was never quite sure if Sera felt anything for him at the time. But then the case divided the two of them into opposing camps, and Worthy realized, even before he knew Sera was engaged to Freddie, that their lives were too different.

Worthy looked at Sera now through different lenses. She was still beautiful, but her beauty triggered no yearning on his part. Instead, he felt pity for her. But if his feelings for Sera were gone, the memory of those feelings wasn't. Four years before, they experienced a kind of intimacy that was only partially based on their working together to find a killer. In looking at Sera now, Worthy realized he needed to maintain a professional detachment even as he felt the desire, almost an ache, to lessen her pain. At the same time, he realized he desired nothing from her romantically.

Sera looked out one of the restaurant's windows. "With everything falling down around my ears, I don't think I've looked, I mean really looked, at those mountains since Freddie came home. When I was little, I called them *my* mountains. I thanked God that he'd made them just for me. But now, I don't know if anything is mine, anything I care about anyway."

"I know when Susan left, I didn't notice the seasons changing for almost a year. And that's not easy when you live in Detroit."

Sera offered a weak smile. "But anyone can see you're happier now, Chris."

Worthy nodded and fell silent for a moment. "Four years ago, Nick said I was someone living in the graveyard of dead marriages."

Sera grimaced. "Maybe I'm stuck in that same graveyard."She sat up straight. "I shouldn't have said that. I know Freddie isn't guilty. I just have to keep reminding myself of that."

Worthy let the obvious go unsaid. Even if Freddie was found innocent, he might never again be the man Sera married.

"How'd you get out of that graveyard?" she asked.

"Maybe not as you might think. I'm not in a relationship, not the romantic kind at least. I'm not sure I'm any good at that. But I finally realized that a lot of my pain was connected with losing my daughter Allyson. Yes, the divorce was a blow, something I didn't see coming, but when Allyson ran away and then returned so full of hate for me, I folded up."

"That's how I feel right now about Felipe."

"Believe me, Sera, I understand. I felt like I was falling down a well with no bottom. I was just going down, down, down. We fall in love with our spouses, but that's something we do as adults, something we agree to do. But we have no choice with our kids. Allyson grabbed at my heart the moment she was born. When she ran away, it broke me."

"But you obviously got past that, Chris."

Worthy looked out the window, sensing that it would be better if the two didn't look directly at one another. "It was painful," he said. "I felt I was being operated on without anesthetic. But, oddly enough, the next case Nick and I worked on together started to repair my relationship with Allyson." Worthy paused again. "I owe Nick more than I can put into words."

"I'm happy for you, Chris." The two sat in silence for a moment, before Sera asked, "What is it you want to ask me?"

"You know me too well. Okay, we both know how this works. Sometimes, the questions we ask as cops of family and friends make them mad. They're thinking, 'If the police are asking questions this dumb, questions so clearly beside the point, then they'll never catch who killed my wife, or son, or sister.'"

"As I remember, I did scream at you four years ago," Sera said. "I promise I won't do that now."

"Back then, I deserved your screams, Sera. I hope I've learned a bit about being more careful, less arrogant."

Sera looked down at her hands. "I asked you to come because you're brilliant, Chris. Okay, you were arrogant back then, but you were brilliant. I hope that hasn't changed."

"Whatever I am, I'm here for you."

Sera began to reach across the table but drew her hand back and looked again out the window. "Go ahead, Chris. Ask whatever you need to ask."

"How much do you know about what Freddie did in Afghanistan?"

Sera shrugged as if she hadn't expected this line of questioning. "Well, I know he worked on high-level interrogations. Apparently, he's...he was one of the best."

"Does Freddie speak the language?"

"A bit, but he mainly works with translators. And some Afghans know some English. I think Freddie is just someone people trust. Why these questions?"

"Before I read the file, I would have assumed most interrogations in a war zone occur in some safe place well behind the lines. So why was Freddie in a place where he could be captured?"

Sera sat quietly for a moment. "What they told me was that they sent Freddie's unit forward when they needed intel right away. Or, maybe they captured someone who they knew wasn't going to live long enough to transport."

Worthy considered the scenario Sera was given by the Army. "Before this last time, did Freddie ever seem conflicted about his work?"

Sera frowned. "He wasn't crazy about being sent back all the time, if that's what you're getting at."

"I'm asking about the interrogation work itself. Do you think Freddie participated in torture?"

Sera shook her head. "No, no. Freddie would never do that, although he said he wasn't allowed to talk in detail about what he did."

Worthy thought for a moment before saying, "Freddie was sent back three times. So what was so special about him that the Army kept calling on him?"

"I don't know, Chris, other than what I said, that he was one of the best. But one time, I heard him complain about that."

"What do you mean?"

"Before the last time, I remember him saying, 'Why me? I just got home.'"

"Did Freddie say that with anger? Or pride?"

"Maybe both. As I said, trust must be the big issue over there, and Freddie was good at talking with people, getting information from them, I mean. Before he went into the Army, he was a pharmaceutical rep."

Worthy tried to imagine the Freddie he'd seen in jail, a man clearly catatonic, selling drugs to doctors.

"Be patient with me, Sera, but tell me again the Army's version of the firefight."

Sera's eyes grew wide. "Version? You don't think the Army told me the truth?"

"What I'm wondering is if you've been told the whole truth."

"Oh" was all Sera managed to say for a moment. "I was told the Taliban overran their base, which was a temporary one up near one of the fronts, that it was touch and go for a while, and then after the threat was neutralized, they saw that Freddie was missing."

"Just Freddie?"

"Well, I was told several other soldiers were killed—US Army, I mean. I don't know about Afghans or the Taliban."

"And Freddie was kept by the Taliban for nearly two weeks before they got him out, right?"

Sera shuddered as from a chill. "The Army said it did all it could to get him back, but two weeks? I can hardly sleep some nights wondering what the Taliban did to him."

Worthy gave Sera a moment to wipe tears from her eyes. "What about the other times Freddie was over there. Did he ever say he was worried about being captured?"

Sera shook her head. "Freddie said his unit was tight and really careful. He gave me the impression that their main worry was walking into a trap. Do you think that's what happened this time?"

"Possibly," Worthy admitted, but a new thought had come to mind. If Freddie's unit was so tight, why hadn't any of them visited him until the night at the bar?

"Why is it so important, Chris, to know what happened before he was captured? Isn't it enough to know that he was tortured?"

Worthy heard the anger in her voice and knew the anger wasn't directed at him. Sera was beginning to regret that she believed so quickly what she was told, that the Army did all it could and the Taliban was solely responsible for Freddie's condition. *No,* Worthy thought, *we haven't gotten to the bottom of this. We're not even close.*

Chapter Eleven

At the military prison, Father Fortis once again endured the pat-down before being seated in the interview room. The wait this time was only twenty minutes, which Father Fortis hoped was a good sign.

When Freddie was brought in, Father Fortis' heart sank. Freddie looked no more connected to reality than he did two days before. The guards escorted him to the table where they handcuffed him again to the metal ring. Freddie's head slumped immediately to his chest, his hair again stringy from being watered down. Father Fortis could see the edge of the paper icon peeking above Freddie's breast pocket. Had Freddie kept it, or had he not even noticed that he'd been given it?

"Do you remember me, Mr. Contreras?"

There was no response, not even a glance up.

One of the guards shifted by the door, a move Father Fortis interpreted as impatience.

"I came two days ago. I promised that I'd come back when I had news about Felipe."

Father Fortis noticed Freddie's head edge back slightly as if sensing he was about to be hit. And behind Freddie's closed eyelids, Father Fortis could detect eye movement. Once again, he realized it was the mention of Felipe that stirred Freddie. Whether the name was a lifeline connected to reality or something that caused Freddie pain, he couldn't tell.

"Felipe, yes, I have news of Felipe," Father Fortis said, watching for the name's effect. Freddie's nose twitched, and Father Fortis thought he detected fear in Freddie as he sat back in his chair.

"Felipe has agreed to go to the monastery. There he'll be safe. I know that's what you would like. Am I right?"

Without warning, Freddie lurched forward, banging his head on the metal table—once, twice, three times before the guard closer to the table pulled Freddie back in the chair. With eyes still tightly closed, as if he could blot out the room, the guards, the handcuffs, and the priest's voice, Freddie made grotesque guttural sounds and flung himself back and forth in the chair.

Father Fortis leaned forward, hoping to decipher meaning in the garbled sounds, but Freddie sounded more like an animal in pain than a human. *What have I done?* Father Fortis thought.

The door opened with another bang and a third soldier ran into the room. With two restraining Freddie as best they could, the third tried to insert the key in the handcuffs, but Freddie's manic movements were now convulsing his entire body. One of the guards was cursing beneath his breath, while another's face was beet-red from the exertion. When the third guard finally succeeded in releasing Freddie's hands, the three lifted the writhing body and ran more than walked him to the door. As the four figures exited the door, yet another guard looked in and with an angry face said, "You wait right here."

Now it was Father Fortis shaking in the chair. His legs felt rubbery, and perspiration was beading on his forehead. For a moment, he felt nausea rising in his stomach, but to his relief, the feeling passed.

Oh God, forgive me, a foolish monk who should know better, he prayed. He felt he deserved to be arrested but accepted that he'd at least be told he could never visit Freddie Contreras again. He thought using Felipe's name was the way to connect with Freddie, but he only caused what he assumed was a psychotic episode.

Five minutes later, the same guard opened the door. "Can you wait a half-hour until Lt. Col. Bratton arrives? She'd like to speak with you."

Father Fortis nodded and watched the door close again. Over and over again, he replayed the scene in his mind. He could see Freddie lurch forward, then hear more than see the horrible sound of the head banging on the table. After that, the scene was all flaying arms, Freddie's previously dead body alive but dangerously twisting and resisting the guards.

So where is Freddie now? Father Fortis thought. *Tied down to a bed? Immobilized by an injection? Is he still grunting and growling?*

Certain of what the psychiatrist would say, Father Fortis tried to find the words to apologize to Sera. *When she hears I've made matters worse, she'll do her best to hide her rage, and I'll be on a plane tomorrow, flying back to St. Simeon's in disgrace. Now what will the judge decide about Felipe? Have I ruined that as well?*

His self-recriminations hadn't abated when, fifteen minutes later, Lt. Col.

Bratton entered the room. It was the first time Father Fortis had met her, and he was convinced it would also be the last. Holding a file in her hand, the doctor took the same chair that Freddie had sat in. Wiping his forehead, Father Fortis braced himself.

"I wasn't sure when Mr. Contreras would begin to surface," Dr. Bratton said.

Father Fortis' jaw dropped. "Pardon?"

"With catatonic-like states, we usually have one of two outcomes, Father. Some disappear within themselves—they enter a cellar in the mind and lock the door behind them. That type of patient can be very difficult to coax out. The other outcome? Well, that's what we hope for. Something gets through, we're not sure how. But whatever it is yanks them to the surface."

"But Freddie was in agony. Anyone could see that."

The psychiatrist nodded. "When patients like Freddie first begin to come back to reality, they often come back screaming."

"It was like the gates of hell broke open," Father Fortis mused.

"I won't argue with that. Did you figure out what was the trigger?"

"I'm pretty sure it was the name of his son. It was when I said 'Felipe.'"

"Are you sure?" Dr. Bratton asked.

"Yes, why?"

"I've brought up his son's name several times in our sessions, but I gotten no reaction. So it was probably something else. What were you saying about Felipe?"

"I came to tell him that Felipe is being transferred out of juvenile detention to a safer place," Father Fortis said, thinking there was no need to identify St. Mary's as that new site.

Lt. Col. Bratton made a note in the file. "That's interesting. From what his wife told me, Freddie seemed very detached from his son when he returned stateside. Perhaps you've put us on to something, Father."

The perspiration on Father Fortis' forehead was replaced by tears. "I can't tell you how relieved I am to hear you say that."

The psychiatrist smiled. "Believe me, I know you've been through a shock. What you witnessed can be very frightening, if you don't understand what you're seeing. No, I'm thinking that something about his relationship with his son began his descent into the state he's in, and now it's possible that his relationship with his son might bring him back. It's obvious that he's quite conflicted about Felipe, but I'd rather we deal with that issue than with his disappearing act."

"I was all set to have you read me the riot act," Father Fortis said. "Now, I'm wondering if there's anything I can do to help."

"There might be, Father, but let's see how Mr. Contreras is tomorrow after the heavy sedation wears off. If his eye movements improve or there's increased motor activity, we'll reconsider his medication to see if we can help him out of himself. Give me a call after tomorrow, and I'll update you."

"Can I tell his wife what happened today?"

Dr. Bratton shrugged. "I wouldn't go into any great detail, and I warn you. Be ready for whatever she says."

"How do you mean, doctor?"

"His wife comes regularly, but we've noticed no change in Mr. Contreras when she's here. She might be angry that her husband does better with you than with her."

After his meeting ended with Lt. Col. Bratton, Father Fortis called Sera and asked her to meet him at a coffee shop just outside the military camp gates. No matter how she reacted, it was his responsibility to tell her the results of his time with Freddie and with the psychiatrist.

They met an hour later, and he saw that Sera looked completely exhausted. He offered a silent prayer that she would take his news as he intended, as the beginning of Freddie's recovery and not a pivotal encounter with Freddie that she missed.

Sera declined his offer to buy her a pastry, saying she wasn't hungry. She would take a water with lemon.

"Do you mind if I have something?" he asked.

She offered a weak smile and shook her head.

He bought two frosted donuts along with a diet soda. When the waitress left, he said, "The diet drink is my little joke."

Sera sighed. "I wish I had your appetite, Nick."

"If you did, you'd be like me, nearly as round as you are tall, my dear."

She rested her hands on the table. "I don't know whether to ask you about Felipe or Freddie."

Father Fortis explained that he would talk to Abbot Peter the next day about Felipe being moved there. "And for Freddie, it's good news, Sera. His psychiatrist thinks he might be starting to come to the surface."He braced himself for an outburst from Sera but was surprised when she seemed to barely react.

After a moment, Sera asked, "How long does the psychiatrist think it'll take for Freddie, you know, to be himself again?"

"She said it's impossible to predict. All the cases like Freddie's she's worked with were different. Some take weeks, some months."He didn't add that Dr. Bratton said others never surfaced.

Sera took a deep breath and exhaled slowly. Resting her head in her hands, she said, "So, it could be long after the trial."

Not knowing what to say, Father Fortis nodded.

The waitress brought their drinks and made a point of saying, "And the diet is for you, as I remember."

Father Fortis smiled. Sera took a sip of her water and rested her head in her hands again.

"I was hoping you'd be relieved with the news." He didn't add that he'd be more comfortable with her anger than her dejected look.

"Confession time, Nick?"

He nodded slowly. "Of course, my dear. Anything you say is safe with me."

She sat back in the booth and looked out the window in the direction of the fort. "I love Freddie, I really do, Nick."

He felt a catch in his throat. "I've never doubted that, my dear."

"He's been a great dad for Felipe and a caring husband. I knew I was one of the lucky ones."

Father Fortis noted the past tense of the verb. "Was" was not what he wanted to hear.

"Freddie isn't gone, Sera, just sick."

"Isn't he—gone, I mean?"

"Worthy and I can't imagine how lonely you must feel, with both Freddie and Felipe locked up."

She nodded slowly. "I sat with Chris over lunch today, and it all came back to me. How he reacted four years ago when I told him I was engaged. I knew we worked well together, but until that moment, I didn't realize he was hoping for more."

Father Fortis sat in silence.

"So, there I was, sitting across a table like this from Chris, and that all came back. And I thought, 'what if Chris and I had gotten together instead of Freddie and me? Where'd we, Felipe and me, be if Chris had become his dad?'"

After a moment, Father Fortis said, "I'd be surprised if that thought didn't cross your mind sometime in the last week, my dear."

"It's hard to unthink something, Nick, and I'm too tired to try."

"It's merely a thought, Sera, a 'what if.' The mind can't help but go there when we're suffering. You're not to blame for thinking it."

"It's just that Chris sometimes has the gift of reading me. I don't want him to know."

"Christopher has changed in the last four years. Even if you told him—and I see no reason you should—he wouldn't take advantage of you. Christopher is a complicated man, but he's a decent man, Sera."

She took another deep breath. "And you're a good priest, Nick. I wasn't sure I could talk about this with anyone, but then I realized you and I never kept secrets from each other."

"Sera, I'm honored that you shared it with me. I can only imagine how tempting it would be to beat yourself up in a time like this."

"My mind keeps thinking someone has to be blamed for all this, and it's easy to settle on me."

Father Fortis felt something stir within him when Sera said that there had to be someone to blame for all that had happened. Then Worthy's words came back to him, that with all that kept happening, he didn't believe in coincidences. So, who then is to blame?

Chapter Twelve

April 4 evening

Back at St. Mary's, Father Fortis skipped the evening service of Compline to take a walk with Worthy. The clouds at dusk were moving like waves across the sky, creating dark shadows on the mountains and the desert floor to the west.

Light and shadow, Father Fortis thought, *like this case.* He let Worthy report first on his meeting with Sera and heard how Worthy's questions about the Army left her more troubled.

"She holding on, Nick, but there's a whole lot more digging we still have to do."

Father Fortis thought back to the exhausted look on Sera's face. "What's our next step?"

"I need to interview the other soldiers from Freddie's unit. We have to find out why Freddie was the only one captured. I wonder who I'll have to beg permission from to do that." Worthy stopped in the middle of the dirt road and looked down at the dust on his shoes. "I've never worked a case where we had to ask permission so much just to do our job. We need permission to talk with Freddie's psychiatrist, permission to talk with Freddie, permission to move Felipe, permission, maybe, for Freddie's fellow soldiers to tell us all they know, and permission for God knows what else. By the time we wade through all the red tape, Freddie will be tried and sentenced."

Father Fortis said nothing until Worthy was finished. He thought again about light and darkness. "I've a bit of good news to share from my time with

Freddie."

"What? Did he sing the National Anthem? Sorry, Nick. It just feels like everyone's handcuffed in this case—Freddie, Felipe, Sera, and now the two of us."

As they walked farther along the road that led away from the monastery, Father Fortis summarized his interview with Freddie.

At the end, Worthy reached down a picked up a stone. He threw it at the last rays of sunlight over the mountain range to the west. "Four years ago, we walked along this very road. That's when we began to crack the case."

"I remember. I thought your theory at the time was completely off-base, but you were just ahead of the rest of us."

"Ahead but still off-base. This time, Nick, I feel like we're lagging way behind. And every time we make a bit of progress on Freddie's case, Felipe's problems come into the picture, and I don't know what I'm looking at."

Father Fortis stopped and looked back at the monastery. "I agree; it's hard to know which of the two cases to focus on."

Worthy tossed another rock, and Father Fortis waited to hear it strike against a boulder. But instead, he heard an animal yelp and scamper away.

"What we know makes no sense, Nick. Freddie is captured and tortured on his last tour in Afghanistan, and when he returns home, the sight of his son freaks him out. So what's the connection?"

The one thing that relieved Father Fortis was seeing his friend so obsessed by the two cases, an obsession that made it unlikely Worthy noticed any strain or awkwardness in Sera's relationship with him. When Worthy worked on the puzzle of a crime, the puzzle worked on him as well.

"Maybe we should just be thankful that we know there *is* a connection between the two cases," Father Fortis said. "The question is, if we keep digging, will we find it?"

"Ordinarily, Nick, I'd say yes. But how certain are we that the Army wants to get to the bottom of this one?"

Father Fortis looked up at the sky and found the evening star. He was familiar with Worthy's tendency to focus with accuracy on the negatives of a case. Sometimes, as in this present moment, that tendency seemed to cloud Worthy's thinking. But at other times, Father Fortis knew, Worthy's negativity preceded one of his breakthroughs. Consequently, he knew better than to try to talk Worthy out of his funk.

"I pray to God you're wrong, Christopher, about the Army. There's no way the two of us—or anyone else for that matter—can take on the U. S. government."

"Then, as much as I hate to say this, it might be better if Freddie stays buried in his head," Worthy said.

The two men turned back and walked silently toward the monastery. The light from the church's windows sent a strong narrow beam in their direction, but Father Fortis was more aware of the darkness he felt all around him and within him. *And Felipe? What happens to him if we don't solve this case?* he thought.

✝

With all the resistance they were experiencing on the case, Worthy suspected the appeal to have Felipe reassigned to St. Mary's would be a tough sell. But in this, he was happily wrong. While it was not surprising that a local judge from the juvenile division would be Hispanic, it was lucky that the judge had twice been on retreat at the isolated monastery. Given the severe beating that Felipe received in detention and given the likelihood that he would likely receive more of the same if sent back, the judge was happy to approve the move, with the stipulations that Felipe be under heavy supervision and the court receive weekly reports of Felipe's progress.

The hospital estimated that Felipe could be released to Worthy and Father Fortis' care in a day or two, which allowed the two of them, in the meantime, to turn their full attention to interviewing Freddie's fellow soldiers.

Worthy suggested they'd make quicker progress if they divided the six names and interview each of them one-on-one. Three lived in and around Albuquerque, one in Santa Fe, another in Laguna Pueblo, and the last in southern Colorado. The murder victim, Ash Burgess, was one of those from the Albuquerque area. The other two from Albuquerque, along with Burgess, were with Freddie at the Milky Way Bar and were therefore of the greatest interest.

Worthy drove from Santa Fe to the car repair shop owned and operated by Cpl. Miguel Rosario's father. The shop, to the west of Albuquerque on Old Route 66, looked as if it might have thirty years before. The cars parked in the lot, none newer than the nineteen-seventies, suggested that classic autos were the shop's specialty.

Worthy was not surprised to find Miguel Rosario working at the shop. Miguel rolled from beneath a mid-sixties Ford Fairlane, his hands and face smeared with grease. When Miguel stood, Worthy realized the man was no taller than five feet six inches, though his muscular arms suggested the soldier would be handy to have on one's side in a fight.

Miguel's father offered the tiny office in the establishment for the meeting. Worthy thought calendars in auto shops with seductive, scantily-clad women were long past, but here he saw a calendar sporting a woman lying on the hood of a convertible. Miguel nodded in the direction of one of the chairs for Worthy while he took one of the other two metal chairs in the tiny office.

After Worthy showed him his credentials, Miguel said, "I don't know if I'm supposed to talk to you, being that I'm a witness for the prosecution, but I'm one of those who believe Sarge should be treated fair and square. So I'll help you if I can."

"I appreciate that, Cpl. Rosario."

"Call me Miguel."

"Okay, Miguel. Let me start with some questions about your relationship with Sgt. Contreras. How long have the two of you served in the same unit?"

"I was assigned to the unit about two years ago. Sgt. Contreras was already in charge of the unit, so he'd been on at least one previous tour."

"And your duties?"

Miguel Rosario raised his greasy hands for Worthy to see. "I'd describe my role as half-time mechanic for anything that would break down—which was a lot—and half-time guard."

"Guarding whom?"

"Those we captured—Taliban, occasionally Al-Qaeda."

"And what was Sgt. Contreras' role?"

"Chief interrogator. He was really good at his job, by the way."

"How do you mean?" Worthy asked.

"He wasn't one of those gung-ho guys who liked to use what we called 'enhanced techniques.' Without being too specific, he might use sleep deprivation, but not some of the other methods. I better leave it at that."

"Did you notice anything unusual about Sgt. Contreras before the day he was captured?"

Miguel Rosario continued to wipe his hands. "It was a pretty tense job, I'll say that. But we all looked up to Sarge. He'd done the work so long that he was always cool."

Worthy wasn't surprised by anything he'd heard so far but knew the tougher questions were yet to come.

Miguel continued to wipe his hands on a rag. "I suspect you want to know about his capture."

"Yes, I do."

"We were in a village near Taliban-controlled parts of Kandahar Province. I guess you could call it a gray zone. Anyway, an infantry unit had picked up one of the warlords who might or might not have been friendly. They called us in to make an assessment, and Sarge realized he knew the head guy—the warlord. Anyway, we weren't in the powwow more than twenty minutes before mortar rounds were lobbed in. Following that, from what we heard later, a force of maybe twenty or twenty-five of the enemy stormed the perimeter. That's when all hell broke loose."

Miguel related this calmly, and Worthy suspected it was an account he gave several times before to the Army. Worthy didn't say anything but waited for the corporal to continue.

"There was a couple of the infantry guys on one quadrant of the camp, and they were the first to be hit. Again, remember we were told all this later. Okay, so remember we're in an interior room, and none of us knows exactly what's coming down until the fighting breaks into where we are. When the dust finally settled, all we knew for sure is that Sarge is gone. Most of the unit was busy repelling the assault on our side of the compound, but Sarge and Ash headed to the other side where others were taking fire."

"When it was discovered that Sgt. Contreras was missing, was a search party sent out?" Worthy asked.

Miguel Rosario shifted his weight in his chair. "Remember, it was about eight or nine long minutes of close-quarter action before it all ended. That's when we heard Sarge was captured. By then...well, by then, it was just too late and too risky to send anyone out. We didn't know how close the enemy was, and there was a chance they'd come back with even more force. I remember we got orders pretty quick to withdraw immediately from the area. War's a mess, lieutenant."

Worthy nodded. Nothing in Rosario's account contradicted the Army's official report.

"What happened to the warlord?"

Miguel shifted in his chair again, his eyes returning to the rag. "What?"

"You said you went there to interrogate a warlord. What happened to him and those with him in the firefight?"

"Oh, I see what you're asking. They all ran toward the insurgents, but the Taliban took them all out."

"In the end, what side did you think the warlord was on?"

"Hell, we never knew. The Taliban could have killed their own. They're butchers. End of story."And as Rosario said that, he tossed the greasy rag on the desk.

Worthy paused for a moment, knowing that was only the end of the first part of the story. "When did your unit return stateside?"

"About six weeks ago."

"When did you hear that Sgt. Contreras escaped and was back?"

Miguel nodded, folding his arms across his chest. "The Army never told us, but we heard about it once he was in the Army hospital."

Although Worthy knew the answer to the question, he wanted to gauge Rosario's response. "How many times did you see him after you all got back?"

"Just the once, the night we met up with our girlfriends or wives at the bar. You know, a reunion."

"The Milky War Bar, right, the night of the murder?"

Miguel nodded.

"You said you were there with your girlfriends or wives. Was Sgt. Contreras' wife with him?"

"No, just Sarge. Burgess came alone, too."

"Did Sgt. Contreras say why he was alone?"

Miguel shook his head. "Sarge wasn't saying anything."

All the questions to this point led to those Worthy thought most crucial to the case. "Besides being quiet, how did Sgt. Contreras look and act that night."

"Geez, I hardly recognized him. He must have lost forty pounds. And there was something in his eyes. It's hard to describe, but his eyes weren't focusing on anything. And when you asked him something, there was this kind of delay before he looked at you."

"And he said nothing?"

"You mean like 'happy to see you guys?'Or, 'can I buy a round?'No, I don't remember him saying anything. But I think he mumbled something at one point across the table to Burgess."

Worthy jotted down a note. "So, tell me about Burgess."

"Ash was Ash. What I mean is, he was a real joker, always teasing. He thought a lot of things were funny that weren't. I don't mean to speak ill of the dead, but I guess I am."

"Can you give an example?"

"Well, that's hard. It wasn't like he told jokes. What was funny to him was goofs or mistakes of others. Like once I tipped over my beer, spilled it all down my pants. Not uncommon, right? From then on, I was 'beer nuts.'"

"How did he treat Sgt. Contreras in Afghanistan? Did he ever push his buttons?"

Miguel Rosario shook his head. "Ash was new to the unit, his first tour. Like the rest of us, he looked up to Sarge."

"What about the night at the bar?"

Miguel's raised eyebrows were all that Worthy needed to know he'd struck a nerve.

"Ash was sitting across from Sarge. I think Ash found the shape Sarge was in as kind of funny. When Sarge didn't seem to understand a question directed to him, I could see that Ash thought this was comical."

"You said earlier that Sgt. Contreras at one point leaned over and said something to Burgess. Any idea what that was?"

Miguel shook his head again. "No. The music was cranked up pretty high, and Sarge's voice was more like a raspy whisper. I guess Burgess understood, but, well..."

"How long was that before the two of them went outside?"

"Hmm. I don't know if I remember exactly, but I remember Ash saying,

'I'm going to take my sergeant out for a smoke.' Sarge seemed okay with that, so that's when the two of them left the booth."

"Just one more question. How long was it before you heard there was a fight outside?"

"I guess it was about ten minutes later when someone came in and yelled for the bartender to call an ambulance. We all went outside, and there was Ash lying in the parking lot face down."

"Did you see Sgt. Contreras at that point?"

"Nope, he wasn't there." Miguel paused for a moment before catching Worthy's eye. "It looks bad for Sarge, doesn't it? I mean, I'm sure going to say he looked out of it; you know, really fucked up in the head."

"Did you notice if Sgt. Contreras or Burgess had a knife with them that night?"

Miguel shook his head. "I didn't notice, but I guess one of them did."

Worthy closed his notebook.

"I'd like to ask you a question," Miguel said.

"Sure."

"I mean, what happens to Sarge if the Army finds him...you know, insane?"

"As far as I know, Freddie will be sent to a military penal institution with a psychiatric ward."

"Freddie? I didn't know that's his name." Miguel sat forward, his elbows on his knees. "For how long will he be in one of those places? I mean, I don't think he knew what he was doing. He just reacted the way we were trained. You know, hand-to-hand shit."

"It will be up to the military court to decide what to do with him if he recovers."

"Life's sure not fair. Ash was an asshole at times, but, well, he must have taken his teasing too far. And like I said, I don't think Sarge knew what he was doing."

"And no one else in your group left the bar after Burgess and Sgt. Contreras left?"

"Not that I remember. I'm sure others from the bar left, but from our group, it was just the two of them."

"So you don't think it's possible that someone other than Sgt. Contreras killed Burgess?" Worthy asked, even though Miguel Rosario had already implied an answer.

"What? Do the police think someone else killed Ash?"

"I'm not saying that. I'm just asking your opinion."

Miguel looked down at his hands. "I wish I could say 'yes,' but in all honesty, it has to be Sarge who did it. He probably couldn't help it, the shape he was in, but I think the Army has it right."

Chapter Thirteen

April 5

The next morning, Father Fortis received a different perspective on Freddie's unit from one of its African-American members, DeShan Durbin. Sgt. Durbin returned to his stateside job of after-school coordinator of recreation at a Boys and Girls Club, which is where Father Fortis found him. To Father Fortis, the man fit what they used to call "basketball tall" in Baltimore where he grew up, and the polo shirt tight to the man's biceps testified that Durbin was at least physically well-suited to his role.

The walls of Durbin's concrete-block office sported photos of grade-school basketball and volleyball teams. There was also what appeared to be a studio photo of two younger boys along with Durbin and a smiling woman next to him.

From information given to them by Sera, Father Fortis knew that Sgt. Durbin was the IT and communication specialist of her husband's unit, the one who kept the unit in contact with off-site command centers in Kandahar Province. Worthy shared Miguel Rosario's impressions of the unit from the previous day, and Father Fortis was eager to hear Sgt. Durbin's version of the firefight and the reunion back in Albuquerque.

"I've been on three tours with Sarge, and I'm damn tired of having my life disrupted just because we're good at what we do. Everyone hears all that bunk about employers being supportive and saving vets' jobs back home, but let me tell you, most of the bosses I've had never got the message. For them, we're taking a vacation."

Father Fortis glanced up at the family photo, acknowledging the one great difference between military service and monastic life. "I imagine the tours are hard on the families as well."

DeShan Durbin picked up a pencil on the desk, only to toss it away. "I've heard the divorce rate is three times as high as for civilians. When I come off the plane, my wife doesn't look like she's happy to see me. She looks like she hates me."

Father Fortis realized he had to do something to shift the conversation away from the man's negativity. "I'd like to talk with you about the unit."

"We're not allowed to say much about our work," Durbin warned.

"Actually, I have a pretty good idea of your roles. I'm more interested in knowing more about the guys in your unit. Can you describe Burgess?"

DeShan Durbin looked up at the ceiling. "Ash was new to the unit, just joined us this last time. I got his sense of humor, so I guess I was one of those who liked him, liked to be around him. He kept things...well, not exactly loose, but kind of alert."

"It sounds like others didn't feel the same about him."

"You're right there. Ash could fillet you with his sarcasm. But I'm black in a white man's world and a white man's Army, no matter what they say. So I enjoyed watching him getting under other guys' skins, especially white skin."

"How did Burgess and Sgt. Contreras get along?"

"Sarge treated everyone the same, which means he expected a lot from everyone. Maybe he expected too much."

"What do you mean?" Father Fortis asked.

Durbin shook his head. "We worked damn hard, and some of the work—without my going into details—is totally exhausting. We could work for days straight. But when we got done with an assignment, Sarge packed things up and acted like it was just another day at the office. The guy might say a quick 'good job,' but that was about it."

It struck Father Fortis that Sgt. Durbin would have been next in command after Freddie was captured. Had he resented the unit's leader more than the others?

"Were you surprised when Sgt. Contreras showed up at the bar for the reunion?"

With a small laugh, Durbin said, "The guy who had a beer with us that night was not Sarge, if you know what I mean. He was wasted, numb from head to toe. My wife said, 'whatever the Taliban did, they fried his brain.'"

"How did Sgt. Contreras get to the reunion?"

"Hell, that's a good question. Oh, wait, Rosario picked him up. It would be Rosario," he said with a grunt.

"That night at the bar, did you notice anything out of the ordinary between Burgess and Sgt. Contreras?"

"I'm saying everything was out of the ordinary. It was a mistake to bring Sarge there, that's for damned sure."

"But nothing between the two of them in the bar?"

Durbin shook his head. "Before Sarge and Rosario showed up, Burgess called Sarge 'broccoli'—you know, like the vegetable? We had a laugh about that, but even Ash wouldn't go that far once Sarge got there."

"It must have been awkward, Sgt. Contreras being the shape he was in."

"I could see it freaked out the ladies. I thought maybe that was why Ash took Sarge out for a breath of fresh air."

"Not for a smoke?"

Again, Durbin shook his head. "Nope, Sarge didn't smoke."

Father Fortis thought it time to repeat some questions Worthy had asked. "And no one else left the booth after the two of them went outside?"

Durbin stared at Father Fortis. "How'd you know we were in a booth?"

"I just assumed you were, based on the few bars I've seen of late."

"Huh," Durbin said, although he didn't look like he believed him. "What did you ask me?"

"If anyone left the booth after Sgt. Contreras and Burgess went outside."

"Oh, yeah, right. No, we were all inside until some guy came in and started shouting about a guy bleeding out in the parking lot."

"Is that when you all went outside?"

"Yup. Not before."

"Do you think it possible somebody other than Sgt. Contreras killed Pvt. Burgess?"

Shaking his head, Durbin said, "Not unless you believe in Afghan ghosts."

Father Fortis thought there was something strange in Durbin's tone of voice, as if he wished he hadn't said that last remark, but Father Fortis didn't ask for clarification.

"Is it your opinion that Sgt. Contreras, numb as you say from head to toe and forty pounds lighter than back in Afghanistan, overpowered Burgess and stabbed him repeatedly?"

"That's what I'm going to say at the trial. Must be what happened. Maybe Sarge had a flashback and thought he was back in Afghanistan. The guy's a psycho, right? People tell me that's what'll get him off."

The callousness of the comment, indeed, the callousness of Durbin's attitude throughout the entire interview bothered Father Fortis. But he understood why Durbin and Burgess got along.

"Well, people tell me," Father Fortis said, not sparing the sharp edge in his voice, "that he'll be incarcerated in a prison with a psychiatric facility."

"But he won't be executed; that's what I mean. Three square meals a day, ping-pong and finger painting—how bad is that?"

That same morning, as the car bumped its way down the unpaved road to St. Mary of the Snows, Felipe pondered his situation. "You always have options"—that was his Dad's advice to him. "When you feel stuck—and at some point you will—don't panic. You always have options."

The memory of Freddie giving him advice hurt Felipe far more than his injuries did. When his Dad came home the last time, he looked like a man who'd run out of options. And Felipe sensed, rather than knew, that he wasn't told the whole truth.

So what are my options? Felipe thought, as he looked around at the desolate canyons and mesas. The safest plan would be to take his punishment and stay put in the monastery. But the thought of being surrounded by old monks praying for his soul nauseated him.

Escape would be another option. He expected there'd be a fence at the monastery, and he figured they couldn't watch him all the time. But any escape would demand planning and would also need help from outside.

"God damn it," the driver, his probation officer, said as the SUV bottomed out on the road.

Not hard to read his thoughts. He thinks my Mom pulled some strings and I'm putting one over on the system. Maybe I am, he thought.

He pictured the three guys he got into trouble with over the last two weeks. They turned on him immediately when the four were picked up for the assault on the homeless guy. There would be no help from them. And where would he escape to, anyway? If he left the state, they would still put a warrant out for him. Mexico was a possibility, but he didn't like his chances of surviving there without a contact.

The third option, requesting to be sent back to detention in Santa Fe, was risky in its own way. Although Felipe hadn't said anything, he knew Lt. Worthy was right in saying his beating was permitted, if not instigated, by someone in authority. He felt a strong urge for revenge on those who attacked him in the shower room. But he knew any chance of revenge would be far off in the future.

With each pothole, each blind curve, Felipe felt the chance of escape growing fainter. He remembered his "life before" as a fading dream. Was this what it meant to become an adult—to lose all hope, to face life looking back with regret after regret?

Finally, the county car drew to a halt. The probation officer grunted something about finding who was in charge and walked toward a low adobe building. Felipe was left alone, and despite all reason, he felt an urge to run back down the rutted road. Instead, he stepped from the vehicle and looked with curiosity around him.

What first impressed him was a tall building, pointed at the roof, constructed mainly of windows. With the cross on the top of a steeple, he assumed the building was a church. Next to it was an adobe wall with a carved cedar door bearing another cross. Above the door were the words "Monastic enclosure—closed to the public."

Other buildings, detached from the chapel, were also made of adobe. But what gradually drew his attention was the sound of the river from farther down in the valley behind some planted vines. *Could there be a boat down there?* he wondered.

Vying with an urge to escape was an awareness that he would be safe here. He wouldn't have to keep looking over his shoulder at every turn. Pecking around on the ground or flying overhead was a variety of birds—blue jays, crows, and hawks—who seemed unconcerned with his presence. He wondered if the birds were tame, but then thought that maybe this was how animals acted when they knew there was nothing to fear.

The next thing he noticed was the absence of antennae or dishes on the roofs of the buildings. *Oh, great. God, I hope they have a library. And I hope they have books beside Bibles.*

From an open doorway in one of the side buildings, the probation officer came out and signaled for Felipe to approach. Grabbing his duffle bag, he thought, *Here goes nothing.*

Chapter Fourteen

April 5

Father Fortis closed his phone and considered the invitation. Lt. Col. Bratton, Freddie's psychiatrist, had asked him to come by her office after four o'clock that afternoon. "Just you," the psychiatrist said.

He was grateful that Worthy didn't take offense at the invitation and even agreed to drive him to the army hospital in Albuquerque.

"I'm betting it has something to do with how you got through to Freddie," Worthy said.

And after the hour drive from the monastery and a half-hour wait in the prison hospital's reception area, Father Fortis discovered Worthy's guess was right.

"Sgt. Contreras seems to be slowly waking up," Dr. Bratton said, her hands forming a tent beneath her chin as she sat behind her desk. "His eyes are following the light, at least to some degree. His blood pressure and respiration are also a bit elevated, which is good news. But he hasn't said anything else."

"Is it possible to predict how long this waking up could take?" Father Fortis asked.

"Not really. It's easier to track a catatonic's physical progress than his mental. But mind and body are related. That's why I asked to see you."

Father Fortis nodded. "Let me know how I can help."

"Good. I'd like you to meet with Sgt. Contreras again."

Father Fortis thought for a moment. "I'm at your disposal, but is there something you want me to say to him or not say to him?"

Dr. Bratton opened a folder in front of her and removed a sheet of paper. She handed it across the desk to Father Fortis.

"We want to identify trigger words. From your time with him yesterday, we know that mentioning Felipe or Felipe's present situation functioned in that way. Now we want to try a list of other words or phrases."

Looking down at the paper, Father Fortis saw a list of words. *America, New Mexico,* and *Santa Fe* were at the top, followed by *Army, soldier, Afghanistan, Taliban, Kandahar Province.* Below that he read *Sera, wife, love, home, Felipe, fishing* and ending with the single work *safe.*

"How do I do this, Doctor? Do I just read the words one after another?"

"No, it's better if you slip those words into normal conversation, though we don't expect Sgt. Contreras to be an active part of that conversation. We're just looking for reactions. It's not a test."

"But it is," Father Fortis said.

Lt. Col. Bratton nodded and said, "Okay, it is, in a way," she said as she stood and walked over to the window. A small cactus on the sill seemed to draw her attention. With her back to Father Fortis, she said, "Before you agree to this, Father, you need to know we're taking a risk. In fact, I would call it a dangerous risk."

"Oh?" Father Fortis said.

"I'm doing this in my role and on my authority as Mr. Contreras' psychiatrist."

Puzzled by what Father Fortis thought was obvious, he said, "I don't understand."

She turned back to Father Fortis but stayed by the window. Father Fortis felt that she was studying him closely.

"I'm not sure Captain Mills, Mr. Contreras' defense attorney, would sanction what I'm asking of you. You see, Father, if you do have some connection with Mr. Contreras, it's possible that his recovery will be speeded up by your visiting him. Now do you see?"

Father Fortis shook his head. "Sorry, I still don't follow."

"To put it bluntly, his defense attorney will have a much better chance securing an insanity plea if Freddie Contreras sits in that courtroom in the shape he's in right now. But if, in the two weeks we have before trial, Mr. Contreras gains a greater hold on reality, the defense will have a harder time portraying him as insane. Put in laymen's terms, Mr. Contreras, with your help, might not look crazy by trial time."

"So what are you asking of me?"

"That you are willing to live with the consequences of whatever happens in the next few visits with Sgt. Contreras. You see, it's my job as a psychiatrist to help my patients recover mental health. On the other hand, a defense attorney's job is to give a client the best defense possible."

Father Fortis sat silently, fingering the pectoral cross hanging from his neck.

"Do you understand the predicament now, Father? My job and the defense attorney's job could be in conflict here."

"Yes, I see that," Father Fortis said slowly.

"Good, then that leaves you with a decision. Helping me, you could be hurting Mr. Contreras' chances at trial. Choosing not to help me will slow Mr. Contreras' recovery, but he'll likely receive an insanity verdict. Given that you're going to have to live with the outcome, what will you choose?"

Oh, God, how do I answer that? Father Fortis prayed, the cross in his hand feeling hot, as if it could burn him.

THAT SAME AFTERNOON, SERA LACEY KNOCKED at the door of the sprawling ranch-style home of the Reverend Daniel Frost and his family. Next door were the massive parking lot and arena-size facility known locally and through its TV and radio ministries sent throughout the world as Bountiful Blessings Bible Church, or the Triple B Church.

A young man of apparent college age answered the door. His hair was cut short, making him look like a younger version of the bald-headed image of Pastor Frost seen on billboards.

"I phoned earlier," Sera explained as she showed the young man her credentials.

"Yes, we're expecting you. By the way, I'm Danny, or Junior," the young man explained in a firm voice before leading her into a sizeable family room. Above the fireplace was a painting that Sera thought she recognized, Jesus standing with a lantern in his hand and knocking on a closed door. Rev. Daniel Frost, looking much as he did on the highway billboards, rose from a leather chair to shake her hand, while a woman whom the pastor introduced as his wife, Naomi, sat next to a young teenaged girl. Each woman's hair was pulled back into a bun. Only the miniature collie, tail wagging as she sniffed at Sera's shoes, seemed happy with Sera's visit.

While Sera shared her sympathy for the family's anxiety and promised the department would do everything it could to find Noah, the four said nothing, the two men nodding, while the mother and daughter looked down at their laps. But after an awkward moment of silence, Mrs. Frost looked up and noted that Sera was still standing. She gestured for Sera to take the other easy chair in the room. Daniel Jr. stood behind the couch, his hand on his mother's shoulder.

"I understand that Noah is the middle child," Sera began.

Rev. Frost replied in a voice a bit too forceful for the size of the room as he nodded to the young man positioned behind the couch. "Daniel Jr. is a sophomore at Oral Roberts University, and Leah is in eighth grade. Noah... Noah is a senior in our high school. Yes, he's only fifteen, but he skipped two grades."

As I assumed, Sera thought. *Noah is either very smart, or he's been pushed.*

"In the last month or so, have you noticed anything different about Noah? Has he seemed more worried or preoccupied?"

Rev. Frost was again the first to speak. "No, that's what makes this so difficult to understand."

Sera looked at the other family members. "Anyone else notice something?"

Daniel Jr. spoke next. "I was home from college about a month ago. Noah seemed the same as always."

"And how was that? How would you describe your brother?"

Daniel Jr. shrugged. "Noah is the quiet one, I guess. He's good in school."

Still addressing the brother, Sera asked, "How about friends?"

The older son yielded the floor to his father. "Noah's best friend is Pedro Morales. Pedro's father is on our ministry staff at Bountiful Blessing. The two boys have grown up together."

"Okay, we'll obviously interview Pedro. How about girls? Does he have a special one?"

"No, no, he's far too young for that," Rev. Frost answered, as if Sera had asked something indelicate if not slightly obscene.

A lot of kids Noah's age are doing a lot more than dating, Sera thought. "And you said Noah attends the church's high school, is that right?"

"Yes. He's been in our program from kindergarten," the father said.

Sera turned her gaze to the mother and sister who so far had said nothing. "Leah, is it?" she asked.

The young girl looked up and nodded.

"Did you notice anything unusual about your brother over the last month or so?"

Leah looked first to her father and then to her mother. The mother nodded. "He took longer on his paper route," the girl said. "When I asked him why, he said I was wrong. But I'm not."

Sera considered the bit of information. "Does your brother have a morning route or an afternoon one?"

"Afternoon."

"And how long does it usually take Noah to do his route?"

"He's back about when 'Pinky and the Brain' comes on. They're repeats."

"I'm familiar with the program. Lately, though, Noah was taking longer?"

"He's never home before the show's over. We always watched it together."

"Maybe he's got more customers," her older brother said.

Leah blushed and looked back at her brother as if she'd been reproved. "Maybe," she said slowly, but Sera didn't think she believed that.

"Mrs. Frost, what can you tell me about Noah?"

Mrs. Frost glanced at her daughter rather than at her husband. "Just what Daniel Jr. said. Noah is a bright boy. He does well in school. Always has."

"What are Noah's plans for the future?"

Rev. Frost cleared his throat before answering. "Noah will attend Oral Roberts, just like his brother. Both Daniel Jr. and Noah have experienced a call to ministry. It's my prayer...our family's prayer that the two of them will take over here at Bountiful Blessings."

The atmosphere in the room shifted with the father's comment. Sera looked at the older son and saw his jaw set, while Mrs. Frost was again looking at her hands in her lap. The collie whimpered a bit and padded from the room. Sera took the chance to probe at bit. "How certain is Noah about that?"

Sera selected Leah's face as the barometer in the room. Leah clenched her hands tightly and shifted closer to her mother.

Rev. Frost's voice was louder as he replied, "Noah made his decision last summer at church camp."No one added to the father's answer.

"What did he want to be before last summer?"

Mrs. Frost looked up sharply at Sera, and Sera wondered if she'd closed down the family or provided an opening. Finally, Noah's mother replied, "He wanted to work out of doors, in nature. But then, as my husband said, he received his calling."

Silence returned to the room. "The call to ministry isn't an easy one, is it, Daniel?" the father finally replied.

"Harder for some than for others," Daniel Jr. said, and Sera felt that the decision for the older son wasn't hard.

She made a note, taking an extra few seconds to write "Noah's future" with a question mark beside it. Although she suspected she knew the answer to any query about drugs, she also knew she had to broach the subject. "So, let me ask this another way. Was Noah under any unusual pressure recently?"

Rev. Frost and his wife answered at the same moment, but their answers were far apart. A firm "no" from the father was not able to drown out a "well, yes," from the mother. Sera ignored Rev. Frost and turned her attention to Noah's mother.

"Please, Mrs. Frost, what did you notice?"

Mrs. Frost didn't look up. Sera understood that if the mother did, she would make eye contact with her husband. "He told me he was nervous about the Bible quiz."

"The Bible quiz?"

Daniel Jr. answered before his mother could reply. "It's for a scholarship to Oral Roberts. It's a national competition, but we're in the West regional."

"Daniel won the regional scholarship two years ago, and placed third in the nationals," Rev. Frost said. Sera waited a moment, to see if it would dawn on the father how mistimed was his expression of pride in his older son. She saw the man's face redden before he said, "If Noah was worried about the contest, he never said anything to me."

"I quizzed Noah the last time I was home. He has nothing to worry about," Daniel offered. "He knows God's Word backwards and forwards."

To Sera, the tone of the two men was identical, as if saying "Case closed. Go on to something else."

Mrs. Frost's voice was so subdued that Sera had to lean forward in the chair. "I don't think it was the contest so much as the TV interview."

"But that's a coup," Rev. Frost protested.

"What do you mean, Reverend?"

"KOKC heard about my two sons qualifying in the competition, about Daniel's winning the regionals two years ago and about Noah being favored this year at the nationals. The station wanted to interview both of them."

Sera thought about the photo of Noah in the file, his eyes squinting shyly into the sun. Noah, the younger son, the one described as quiet, the one who perhaps preferred to be out in nature than in the church. Was he always in the shadow of his brother?

"Mrs. Frost, what did Noah say about the TV interview."

The mother waited so long to answer that Sera thought she might beg off answering the question. But then, Leah reached over and squeezed her mother's hand.

Mrs. Frost looked up with a weary face. "I don't know if it was anything Noah said. I just felt that my son...our son isn't as comfortable as Daniel Jr. with the spotlight. He takes after my side of the family, I guess."

"Naomi, the interview is a coup," her husband repeated. Turning toward Sera, the minister asked, "Lieutenant, are you Roman?"

"Are you asking me if I'm Catholic?" Sera replied, initially confused by the question. Rev. Frost had emphasized the word "Roman" as if it were a disease. "How is that relevant?" Sera asked.

"Then I assume you are. Bountiful Blessings ministries is a beacon of light in New Mexico."

Which makes Catholicism what—surrounding darkness? Sera thought.

You have to understand, we're a Christian alternative in this state. But we're still a minority, even though we're growing rapidly."

Sera waited for the "Praise the Lord" she'd heard from TV evangelicals before, but none followed from Rev. Frost.

"So you see, Lieutenant," Daniel Jr. added, "the TV interview would draw attention to Bountiful Blessings and what we're about."

Sera noted the "we're." Daniel Jr. obviously counted himself as already part of the program.

"Frankly, Lieutenant," Rev. Frost said dryly, "I'm beginning to sense something off-base in these questions. They suggest there's something in our family that caused Noah to run away. Noah never ran away before. None of our children have."

Mrs. Frost flinched, as if she were the true target of the complaint. *Maybe she is,* Sera thought.

"Rev. Frost, this is not my first missing teenager case. The questions that I'm asking are quite standard, I can assure you. We need to establish the pressures that any teen who runs away was experiencing."

"We believe Noah was lured away by someone," Rev. Frost pressed on. "Are you even considering that possibility?"

Sera thought it likely that this was not the Reverend's main worry. This was his preference, his hope.

"Has Noah talked about someone he's met recently?"

The room was silent. Sera moved her gaze from one face to another. Slowly, they all shook their heads.

"Was Noah part of any group, outside of school and church, I mean?"

Another moment of silence before Rev. Frost answered, "Just his paper route, I believe."

Sera considered the answer. She would understand if Noah hadn't told his family of a relationship outside the tight family circle, someone maybe on his paper route, his one link to life in Santa Fe outside of Bountiful Blessing Bible Church.

As Sera left the Frost home, she heard Rev. Frost's last words to her at the door. "If you can keep this out of the press, we'd much appreciate it."As she drove off, she realized that, for nearly an hour, she'd focused on someone other than Freddie or Felipe. If Captain Cortini would consider this a victory, why then did she feel guilty?

Chapter Fifteen

April 6

Worthy awoke the next morning with a change of plans. With Rosario and Durbin already interviewed by Father Fortis or himself, three names remained. Two who'd been at the reunion party hadn't yet been interviewed, while the final member of the unit, Pvt. Padilla, wasn't present at the Milky War Bar.

But Worthy was curious about another name, a name not on the list of soldiers but still a name in the file. Sally Fremont was Burgess' ex-wife, who dropped her married name after the divorce. And, she lived in Santa Fe.

He found her name and number online and decided to start with her, sensing that unless their divorce had been unusual, Sally Fremont would respond candidly to questions about her ex.

Sally Fremont answered the phone and, hearing Worthy's request, agreed to meet him at a coffee shop in the center of Old Santa Fe near the cathedral at eleven a.m. Worthy arrived early, not certain how difficult parking would be in the touristy area. He sat at a table outside and looked across the square at the massive church. He was surprised to see a building that looked alien to its surroundings, made of stone, not adobe, and gothic in design. The influence of someone in the past had superimposed northern European design on the otherwise Hispanic square.

A blond woman in her late twenties, in jeans and a top that looked expensive, approached his table and introduced herself as Sally Fremont. Worthy stood to shake her hand and then gestured to the other seat.

"What can I get you to drink?" Worthy asked.

"I won't say no to a chai latte. Thanks," she said.

When Worthy returned to the table with the drinks, he pondered how to begin the conversation. Sally Fremont solved the issue for him by saying, "Please don't feel that you have to express condolences for Ash's death. We didn't have an amicable divorce."

"How long have you been divorced?" Worthy asked.

"Just over a year. It would be longer, but his mother dragged it out."

"She's a lawyer, right?"

"That's a nice word for it. She stalled everything just out of spite. She thought I was trying to get money out of Ash. But I think she knew I just wanted to be free of him."

"Tell me about your ex-husband."

Sally Fremont took a sip of the tea and looked at the cathedral in the distance. "Ash could be a real charmer. He charmed my family, and I suppose he charmed me. Do you know the Janus figure, Lieutenant?"

"The god with the two faces?"

"That was Ash. I don't mean he was a god, but he was two persons, and they weren't alike at all. Even some of my best friends from college thought I was crazy when I told them about the 'other Ash,'" she said, making quotation marks with a gesture. "That was before we were even engaged, so I have no one to blame but myself. But the happy Ash was just so damned fun to be with."

"So, tell me about this dark Ash."

"He never hit me, if that's what you're thinking. I thought he was about to once, but I told him I'd walk out if he ever did. But he could hurt me worse than any punch with his words."As she looked at Worthy, he could tell the pain was still fresh. "I've never met anyone who could push me—yes, it felt just like he was literally pushing me. It's hard to explain."

"Maybe like his lawyer mother?"

Sally's eyebrow shot up. "You can say that again. But he had his Dad's charm, so I guess I thought I could bring out that part of him. Sometimes, I thought I did, but then it would be like a light switch, and, well...it wasn't pretty."

"I take it the marriage ended before he went into the Army," Worthy said.

Sally nodded. Worthy could see the beginnings of frown lines on what was still a stunning face. Mementos of feeling pushed around by her ex?

"I was surprised when I heard he enlisted. It wasn't like he was unpatriotic, but I wouldn't describe him as rah-rah, pro-America, either. But Ash was always working some angle, and I couldn't figure out what that was with the Army."

"Would you be surprised," Worthy said, "if I told you that Ash was written up in boot camp for breaking another soldier's arm?"

Sally sat wide-eyed. "Really? He actually hit someone?"

"More like he twisted the other guy's arm until it broke."

Wincing, Sally shook her head. "I wonder if he ever thought of doing that to me."

Worthy let the question hang in the air before asking, "You said that Ash was always working some angle. How do you think he'd do having someone in authority over him?"

"I take it you mean the sergeant who's charged with killing him."

"Or practically anyone, since your ex was a private on his first tour of duty."

Sally sat quietly for a few moments before Worthy saw the tears. "Sorry," she said. "I couldn't stay married to Ash, but that doesn't mean I didn't love him."

Worthy didn't intrude on her grief.

"Some people, you know...you hear they died, and even if they were young, you think, 'Okay, they're the type to die.' But Ash was like a meteor, this flash of something. Energy, maybe. It's hard to believe he's really gone."

She pulled a tissue out of her purse and quietly blew her nose. "Did you ever see the film *The Talented Mr. Ripley*?"

"With Matt Damon?"

Sally nodded. "After my divorce, my brother sent me the DVD. I guess twins sometimes know each other pretty well, because my brother thought I'd see Ash in the Ripley character." She dabbed at her eyes. "My brother was right. A charmer always looking out for himself—no holds barred."

"When you read what the police believe happened that last night at the bar, what did you think?"

"Oh," she replied, shaking her head. "I was gut-punched. I felt guilty, and I guess I still do."

"Why? You couldn't have done anything to prevent it, could you?"

"That's just it. Could I have done something? If Ash and I were still together, I'd have probably been with him and the others that night. Maybe I'd have sensed that he went too far with the other guy."

"That's what you think—that Ash went too far?"

Sally nodded. "I'd bet money on it. And if the other guy felt he was being pushed around, and if he was wacky enough—which I gather from the papers he is—then I'm almost positive that's what happened. Ash finally met someone who wasn't going to take it."

✝

After the interview with Sally Fremont, Worthy drove across town to meet up with Father Fortis, who spent the morning paying his respects to the Orthodox priest of the city. The two found a park along a stream bisecting Santa Fe, where Worthy summarized his interview with Burgess' ex-wife.

"I'm curious, Christopher, why you interviewed her before the other two soldiers in the unit."

"Just a hunch, Nick, but I'm glad I did it. His unit seems split on Burgess—was he stirring things up all the time in Afghanistan or keeping things light?"

You don't think the ex-wife was biased against him?"

"That's not how she came across to me. I think she saw him clearly. Maybe she's the only one who did."

"Hmm. So this is part of your getting to know the victim, right?"

"I guess so. You know how unpopular I can be when I say that the victim might have invited his own death, might have opened the door to his killer, so to speak. That's why I don't share that theory with too many people."

"But it's different in this case, isn't it? The police and military think they know who killed Burgess," Father Fortis said.

"And they think they know why. But we both know they're not always right." The two waited for a couple walking a dog to pass before continuing. "She called her ex 'Janus,'" Worthy said.

"Janus? Isn't that the myth about the two-faced god?"

"Yep. Burgess could be charming, and he could be a bully. We know for a fact that Freddie and Burgess were fighting in the parking lot, but I think a guy like Burgess had more than one person tired of his lip."

"Someone else in the parking lot? If so, that would explain why Freddie didn't know about the knife and why it was never found," Father Fortis added.

"But the unit members we've interviewed said no one else left the table. It's hard to imagine a stranger just happened to walk by and knife Burgess." The two sat in silence, as if they'd reached a dead end, before Father Fortis said, "Which brings me to my news—actually, to my decision."

"Oh?"

"I'm struggling with something Dr. Bratton asked me."

"Let me guess. If Freddie gets better, his lawyer will have a harder time getting him off with an insanity plea," Worthy said.

"There you have it, my friend. Freddie not remembering about the knife will be interpreted by the court as a convenient lie."

"So, Nick. If someone else knifed Burgess in the parking lot after Freddie wandered off, we're going to have to discover who that is, and discover that before the trial."

Chapter Sixteen

April 7

Father Fortis sat nervously beside Lt. Col. Bratton as the two waited for Freddie to be brought into the interview room. *Will he look different,* Father Fortis wondered? *Do I want him to look different?*

Although handcuffed as before, Freddie was escorted into the interview room by only one guard. The guard was no longer dragging Freddie as much as guiding a man now capable of walking on his own. But Freddie's gaze still looked unfocused as he was seated and handcuffed to the ring on the table.

"Good afternoon, Sergeant," Lt. Col. Bratton said.

There was no response from Freddie, though his eyes wandered around the room. The psychiatrist made a note and gave Father Fortis a nod.

"I hope you remember me, Freddie. My name is Father Nick. I've visited you before."

Freddie said nothing, his gaze remaining unfocused.

Father Fortis took a deep breath and continued. "I want you to know that Felipe was moved today. He'll be safe at the monastery."

When he said the name "Felipe," Father Fortis noticed a slight wrinkle on Freddie's forehead. When he said the word "safe," he saw Freddie strain against the ring on the table.

Is he trying to break away, or does that mean something else? Father Fortis thought. He looked back at Lt. Col. Bratton for direction.

"I'd say you look better today," Dr. Bratton said. "There—you looked up just for a moment. I think you want to speak to us, Sergeant, but something's stopping you. Please know we can be patient. You *will* speak, Sergeant, when the time is right."

Freddie didn't respond to this assurance and gave no indication if the psychiatrist's words were welcome or not.

When Dr. Bratton nodded again, Father Fortis sat forward, his meaty hands just a few inches from Freddie's. Instead of pulling away, Freddie's hands seemed to relax, and his eyes were clearly on Father Fortis' hands.

On cue, Dr. Bratton also sat closer to the table and rested her hands on the other side of Freddie's. Freddie's hands edged away, bringing them even closer to Father Fortis'.

Bratton rose and, glancing again at Father Fortis, said, "Excuse me for a moment. Please continue, Father."

Freddie's hands stayed where they were, and Father Fortis tried to remember the words from the list he was supposed to say. He felt growing tension in his throat, aware that he wouldn't know which words affected Freddie until he pulled away or began screaming.

After a moment of near panic, he began to pray softly.

Our Father, who art in heaven;
Hallowed be thy name:
Thy kingdom come, thy will be done,
On earth as it is in heaven.
Give us this day our daily bread,
And forgive us our trespasses, as we forgive those who trespass against us;
And lead us not into temptation, but deliver us from evil.

He made the sign of the cross and, in a lower voice, uttered the benediction before looking up. Freddie was still not looking at him, but tears streamed down his cheeks. Father Fortis knew that Dr. Bratton was observing everything from the next room and was maybe even videotaping what was occurring.

From his seminary training, Father Fortis knew that there was a great chasm between how American society sees tears and how Orthodoxy views them. What is embarrassing for Americans, especially men, is considered a divine gift in his faith. That was how he interpreted Freddie's tears and hoped that his calm reaction gave Freddie a sense that the tears were welcome.

Father Fortis rested his hands lightly on Freddie's as he did the previous time. But Freddie didn't scream this time. Instead, Father Fortis could see Freddie's lips part, as if he were trying to say something.

Father Fortis squeezed Freddie's hands, hoping Freddie knew, even without words, that his message was heard.

"Freddie, may God bless you and protect you."

✝

THAT AFTERNOON, FELIPE FOUND THE CHAIR in the monastery's chapter room to be uncomfortable. *Maybe that's deliberate,* he thought. *Maybe these guys like to suffer.* He scooted his chair up to a table made of long planks and waited.

He was surprised on his first day at St. Mary's to be mostly left on his own. Brother Abram came around to his room in the guesthouse to pick him up for meals, but other than that, Felipe was given the rest of the day to settle in.

And Brother Abram was a second surprise. Maybe he thought monks would all be old—and many of them at the basic supper of the previous evening were—but Brother Abram appeared to be in his thirties. Even more surprising than his age was the fact that the monk was clearly in good shape. He wore running shoes that looked like they were used for just that—running.

Now, Felipe waited alone in the room for Brother Abram and whoever else would be his jailers. He wondered if the two men he met in detention and in the hospital, the policeman from Detroit and the monk from Ohio, would be at the meeting.

Felipe knew that the judge expected his mother's two friends to forward daily reports about him. But he hadn't seen the two at meal time at St. Mary's, leaving him to wonder how closely they would watch him.

Felipe doubted if he was ever in a quieter room. In detention, someone was always yelling or screaming, and even at home, the TV was usually on.

Finally, the door opened and two monks, the first being a stranger, the second, Brother Abram, entered the room. The first monk looked a generation older than Abram with a face that looked neither angry nor welcoming to Felipe. He just looked.

The two monks sat on the other side of the table and, for a moment, no one spoke.

Finally, the older monk said, "I'm Father Peter. I'm the abbot of St. Mary's."

Felipe could think of nothing to say, so he remained silent. *This is their show,* he thought. *I'm just here to figure out what I'll do next.*

"Life in a monastery is a bit opposite of life outside," the abbot said.

If Felipe was supposed to reply with "What do you mean?", he wasn't going to play the game.

"When do you usually go to bed, Felipe?"

"Depends. Usually by midnight."

"We go to bed at 8 pm. When do you get up?"

"As late as I can," he said.

"We're up at 2:30 am."

"Holy shit," Felipe said before regretting his choice of words.

The abbot showed no reaction. "Your schedule doesn't have to match ours. You'll work a standard eight hours from eight a.m. to five p.m. with an hour for lunch. The monks will have eaten breakfast hours before that, but cold cereals and fruit will be left out for you before you start work. But there is something far more important than St. Mary's schedule that I want you to think about. We work the hardest when no one else is watching us."

If that was intended to raise Felipe's curiosity, it did. "How can you tell if someone's doing that? Are you spying on each other?" he asked.

The abbot smiled at Felipe. "Do you know what a 'tell' is, Felipe?"

"Yeah, it's when a guy does something that gives away his poker hand, lousy or good."

"So most days, monks work alone, no one around. Now imagine you're in my place, and you come upon another monk. The monk is working feverishly, really breaking a sweat. It's like the monk is working out in the gym. What would be your first thought?"

"That the guy saw you coming."

"Precisely. Now, consider another scene. Imagine you come upon another monk, and what does he do? He stops work to talk, gets a drink of water, and sits down to pet Loco, our faithful German Shepherd. Now what would be your first thought?"

Felipe wasn't sure what to make of this guy and his riddles. But then again, Brother Abram wasn't what he expected either. No one in the room spoke, and Felipe realized he was expected to answer. "I guess I'd think the guy was probably just doing his job," he said.

"That's what I think too," Abbot Peter said.

Felipe saw the abbot look to Brother Abram as if something important had been established.

"So, what kind of work will I be doing?" he asked, to change the subject.

"St. Mary's has hundreds of acres. There's a lot of upkeep. By the way, can you handle small machines, like Bobcats?"

"I've got a driver's license, and my Dad...well, he let me drive a Bobcat once."

"Good. To answer your question, you'll work with Brother Abram. Abram is head of grounds keeping. He'll bring you to your work site for the day, answer any questions you have about what you're supposed to do, and then see you again at noon when he brings your lunch. He'll come back again at five p.m. to check your work and fetch you for dinner. So, you see, he'll leave you to it."

'Leave you to it.' Are these guys serious? After a moment, he realized that the abbot and Brother Abram didn't trust him so much as they knew the monastery was large and the Bobcat a poor means of escape. Even if he was assigned a site near the monastery's boundary and he managed to drive the Bobcat off the property, where would he go?

He thought of another bit of advice that his Dad gave him when he was younger. He'd taken out Dumas' *The Count of Monte Cristo,* intending to read it for a book report assignment in middle school. But the book was long, and he wasn't more than fifty pages into it with only a few days before the book report was due. His Mom took him back to the library where he picked out a much shorter book to read. Coming home, he made the mistake of telling Freddie that he "solved his problem," as he started for his room to play a video game. Freddie stopped him and said, "No, you haven't solved your problem; you've only changed it."

He'd hated his Dad saying that at the time, mainly because it was the truth. But he hadn't forgotten the insight. In his mind, being at St. Mary's instead of juvenile detention had clearly changed his location, but it hadn't solved his problem. And what was that deeper problem? That he had nothing to look forward to in life.

Chapter Seventeen

April 7

Although Sera had passed the Bountiful Blessings Bible complex many times out on the west side of Santa Fe, she never before had reason to enter either the church or the school. The students at Triple B high school, as it was known, were not likely to end up in gangs or flirt with drugs. Thus, in her prior days in searching for missing youth or working in homicide, Sera never crossed paths with anyone from the Christian school.

The attendant at the gate accepted her ID and took a few minutes to write down information from it in a notebook. From the gate, she drove down a long driveway that led to parking lots flanking a low set of cinder block buildings. The American flag and a blue and white flag with a cross shared matching flagpoles. The sign over the visitors' parking spaces read "The Home of the Crusaders."She wondered what the growing Muslim population of Santa Fe thought of the sign, not that Muslim children would ever attend Triple B high school.

She walked through the front doors of the main building and approached a reception desk. A large cross, without a Christ hanging on it and superimposed on a flat map of the world, filled one wall. From a center pin positioned over Santa Fe, blue and red strings radiated out to sites in the Far East, Central and South America, and Africa. Below the map was a large sign, reading, "Go into all the world and preach the Gospel."

Sera showed her ID again and explained that she had an appointment with Rebecca Horvath, Noah Frost's advisor and social studies teacher. The

Anglo receptionist pointed to a cluster of soft chairs for Sera to choose from while the receptionist said she'd inform Mrs. Horvath of Sera's coming.

While Sera waited, a loud bell rang, and students flowed out of their classes. The hallways erupted with sound, happy sounds to Sera's ears. The students were in uniforms, the girls in jumpers that came down to their knees, the boys in khaki slacks and polo shirts. The school's logo, the word "Crusader" below a cross, was on both the shirts and the jumpers.

Out of curiosity, she studied the students, wondering if she would see Hispanic faces. While most of the students were Anglos, Sera estimated that a small number looked Latino.

But what surprised her more was the absence of cellphones in the students' hands. She assumed from what Felipe had told her that all students at his high school consulted their smartphone as soon as they left class. Not at Triple B high school, she concluded.

As the students were opening their hallway lockers or entering other classrooms, a short woman approached Sera and introduced herself. Rebecca Horvath's skirt also came precisely to the knee, and her blouse was buttoned to the neck. The woman's expression changed from a worried look to a smile, leading Sera to wonder if Mrs. Horvath feared Sera would come to the school in police uniform.

In Rebecca Horvath's office, Sera sat in one of the two chairs positioned on the other side of a desk. Above the desk were group photos of students as well as another empty cross.

"How long have you taught at Triple B?" Sera asked.

"I'm in my fourteenth year," Mrs. Horvath said in a soft voice.

"So you know Daniel Frost, Noah's brother."

With her hands folded in front of her, Rebecca Horvath nodded. "I've taught both boys, though I know Noah better."

"Noah's been gone over a week, now, and I can imagine that everyone at the school is worried."

"Yes, it's all students talk about. The teaching staff, too, for that matter."

If Rebecca Horvath represented the faculty of the school, Sera could see that the staff was indeed worried. Sera doubted if the school dealt with many runaways, and Noah, the son of the church and school's founder, would undoubtedly be causing even more concern.

"What can you tell me about Noah over the past month or so?"

Rebecca Horvath seemed ready to reply, but then stopped and coughed. A silence lasted longer than Sera thought normal.

"Mrs. Horvath, does Rev. Frost know you're speaking to me?"

The teacher avoided eye contact but nodded. "He said I was to go ahead."

"But you expect him to want to know what we discuss about Noah?"

The woman just looked down at her lap. "He reminded me how worried the family is, how they want answers, how they want Noah to come home as soon as possible."

"Mrs. Horvath, what you tell Rev. Frost is up to you and your conscience, but you can be sure I'll share nothing of what we talk about."

The teacher placed her hands on the desk, her fingers locked together. "Yes...yes, I understand."

"Mrs. Horvath, tell me what you thought when you first heard that Noah ran away."

The teacher shook her head slowly and sighed. "Noah is a wonderful child, or should I say a wonderful young man? But he's very sensitive and very quiet."

"More so lately?"

"Noah was a student in one my classes each of the last three years. He's very bright and such a pleasure to have in class. He's a true joy," Mrs. Horvath said with a smile that disappeared almost immediately. "This year, his senior year, I do believe he's burdened with something."

"Did he ever tell you that over the summer he felt a call to the ministry?"

Mrs. Horvath jaw dropped, obviously surprised by the question. "Last year, he told me he wanted to work out of doors, maybe as a conservation worker."She seemed to ponder what Sera had shared before saying, "Really, the ministry? But he's not at all like his brother, Daniel."

"Did he ever talk about a Bible contest that he entered?"

"He didn't have to. The faces of those enrolled in the contest are displayed in front of the principal's office. So yes, I knew about that."

"You describe him as sensitive and quiet. Do you think Noah felt any pressure to be in the contest?"

Rebecca Horvath sighed heavily again and didn't answer for a few moments. "You have to understand that pastors' families often consider everyone in the family to be in ministry."

"And Rev. Frost is one of those families," Sera said, a statement, not a question.

Mrs. Horvath nodded. "Both Daniel and Noah play the trombone, the same instrument that Rev. Frost plays. Some Sundays, they play as a trombone trio with the daughter accompanying on the piano."

Sera wondered why Rebecca Horvath shared the detail, but then thought she understood. "Am I right to assume Noah didn't enjoy that?"

Mrs. Horvath pursed her lips and closed her eyes. In a shaky voice, she said, "I think Noah loathed that."

"And Daniel?"

"Daniel is born to be a minister. He is his father's son."She paused for a few moments before adding, "Of course, Noah is also his father's son, but Daniel and Noah are so, so different."

"Except that Rev. Frost told me Noah received a call to ministry last summer at church camp much like his brother. And Daniel said that Noah was prepared to do extremely well in the Bible contest."

Tears formed in the corner of Mrs. Horvath's eyes. "This school, the church next door, the twelve hundred families that are on the rolls of Bountiful Blessings—all this is because of Rev. Frost. God has worked mightily through him. Yes, he's a very commanding person, but none of us doubt he's been used by the Lord in Santa Fe."

"Help me understand your tears, Mrs. Horvath."

The teacher opened a desk drawer and withdrew a tissue. She dabbed at her eyes and took a moment to collect herself. "I keep saying the same thing over and over again, that Noah is a quiet child. That can be a gift that goes unappreciated in some families. Oh, my, what am I trying to say? I'm sure the Frosts never meant harm, but I sometimes thought...I've sometimes worried that Rev. Frost misunderstands Noah, that he takes his son's natural reserve as Noah not knowing what he wants in life."

"Which could lead to a very commanding person superimposing his wishes on such a child."

"But with godly intentions," Mrs. Horvath said, in retreat from what she previously said.

"How about his mother? Do you think she listens to Noah?"

"Yes, yes I do. I think the two of them are very close. Naomi must be terribly anxious. Where could Noah possibly be?" the teacher asked, as if she sensed the question that tortured Mrs. Frost. "That's the hardest part of this for me to understand—that Noah would do something to cause his mother such worry."

Sera thought about what the teacher hadn't said, that Noah might not be so concerned about his father's feelings. She flipped her notepad to the next page. "Noah's sister told me that Noah recently took considerably longer on his afternoon paper route. Do you think he could have been meeting someone, someone outside of Bountiful Blessings?"

"But for what reason?"

"I've ruled out drugs, but I'm asking myself the same question."

"Maybe...no, no."

"What?" Sera asked.

Mrs. Horvath looked up again at Sera, her face brightening for a moment. "Maybe he met someone he could talk to, someone who understood him."

The teacher's words bored into Sera, sending a shiver down her spine. Was that what her son Felipe did? When Freddie came home so broken and she was so obsessed with trying to help her husband, was Felipe forced to find someone outside the family to talk to, someone he hoped would understand him?

Chapter Eighteen

April 8

Sera kept busy the following day working on the Noah Frost case. Worthy called that morning and proposed that the three meet that evening for updates. Sera chose "Maria's," a restaurant in Santa Fe with not only exceptional food—if anything could give her back her appetite, it would be Maria's homemade tortillas and flan desserts—but one with tables in a back room where the three would have more privacy.

What do I feel? she asked herself as she combed her hair that morning. She was thankful that the fantasy about Worthy had subsided. Nick was right. Given the uncertainty of Freddie's future, her mind had played the "what if" game on her. That left the bottomless grief she felt with the other "what if" scenario—what would Felipe and she be like if Freddie had been killed in Afghanistan? And there was something else roaming around in her mind, something nameless to this point but which gave her a feeling of dread.

She returned to Triple B high school earlier that afternoon where she managed to have Pedro Morales, whom the Frosts had identified as Noah's best friend, excused from a P. E. class to talk with her.

Pedro Morales was the type of teenager who found sitting calmly in a chair a challenge, and Sera thought their time together might go better if she talked with him after his P. E. class. His fingers drummed on the table between Sera and him, and he had a habit of sucking air into his mouth with a low whistle. Beneath his school uniform shirt, open halfway down, he wore a T-shirt indicating he was a member of the school's wrestling program.

"I've been told you and Noah Frost are close friends," Sera said as a beginning.

"Yeah, I guess so. I mean, we're friends, but Noah is more the brainy type."He smiled and added, "while I'm both brain and brawn."

And cocky, Sera thought.

"When was the last time you saw Noah?"

Pedro sucked in air more noisily as he paused. "At youth group, Sunday night almost two weeks ago."

"So at church, not here at school?"

"Yep, yep," he replied. The boy was making a fist with his right hand and relaxing the grip, making his forearm muscles jump. But he seemed unconscious of the action, and Sera chalked it up to his antsy nature.

"Did you notice anything out of the ordinary about Noah that night? What I mean is, was he quieter than usual or maybe nervous?"

Pedro squirmed in his chair, and now one of his feet tapped the floor rhythmically. "Noah is always quiet. Almost creepy sometimes."

"Was there anything about the program that night at church that might have upset him?"

"You mean because our leader made us form a circle and pray for Noah to do well in the Bible quiz?"

Sera remembered the picture of Noah that his mother and his teacher had drawn. Yes, that could have made him nervous.

"Did Noah also pray?"

"Nah, he wouldn't have wanted to pray about himself. He's kind of a loner if you know what I mean."

"Yes, I think I do. Why do you think Noah ran away?"

"Search me. Look, I don't know who told you we're close friends, but that's not exactly true."

Sera wondered if there was any point in continuing the conversation. Pedro was clearly not concerned about his missing "not best friend."

"Over the past two or three months, did Noah seem different from before?"

"I've never figured out how his mind works, but he'd say some things that just come out of the blue."

"Give me an example."

Pedro's head bobbed back and forth. "I remember before Christmas, he came up to me after youth group and asked if I wanted to be a minister like my dad."

"What did you tell him?"

"To be honest, I told him being a preacher seemed like a pretty good gig. I mean, look at Noah's dad. He's got something pretty sweet here."

Sera sensed that Pedro might have heard some of that from his father, a minister on Triple B's staff who was lower down the ladder of responsibility and salary.

"Anything else? Maybe something in the last month or so?"

The boy considered the question and then nodded. "Yeah, he comes up to me in the hallway here at school about three weeks ago and, without any warning, asked if I ever regret that my father converted from Catholicism. I think the way he put it was, 'do you wish you had grown up Catholic?'"

"That was it? No explanation?"

"Nope. I told him I wouldn't do all that kneeling and playing with beads and crossing myself for a million bucks."

The boy seemed to have no awareness that Sera, an obvious Latina, was probably Catholic.

"If you had to guess, why do you think he asked that?" Sera posed.

"I don't know. Was he jacking me around because I'm Hispanic? Could be. Like I said, I don't understand the guy."

"So you have no idea where he might have gone?"

"I do know that he's really good at orienteering; you know, using a compass? I'm not worried about him because wherever he is, I don't think he's lost."

At Maria's, Sera sat in the waiting area for Worthy and Father Fortis to arrive. In the wait, the question returned, *what am I feeling now?*

As she watched families come in with small children, the answer to the question slowly surfaced within her. Grief was always present, like an open wound just below her throat, but she now realized that she was also angry.

Okay, so I'm angry. What am I angry about? Part of the answer to that question was easy: what am I not angry about? She was angry about what had happened to her husband and then her son. She was angry that she felt so guilty about being able to fix neither problem. And, even with Worthy and Father Nick doing all they could, she was angry at the slow pace of progress on Freddie's case. The trial date was rushing at her like a thunderstorm in the desert, and she wondered how much would change about the case before the trial in twelve days. Were they any closer to finding even one shred of evidence that Freddie was innocent? Granted that Freddie seemed to be building some connection with Nick, Freddie still hadn't said one recognizable word.

But as she sat in the restaurant, waiting for her two friends, Sera realized the most frustrating experience of late was being shut out of Felipe's case. Nick had worked it out with the abbot of St. Mary's for Felipe's transfer, and all that was required of her was her agreement.

Once she admitted that, she could see how thoroughly she was being sidelined with Felipe as well as Freddie. Nick now met with Freddie—the psychiatrist had instructed her not to come—while Chris was the one mainly conducting the interviews with Freddie's fellow soldiers.

Damn it; I invited Chris and Nick to help me, not make all the decisions, she thought. Wasn't this very dinner, set to update her on both her husband and son, proof of a key fact—she was holding back both her husband and son?

Captain Cortini had advised her to leave Freddie behind and focus on saving Felipe. Although his words arose within her, in her darker moments, as a temptation, she was usually able to push that temptation down. But now, weren't Chris and Nick, like Cortini and Dr. Bratton, leaving *her* behind in their attempts to offer help?

And in the back of her mind, though increasingly present, was her worry about Noah Frost. No one had yet uttered the word "suicide," but Sera, with each day, wondered if that could be the cause of the silence. The sensitive young man was now gone for well over a week. Would she awake one morning soon to learn that a teenage boy's body was found, his wrists slashed?

As happened unexpectedly at the end of her interview with Mrs. Horvath, Noah's teacher, Sera found it impossible not to think of Felipe while she was trying to understand Noah. Both were teenagers, but on the surface, the two were so very different. Felipe was belligerent and acting out; Noah had been passive until he ran. Noah was studious; Felipe no longer seemed to care about school. Felipe was safe for the time being, while odds were that Noah had put himself in some danger.

Yet the similarities of the two boys were what haunted her. Both seemed to feel trapped in their lives by circumstances beyond their control. Both were damaged by their families, especially by their fathers. Both also broke away, but in ways that solved nothing.

Sera tried to put herself in Noah's place. Having found the courage to run away, where would he go? Did he make a new friend, someone outside the bubble of Triple B, someone who was aiding or even hiding him? If so, assuming the comment by Noah's sister was accurate, that new friendship formed recently.

Sera took her notebook from her purse and looked over the next steps she'd jotted down after her two interviews at Triple B high school. Much as she didn't look forward to the task, she knew she had to interview Noah's customers on his paper route. She didn't believe one of them was hiding Noah, but one of his customers might have noticed something out of the ordinary about Noah in the last weeks.

On a second page, she reread other important questions to the case. Was Noah thinking about escaping for days, weeks, or maybe even months? Were the added minutes to his paper route devoted to buying food, water, and other supplies, or did he do something else during those minutes?

Her thoughts returned to Felipe and how her son differed from Noah Frost. To survive even the last eight days, Noah must have had a plan, while Felipe probably beat up the homeless man on an impulse.

She looked up just as Father Fortis and Worthy came into the restaurant. Her focus on Noah had taken the edge off her anger, but only the edge. Rising, she accepted a hug from Father Fortis and a brief arm around her shoulder from Worthy.

A hostess escorted them in the direction that Sera indicated. As she passed table after table of patrons, she wondered what had brought them to the restaurant. Maria's was her family's place for celebrating something. Was that what brought the families she passed, even as she feared her own family would never celebrate again? Were some of the couples on a date, as Freddie and she once were in coming to Maria's? Was there anyone in Maria's who felt as broken as she did?

"First, tell me about Felipe," she said after a waitress poured water and left.

Father Fortis explained the ground rules and duties that Felipe had been assigned at St. Mary's. "Brother Abram gives us a report every evening. Felipe seems to be adjusting about as well as anyone could hope. I think the way Brother Abram put it, 'Felipe's quiet and checking out the situation.'"

"I didn't think they'd trust him that much," she said. "I suppose I was hoping that someone would watch him all the time."

"The abbot made it clear to both of us, and I'm sure he said the same to Felipe, that he heads a monastery, not a reform school," Father Fortis explained. "But the abbot and Brother Abram—and I should add, we also—think Felipe will stay put. St. Mary's is fifteen miles isolated down a dirt road, and the communication to the world outside is by a single landline in the cloister area or by the monastery's computer. And no one is going to give Felipe the password."

"Have you seen Felipe yourselves?"

Both men nodded. "Briefly, usually in the morning before he's sent out to work," Father Fortis said. One morning, we had breakfast with him. He's still pretty quiet." After a moment, he added, "After Felipe settles in, you should come out to see him."

"Assuming he wants to see me," Sera said. "I'm sure he still blames me for his attack back in detention."

Father Fortis nodded. "When a person is in pain or confused—and I think Felipe is both—such a person will dump on someone close to him. And yes, Sera, that's you."

The waitress returned and asked if they were ready to order. Until she began to read the menu, Sera hadn't realized she was hungry. Of late, she mainly felt her stomach so knotted that she could hardly stand the thought of food. But somehow, being angry now eased that knot.

Yet, after ordering and while waiting for their food, the knot in her stomach returned as she realized, guiltily, that she hadn't asked about Freddie. *This is my life now. Peace of mind lasts no longer than a moment.*

Overruling her guilt, she let her friends eat their dinners without pumping them for information. It was therefore after the plates were cleared and coffee brought when she broached the subject of Freddie.

"Dr. Bratton believes he's surfacing," Father Fortis said. "He's not speaking yet, but he makes eye contact and walks on his own."

"I need to see him," she said hurriedly, as if Father Fortis were preventing that.

Father Fortis nodded. "Of course, my dear. Yes, I think you should see him. Why don't you contact his psychiatrist to see what she says?"

Sera sat back abruptly in her chair as if hit. "You don't think she'll let me see my own husband? You think she has a right to refuse me? Everyone seems to forget that I'm his wife." She looked directly at both of them and was aware she raised her voice only when she saw those at a nearby table look over.

She groaned before adding in a quieter voice, "Sorry, you guys. I'm sorry. Forgive me for saying that."

"No need to apologize. None of this is fair to you," Father Fortis said.

A spit of anger welled up within her. *Why did Nick have to be so understanding?* She looked down at her cup of coffee and slowly shook her head. In a tired voice, she said, "I should be glad about Freddie. Instead, I want to throw this cup at that wall."

Father Fortis opened his mouth, but then paused and looked away.

"What is it?" she asked.

Father Fortis turned and seemed to be studying her face. "Maybe we should wait until after we leave."

"God, Nick, I didn't say anything during dinner, so now you have to tell me."

Father Fortis looked over at Worthy who nodded.

He wet his lips and said, "It's good news about Freddie," Father Fortis said. "Unless there's some setback, Freddie is, as I said, surfacing. No one knows how long his recovery will take, but there's a decision about Freddie that only you can make, Sera."

Sera spit out her reaction. "Oh, that's sweet! First, I'm not allowed to see my own husband, and now you say *I* have to make what's obviously, from your face, a major decision concerning Freddie?"

Worthy sat forward and froze Sera with his stare. "That's exactly what Nick is saying, so stop reacting to every word he says, or this is going to be one helluva long night. Can you do that, Sera?"

She looked up at the vigas on the ceiling. *Correction: I don't want to throw my coffee at the wall; I want to throw it in Worthy's face. How did I ever think Worthy and I could work out?*

Worthy had spoken to her in that icy tone of voice once before, four years ago, and while she felt humiliated then as she did now, she realized Worthy could have made things harder on her. He could have threatened that Father Fortis and he would walk out on her if she didn't pull herself together, but he hadn't. Instead, he said she could make this a long night. Wasn't that a subtle promise that the two men intended to see it through?

Slowly, she nodded and mouthed a silent "okay." Both Worthy and she sat back in their seats.

The waitress poured more coffee and left the three in silence. "Let's go to your place, Sera. This isn't the place to talk about Freddie." Then, as if Worthy sensed that she wouldn't be able to bear the silence, he asked. "What do they have you working on?"

Okay, she thought. *I can wait a few minutes more.* "I'm back in missing persons. My captain felt it awkward with me in homicide, while my colleagues put the case together against Freddie. Anyway, I'm looking for a teenaged boy. It's one you might find interesting, Chris. Maybe you too, Nick."

Worthy groaned. "Not another religious one."

Sera nodded and then shared her discoveries about Noah Frost and her impressions of the Frost family.

Worthy shook his head at several points. "Someone told me there's a support group for P. K.s," he said.

"P. K.s?" Father Fortis asked.

"Preachers' kids or pastors' kids. I think there's also one for missionaries' kids," Worthy explained.

"One more reason I'm grateful for celibacy," Father Fortis said.

"I want to ask you something, Chris," Sera said. "No one has said anything, but do you think it's possible my runaway could have considered suicide."

Worthy sipped at his coffee before replying. "I think it depends on how exposed, how naked, the kid felt. My Dad would pull the same trick: putting us kids on stage, usually when he felt vulnerable, job security-wise, I mean." Worthy rolled his eyes. "When I applied for part-time jobs in high school, employers would ask me if I had other work experience. I remember thinking I should say that I'd been in sales from the day I was born."

Sera nodded. "I think that's how Noah feels. But you didn't exactly answer my question, about suicide, I mean."

"I know, but the fact that his body hasn't been found could be a good sign. It sounds more like he's trying to break out of the box."

"I call it 'the bubble,' but it's the same idea," Sera said. "Whether box or bubble, what bothers me is that I don't see how he's taking care of himself."

"Is it possible he has a friend, someone who's helping him?" Father Fortis asked.

"That's just it. The only friend his family and his teacher know about is at the school run by his father. And this kid doesn't even seem to care that Noah has taken off."

The three sat in silence for a moment before Worthy said, "You did say he might have a secret life. Someone he's met on his paper route."

"So far, that's the closest thing I have to a clue. Something he did or someone he met accounts for thirty to forty-five extra minutes when he was delivering papers."

"Have you walked his route?" Worthy asked.

Sera felt her face burn. "Give me a break, Chris. I just got the case."

"That's not what I mean. What I'm saying is that I'd be happy to help with those interviews. As you said, this kid and I have some things in common."

Now I wish I could throw the coffee into my own face, Sera thought. "I'd be grateful for any help you can give me," she said ruefully.

"No problem. Just so long as I don't have to talk with the kid's father. I'd probably punch him in the mouth."

Chapter Nineteen

Returning to Sera's home, the three sat around the kitchen table. Worthy glanced over at the refrigerator, spotting a collage of photos of Freddie, Felipe, and Sera from happier days. One photo showed Felipe in his Little League uniform, which he remembered seeing on Sera's desk at the police station four years ago. He thought of the photos of his own family that still lined the walls of his cabin in northern Michigan. *Is it hope or sorrow that makes us preserve happy reminders of the past,* he wondered?

"I think I'm ready," Sera said, her hands folded in front of her on the table. "What's this decision I have to make about Freddie?"

Father Fortis sat forward, reducing the distance between his own hands and Sera's. "It's about the next twelve days leading up to the trial," he said. "That seems short to us, but Freddie could be much better by then. What I mean is, he could be communicating in some way, and if that's the case, he could be capable of testifying in court. And that would mean he would be cross-examined."

Sera looked puzzled. "I don't see how this involves me making a decision."

"It's this way, Sera," Worthy said, "Dr. Bratton and Nick can do what they can in the next twelve days to help Freddie return to reality—to you and Felipe—or they can leave him as he is now. Here's the problem: the more Freddie is able to respond appropriately to questions at trial, the more likely the insanity plea will be taken off the table. He'll be tried straight up for murder."

From Sera's changing expression, Worthy could see that she understood the situation. If he was in her situation, he wondered what he would decide. Even if he fought for Freddie's innocence, as Sera was fighting, wouldn't he count on the insanity plea as a safety net? But if that safety net was removed, Freddie would be found either innocent or guilty.

"Freddie didn't kill Burgess; I still believe that," Sera said, her jaw trembling. "But how can we prove that, especially in twelve days?"

"We have no alternative but to find who really did stab Burgess," Worthy said. "Someone was in the parking lot that night watching the fight, saw Burgess get knocked out. That person or persons saw Freddie wandering off and then took the opportunity to commit the murder."

"You think it's one of the other guys in his unit, Chris?" Sera asked.

"Maybe, but that means the person most likely to have seen the real killer is Freddie."

Sera closed her eyes. "I think I get it," she said. "If we're to clear Freddie, he needs to tell us what he remembers about that night. But if Nick and the psychiatrist bring him back so he can answer questions, and Freddie doesn't remember...."

Father Fortis reached over and cupped her hands in his.

"...then he'll be found guilty," she said, finishing the thought.

APRIL 9

WORTHY HAD DEBATED IF THERE WAS any point in meeting with Pvt. "Coco" Padilla, another member of Freddie's unit in Afghanistan, before he met with the remaining two who lived closer to Santa Fe. Pvt. Padilla was a member of the Laguna Pueblo and still lived on pueblo land forty miles west of Albuquerque, which made Worthy's trip from Santa Fe a good one hundred miles one way. The distance wasn't the only reservation Worthy had. Pvt. Padilla wasn't present at the reunion at the Milky Way Bar the night of Burgess' murder, so he wondered what light, if any, she could shine on the murder.

Yet, as Worthy drove south on I-25 on the stunning spring morning, he realized there was something more than intuition goading him. He understood as soon as he left the outskirts of Santa Fe that he needed some time alone. The problem was this: the longer he was with Sera, the more her desperation and fear were becoming a kind of obscuring filter. He was used to victims' families asking questions for which he had no answer, but this case was different. With Sera, the desired outcome—Freddie is found innocent, and, once that is proven, Felipe gets his life back on track—was stated in her first letter and hadn't changed.

But Worthy knew that the outcome to a homicide investigation could never be determined beforehand. Wasn't this what he detested most in Phillip

Sherrod, his nemesis in the department? Sherrod looked at the crime scene, determined the most likely theory, and then went about gathering evidence to substantiate that theory. Sherrod could boast that, when he was right, he usually nabbed the killer quite early in the investigation, something Worthy would never be accused of. For Worthy, the most basic guideline of homicide investigations, a tenet so obvious that it was quoted on all TV crime shows, was that the evidence had to be given free rein, pet theories be damned—even Sera Lacey's pet theory.

As Worthy drove south toward Albuquerque, he gave himself permission to let his thoughts have that same free rein. On his left, the foothills leading to the Sangre de Christo Mountains formed a kind of wall. *If I'm going to concentrate on Freddie today,* he thought, *I'm going to have to place both Sera and Felipe on the other side of that barrier.* To the right of the highway were the miles of desert filled with mesas and bisected by the Rio Grande Valley. The openness of that vista, the fact that he could see twenty to thirty miles unobstructed in that direction, was exactly what his mind needed.

Today, he would rely on a mental trick he'd learned over his years of homicide investigation, helpful especially in cases where he was too enmeshed in the details of the investigation to see things clearly. His mental trick was to picture himself higher and higher above the case at hand, floating free of its nagging questions. In his imagination, he would float upward, now floating above the date on the calendar. He would drift, above the decade, then above the century, ascending until he felt suspended above time itself.

It was from this exalted viewpoint, what he knew some called a "God's eye" perspective, that he would sometimes see what he'd overlooked in a case.

He glanced again to his right and the area of the Rio Grande River. From the southbound lanes of the interstate, he could see centuries-old adobe churches, evidence of when Spain first put its stamp on the land.

As he drove farther south toward Albuquerque, he passed pueblos that witnessed to the centuries before the Spanish conquistadors. At the Acoma Pueblo that he visited with Sera four years before, the two of them had descended from the mesa on a worn pathway that was over a thousand years old.

From that same trip four years before, he also remembered Sera pointing out petroglyphs, primal symbols left on rocks by the mysterious Native American peoples who predated even the pueblo peoples. And eons before that, dinosaurs had roamed this same area.

What does this perspective offer me? he asked himself. The answer came to him in a matter of seconds: everything he saw from his high vantage point testified to one truth—life is violent. There was the geologic violence of the mountains and the river. There was the violence of the age of the dinosaurs.

There was the violence of the petroglyph tribes who had to be ready to kill to avoid being killed. The same was true of the Pueblo Indians, first fighting one another and marauding tribes, then the Spanish.

If the land before his eyes had wisdom to shed on this case, it was that the pain and sorrow experienced by Sera, Felipe, and Freddie were part of a much greater saga. Society paid Sera and him, as police officers, to keep the violence and chaos at bay, to maintain a level of peace and civility that could be labelled "normal."But what was normal was only veneer deep. Eruptions that broke through the thin membrane, such as what had happened to Freddie, then Felipe and Sera, or what had happened to an innocent nun four years before, were proof, to Worthy, of the violent heart of everything. The paradise of Eden had never been anything but a fantasy, dreamt up by the broken hearts of our ancestors. No, the human story began not the primeval peace of Eden, but the scheming of Cain to kill his brother, Abel.

And that view of reality, Worthy understood, was the true reason he could no longer believe in a God. He thought of the ancient notion that innocent blood cried out from the ground. What a cacophony would result if the landscape he was passing could speak. And when had a loving and caring God ever answered those cries?

With this insight, Worthy saw the quagmire enveloping Freddie Contreras in a new light. There was no mystery about why the Taliban had attacked the Army base in Afghanistan. That was war. And there was no mystery about why Freddie was interrogating a warlord at that same moment. That also was war. Had Freddie died in that firefight, that too would not have been a mystery, for that too would have been war.

From this vantage point, Worthy could also understand what had happened to Felipe. The horrors of war flew back with and within Freddie, and those horrors tore his family apart.

But the violent heart of everything failed to explain one aspect of Freddie's case. And that troubled Worthy. How was it, in a firefight in the midst of a war zone, in hand-to-hand combat when so many were killed, that Sgt. Freddie Contreras was abducted by the Taliban, not killed?

Chapter Twenty

Unlike Acoma Pueblo, which had the privacy of being twenty miles off the freeway, the Pueblo of Laguna, with a whitewashed church at the crown of a hill, could be seen from the freeway. Worthy exited the freeway and drove through a gate before stopping at a building with tribal police SUVs parked in front.

It was now noontime, and Worthy wondered if anyone would be on duty. But inside, behind a sliding window sat a Native American officer who was worrying a toothpick from one side of his mouth to another. The officer, with eyes that studied Worthy carefully, waited for the visitor to initiate the conversation.

Worthy removed his ID from his shirt pocket and laid it on the counter. The officer rose, walked to the window, and studied the ID before offering his hand to Worthy.

"How can I help you, Lieutenant?"

Worthy read the nameplate on the man's camo shirt. Police Chief Aron Monee, Laguna Tribal Police.

"I'd like to interview a resident, Coco Padilla," Worthy said.

"Don't think Coco's been to Detroit. I'm her uncle on her mother's side, you see, so I'd know."

Worthy explained his presence in New Mexico and then his interest in the chief's niece.

"So, Coco's not in any trouble," Chief Monee stated more than asked.

Worthy could tell the police chief was determining how much "help" he would give. No doubt, the chief had all too frequently faced police from Albuquerque or elsewhere who resented their impotent authority on the pueblo. Worthy had seen the same wariness four years before on the faces of the tribal police at Acoma.

"No, sir, I'm working on the defense of Pvt. Padilla's sergeant. Maybe you read about the murder in Santa Fe."

Chief Monee gave Worthy a quizzical look. "Something fishy about that," he said.

"How so?" Worthy asked with keen interest.

"Two short columns in the newspapers? That's it?"

"Good point," Worthy admitted.

"So, because it was Coco's unit, I looked more into it. Officially, I mean."

"Did you find anything that I should know about?"

Chief Monee took his time before answering. "I served in Uncle Sam's Army myself in Gulf War One. So, it's pretty clear to me when the government wants to control the message."

Worthy nodded. "I can't disagree with you there, but we still have eleven days before trial."

"What's the Army trying to prove?"

"Unless there's some new development, they're going for an insanity plea."

Chief Monee whistled. "No lie? Yeah, I can see that. Best for the public to think soldier-on-soldier violence here in the States is plain crazy. The Army wouldn't want people fearing their Jimmy and Johnny, just home from Iraq and Afghanistan, going berserk."

Worthy decided to put the cordiality that the two had established to the test. "Hope you don't mind me asking, but how was your niece when she came back?"

The fellow officer broke eye contact with Worthy as he removed the toothpick and seemed to study it. "No different. Coco's hoping not to go back, but that's normal. No, Coco is Coco."After a pause, he threw the toothpick into a wastepaper basket and added, "I'll just call her, let her know you're here."

Worthy understood the message. The police chief was not going to let his niece be surprised by Worthy's visit. But Worthy also spotted the giveaway of the toothpick. Pvt. Padilla came home changed in some way, and her uncle was protecting her.

Perhaps because of the warning, Worthy found the interview with Pvt. Padilla less helpful than his talk with Police Chief Monee. Pvt. Padilla looked no more than twenty, but he also understood that he might be off by as much as ten years. She'd obviously had her hair cut and styled since her return, the one side shaved close to the skin, the other side with hair in a short braid down past her ear.

Pvt. Padilla explained that she was invited to the reunion at the bar but thought the distance was too much given the state of her car. When Worthy asked if she was shocked when she heard about Burgess' murder and then her sergeant's arrest, she nodded impassively but did not offer an explanation.

Her view of Ash Burgess was also neutral. She said she wasn't close to him. He was"cocky" she said. "It was Burgess' first tour," she said, as if that explained her distance from him. Sgt. Contreras she described as a first-rate soldier, a "solid guy."

At times during the interview, Worthy waited to see if Pvt. Padilla would say more about Burgess or Freddie, but she seemed comfortable with the long silences. It was only when Worthy asked if she thought it possible that someone other than Sgt. Contreras killed Burgess outside the bar, that he noticed Pvt. Padilla, unconsciously mimicking her uncle, looking away from Worthy's gaze.

In a flat voice, she said, "Can't say I thought about it. As I said, I wasn't there."

"So you don't expect to testify at the trial?" Worthy asked.

"No."

"Do you plan to attend the trial?"

Again, she shook her head. "No, I don't."

Worthy left the encounter, impressed at how Pvt. Padilla tried to give nothing away. But even without a toothpick, she did.

Chapter Twenty-One

April 9

Mealtime at the monastery was far different from what Felipe had experienced at home and in the detention center. He was expected to have his own breakfast and then wait for Brother Abram to bring sandwiches to his work place for the day. That meant Felipe didn't see the rest of the St. Mary's community until the evening meal.

Given what happened to him at the juvenile detention center, his natural reaction at the monastery was, at that meal, to assess the monks sitting around the horseshoe-shaped table in the refectory. Several looked Asian, while a few more seemed Hispanic. Although about five of the monks were in their thirties and forties, Felipe felt it unlikely they posed a threat to him.

Felipe thought back to high school and middle school, trying to remember a time when he felt no need to identify the bullies and stay clear of them. Was it possible that he really had nothing to fear at St. Mary's? He remembered the case his mother worked on four years before, the brutal, ritual murder of a nun staying at this same monastery. Perhaps, he thought, there's no safe place in this world.

But after his first day of work, light work in the monastery's tool shed because of his injuries, he noticed again that the birds and squirrels around St. Mary's showed no fear. He adjusted his observation—perhaps there's no place safe in this world for humans. He would keep on guard at St. Mary's—just in case there was a dark side to the place.

April 10

The next morning, Father Fortis rose awkwardly from his knees in the chapel of St. Mary's. As he often thought, there is prayer and then there is prayer. The prayers that gave him no relief were those he offered when his mind couldn't stop racing, especially when he felt engulfed by a problem. The prayers that he knew accomplished what prayer is meant to accomplish were those in which he was able to offer his concern and then sit in silence of mind and heart. It was in that blessed silence when he often felt a door open, offering him a way forward.

His prayers for the upcoming time with Freddie and Lt. Col. Bratton were of the first type and left him feeling no less troubled than when he first dropped to his knees. His prayers were focused on the decision Sera made, for him to work with the psychiatrist and do whatever was necessary to bring Freddie back to himself.

"If I let them lock Freddie up in a psych ward, that's as much as saying I think he killed the man," Sera said.

Is that the right decision? he asked himself. The night before, as Worthy drove the two of them back to St. Mary's, they continued to talk about Sera's decision.

"What if Freddie doesn't remember anyone else in the parking lot that night?" he asked Worthy.

"I think it's more than a 'what if,' Nick. Given the amount of his own blood at the scene, I think he focused on one thing—surviving the beating. But I know what you're really asking—should we have advised Sera to take the insanity plea? Listen, Nick, in the end, that's not for us to say."

"But if we can't find the real killer?"

"If Freddie is coherent, he'll have to make a strong case under oath that Burgess was alive when he left."

"Aren't we forgetting the confession Freddie made, Christopher?"

Worthy shook his head. "I think Freddie was descending into the catatonic state when he made that statement. We don't know what he'll say if and when his head clears."

Father Fortis made the sign of the cross a final time as he retreated from the chapel and reconsidered his friend's comment in the car. *We don't know what he'll say if and when his head clears.* The nightmare image that kept intruding on his prayers was Freddie at trial, able to talk and answer questions, but instead of exonerating himself, confessing all over again to Burgess' killing. That would land Freddie with a life sentence in a military prison, if he were lucky, and the three of them—Sera, Worthy, and himself—would know that their best intentions had brought about that verdict.

"Lord, have mercy," he whispered as he walked unsteadily down the hallway.

Later that morning, Father Fortis' prayers seemed more successful. While there was no certainty, a memory strengthened his belief that Sera made the right choice. The memory was of Freddie's trembling hands when he held them on his last visit. In remembering that, Father Fortis felt certain that the person who least wanted to accept the insanity plea was Freddie.

That afternoon, to Father Fortis' relief, Freddie walked into the jail's interview room, escorted but without needing physical support, even though he walked with a very slow gait. He was also looking up, though seemingly dazed by his surroundings.

Seated next to Lt. Col. Bratton, Father Fortis waited for Freddie to meet his eye. *Will he know me?*

"Freddie, it's Father Nick. I've visited you two times before."

Freddie's brow furrowed as he looked from Father Fortis to his psychiatrist and then back to Father Fortis.

He's trying to remember, Father Fortis thought. *Come on, Freddie.*

Slowly, Freddie shook his head and dropped his gaze to his handcuffed hands.

"I'm a friend of Felipe," Father Fortis said. "I came before to tell you that Felipe is safe."

Freddie's head rose at that point, and he stared at Father Fortis. His mouth opened and closed several times, but Freddie only grunted.

The psychiatrist sat forward. "Sgt. Contreras, we can see you want to say something."

Freddie didn't alter his gaze, and Father Fortis couldn't tell if Freddie heard the psychiatrist. Freddie's mouth continued to open and close, but again he only grunted. Dr. Bratton touched Father Fortis on his arm. Father Fortis looked over and the doctor nodded.

"Freddie, blink if you are trying to say something to us."

Now Freddie sat forward and looked pleadingly at Father Fortis as he blinked repeatedly.

"Sgt. Contreras wants to say something to you, Father," Dr. Bratton said.

Freddie continued to stare at Father Fortis. The look was so intense, the blinking so severe, and the moaning so disturbing that Father Fortis looked over at the psychiatrist for further guidance.

"Father, what do you think Sgt. Contreras would say to you if he could?"

Dr. Bratton asked.

Father Fortis blanched. *If I knew that....* He offered a silent prayer and made the sign of the cross.

As Father Fortis completed that gesture, Freddie rose awkwardly from his chair, his shackled hands straining at the ring. His eyes bulged, his mouth gaped widely. "Aar...Aar...Aar," tumbled from his lips.

Father Fortis was mesmerized by what he was observing. What did it mean?

"I'm sorry, Freddie. I wish I knew what you're trying to tell me."

"Ask him if it's connected with you making the sign of the cross, Father," Bratton said.

Instead of repeating the question, Father Fortis slowly crossed himself again.

"Aaba...Aaba...Aaba...Bap...Bap," Freddie uttered.

Father Fortis had no idea what the garbled words meant, but it was clear that his gesture triggered Freddie's reaction. He looked again at Dr. Bratton. "Do you think Freddie might be able to write what he's trying to say?"

As if Father Fortis had issued an order, Bratton opened her briefcase, pulled out a legal pad and pen, and laid them on the table in Freddie's reach. Freddie slowly sat down, but he gave no indication that he even saw the writing materials.

After a few moments, the psychiatrist said, "Sgt. Contreras isn't quite ready for that."She took back the pad and pen.

Freddie's eyes were now downcast, and he looked exhausted by his effort to communicate. Father Fortis also felt defeated.

"Freddie, the words are coming. You know that, and so do I. I believe you understand every word we're saying, and I can only imagine how badly you want to speak. I will be back tomorrow, Freddie. I promise."

Freddie didn't look up, and his hands rested limply on the table.

"Sgt. Contreras, I would like to speak to Father Fortis alone, if we're done for the day," Dr. Bratton said.

Again, Freddie gave no indication that he heard the psychiatrist's words.

After Dr. Bratton nodded to the guards by the door, one of them came forward to release Freddie from the ring on the table. Freddie rose, again a bit awkwardly, and dutifully walked alongside the escort out of the room.

"I feel like a failure," Father Fortis said. "He was trying so hard."

"If you saw other cases like this, Father, you'd know that today was anything but a failure. Sgt. Contreras is close, very close."

Father Fortis tried to believe Dr. Bratton's words. He, too, felt wrung out, as if he'd run for miles in the desert. "What is it you wanted to say to me?"

"I have a legal responsibility to let his attorney know that Sgt. Contreras is close to speaking again."

"I don't see a problem with that. Am I missing something?"

Dr. Bratton pursed her lips and frowned. "His attorney will then be under a legal obligation to let the prosecutor know. He can't legally withhold that information."

"That's going to pose a problem, I assume."

"More than one, Father. The prosecutor will undoubtedly send a psychiatrist of his own to assess Freddie. Once that happens, the prosecutor can submit new charges to the court against Sgt. Contreras. So we have to hope that Sgt. Contreras has a compelling version of events the night of the murder. And most of all, we have to hope he withdraws his confession."

Father Fortis nodded slowly. "I wish I had a better idea how I can help."

The psychiatrist rose from the table and closed her briefcase. "Think of it this way, Father. Sgt. Contreras wants to say something to you in particular. Maybe it's about Felipe, maybe it's about Afghanistan, I don't know. Before tomorrow, try to figure out what that could be, because unless Sgt. Contreras senses that you understand, he will likely feel that we're on the other side of a locked door."She looked up and caught Father Fortis' eye. "And if I'm right, Freddie believes you alone have the key to that door."

Chapter Twenty-Two

April 10

Late that afternoon, Sera opened a city map to show Worthy the area covered by Noah Frost's paper route. All together, Noah had fifty-four customers on three parallel streets not far from his home. Dividing the list meant that Worthy and Sera would each try to contact twenty-six customers, with both of them asking if customers noticed anything unusual about Noah in recent weeks.

"We should also ask which customers were getting their newspapers at the regular time and which weren't," Sera suggested. "I don't assume that all the customers will notice something like that, but older people might."

"Excellent idea," Worthy said, relieved that Sera was concentrating on the case at hand. "If he met someone while on his route, that will help us pinpoint where that meeting occurred."

"And if everyone received their papers at the normal times, then we know Noah's meeting happened after he finished his route."

That first afternoon, Worthy found ten of fifteen customers home, but he had a sudden inspiration that they could both save time by talking with a few at the beginning and a few at the end of their two halves of the list. By that method, he could establish if the early ones received their papers at the usual time and the latter ones received their papers delayed or at the usual time. He called Sera to explain his plan, and she agreed to do the same.

The homes in the subdivision were mostly adobe, at least on their exterior. Most looked like they were built in the last twenty years with several being significantly older. They were compact, though some were enclosed by a wall with a gate in the front. Cacti and various colored rocks filled the space that would be lawn in Detroit.

The result of his canvassing efforts was uniform: none of the customers Worthy spoke with remembered receiving their papers late. He was tempted to dismiss this as insignificant, given that most of those he spoke with admitted they wouldn't notice a delay of thirty to forty minutes. But that was before he spoke to Mr. Arlo Hunt, an elderly man at the end of Worthy's list, who proudly stated that he was always sitting on his porch when the afternoon paper was delivered.

"I have a nice little conversation with Noah every day," Mr. Hunt said. "He's as regular as clockwork. A very responsible young man, yes sir. He's been sick of late, I take it."

Worthy ignored the subtle attempt for information and asked if Noah had seemed any different of late.

"He's been in a bit of a hurry, I'd say. Like he was on his way somewhere."

Worthy nodded, thanked the man, and after leaving called Sera. "Any luck?"

"I think so," she said. "I'm two blocks over at the corner of El Monte and Figueroa. Meet me there as soon as you can."

Worthy walked to Figueroa and turned right. Down the street, he could see Sera looking in one direction and then another.

When he got to where she was standing, she said, "Up to this point, Noah seems to have been keeping to his usual schedule. But two people over there in the next block told me their papers have been coming later than usual. So, if their memories are good, this is where he took a detour."

Worthy figured Noah wouldn't have retraced himself on his route, so he looked in the other three directions. His heart sank when he noticed a strip mall three blocks to the left of where Sera and he were standing. "Think he went there?" he asked.

"Could be. I don't see much else except a church down a side street. I have a hard time thinking Noah went there."

"Yeah, me too. I think this kid is trying to run away from religion. The shops are probably still open, so let's split them up and show Noah's photo."

They walked back to the car and drove down to the strip mall parking lot in front of a used book shop, a liquor store, a men's clothing store, a tanning salon, and a Goodwill store.

With Noah being only fifteen, they decided to skip the liquor store. Sera also doubted Noah frequented the tanning salon but said she would inquire anyway as it was next to the Goodwill store. Worthy took the men's clothing store and the used book shop.

It took Worthy only a few moments to learn that Noah was unknown to those working in the men's clothing store, though the manager did his best to convince Worthy to take advantage of a sale on sport coats. In the used book shop, however, the husband and wife owners said they recognized Noah from the photo. They thought he had browsed the shelves more than once or twice over the last months.

"Do you happen to remember what types of books he was interested in?"

The husband shook his head, leaving his wife to speak for both of them. "He didn't seem interested in the used comics and graphic novels." She gazed down a different aisle and added, "And I don't think he went down the sports aisle. That's kind of odd, isn't it? I mean, for a boy his age."

Worthy nodded. The woman seemed to have a better idea what her customers didn't like than what they liked.

"And you say he visited only occasionally?"

The woman looked at her husband, who shrugged. "We have to keep an eye on the kids. Sticky fingers, I mean. I would say he was in three times at the most, and the last time was over a month ago."

That didn't seem to match what Noah's sister recalled, but Worthy wondered if Sera had found another haunt or two of Noah's. Two or three shops of interest to Noah over the last month might account for his more recent change of routine, though Worthy, remembering that Noah had his route for more than two years, couldn't see why such a change happened only recently.

He thought back on his own teenage years. He remembered becoming uncomfortable not only with being known as a minister's kid—"Chris doesn't smoke" and "Don't you know; Worthy doesn't swear"—but also with becoming more curious about the different lives his classmates lived. Was Noah Frost like he was, a preacher's kid attracted to the world that existed outside his father's church?

On a hunch, he stepped into the liquor store and found the cashier, a woman heavily made up with fire-red hair, sitting behind the counter, reading *People* magazine. He showed her Noah's photo and asked, "Did you ever see this boy lurking outside your store?"

Looking up, the woman said in a flat voice, "You a cop?" It was then that Worthy noticed the tear tattoo below her left eye, a hint that she'd spent time in jail.

"I am, but I'm from Detroit. I have no jurisdiction here."

The woman eyed him warily while Worthy held the photo in front of her. She looped a strand of her hair, stiff as a brush, behind her ear as she finally complied.

"Maybe. What's he done?"

"He's a runaway. Been gone a little more than a week."

"Good for him. I'd like to get the hell out of here myself."

Worthy thought of all the people in Detroit who, upon hearing that he spent time in Santa Fe, confessed how much they loved the Southwest and wished they could retire there. Everyone wants to be somewhere else, he thought. But if a person's life sucks, it will eventually suck anywhere.

"So, have you seen him?"

The woman looked past Worthy. "I guess I ran him off a couple of times."

"What was he doing?"

"Standing out there, just staring at the displays in the window. Not good for business."

Worthy looked back at the front window. Whisky and other hard liquors were lined up along with boxes of cigars. Yeah, Worthy thought, I bet Noah was fascinated by those bottles.

"But he never came in," the woman added. "Nobody underage gets through that door."

Worthy doubted this was true but thought it true in Noah's case.

"How often did you say you ran him off?" he asked.

"A couple times; I don't remember."

"Recently?"

"Two weeks ago? Hell, it's hard to remember shit like that."

Worthy thanked her and stepped outside. Both shop owners who recognized Noah indicated they saw him only sporadically. Noah's sister said her brother's extended time on his paper route had been more consistent than that. What was clear to Worthy was that Noah Frost began exploring the taboo world of his father. Had he run away to disappear into that other world?

When he met up with Sera, Worthy heard that Noah occasionally stopped into the Goodwill store as well. One of the older workers, a vet with an arm missing, thought he'd seen Noah several times in the store over the past months.

"The employee works only part time, so he wasn't sure," Sera said as they walked to the car. "And he thought the last time was three weeks ago."

As Sera started her car, Worthy asked. "When you put all the stops together, does it match what his sister said?"

Sera rubbed her forehead. "The answer to that is 'yes,' if his sister exaggerated. She seemed angry that Noah had changed his routine."

"But if she's telling the truth, then what?"

Sera looked over at Worthy. "Then I guess we missed something. Or else...."

"Or else?"

"Or else it wasn't the shops that held his interest, but something or someone else."

"So an accomplice then, someone unknown to his family," Worthy said.

"That would explain a lot—how he's surviving, how he travelled to wherever he is."

Worthy looked out at the sunlight edging up the mountains ahead of them in the early evening. "I wonder," he said.

"What?" Sera asked.

Worthy glanced over at Sera. Would what he would say next cut Sera to the core? Yet, it had to be said. "Given Noah's background, I see him as an innocent. Sheltered, you know? What if he got with someone who's a lot more street-savvy than him?"

Sera exhaled slowly and was silent for a moment. Worthy wondered if she had put the two images together, Noah being pulled in by someone like Felipe.

"I think it's time to contact the media and get Noah's photo out there," she said. "To hell with his Dad and his need to keep this out of the papers."

Dear Allyson,

I got your e-mail, and I'm glad to hear about your good performance review. From what I know about the FBI, they don't tend to flatter their folk, so a double congratulations. Now that you're twenty-one, I hope you toasted yourself.

I know I should apologize for not e-mailing sooner, but you know that I'm a Luddite, as you once called me. Technology and I aren't on much better speaking terms than when we were together in Venice. So, I guess I have the choice of apologizing for writing by snail mail or being one of those prigs who argue that the handwritten letter is classier. I'll let you decide.

In answer to the question in your last e-mail, no, I have no idea if we're near the end of this case, at the halfway point, or still at the beginning. I suppose I won't know that until the case is solved and I can look at where we are now in retrospect. What I do know is that I'm at the stage in this case when my approach changes. I feel myself turning inward, savoring the times I can be with my own thoughts.

You know better than almost anyone how this need in me can cause problems for others. You saw me pull back too many times not to feel that I disappeared as a father. I wish this weren't my need as an investigator, but I know it is.

I take some comfort remembering you did something like that on the Venice case. If, in fact, you inherited this tendency from me, I warn you in advance that others won't always understand this about you.

Please know I'm trying to describe this behavior more than justify it. I wish I felt otherwise, but at a certain point on a case, I realize that all the energy that is needed for me to keep others informed and to be a "good colleague" (you could substitute "good husband" or "good father") is energy taken away from the case.

Sometimes, I think my middle name should be "Ponder," because that is what I need to do at this point on a case. As I see myself doing this on this case, I hope this pondering will lead to a more productive angle on the case. God knows we need a breakthrough, because so far the issues of this case—actually, these two cases—are all tangled up with one another. Yet, I know that both Sera Lacey and Nick might need me to come out of my shell.

What I appreciate right now is that Nick isn't like me at all. It's not just that he's an extrovert and I'm not, or even that he somehow accepts my need to turn inward. Nick is put together so that he can be talking with someone and at the same time be hearing the undertones of the conversation. Not me.

Speaking of Nick, he sends his love. Please know that he is almost as proud of you as I am.

Love,

Dad

Chapter Twenty-Three

April 11

Just when Felipe's days at St. Mary's seemed versions of the first, with him working in the tool shed, Brother Abram disrupted the pattern to drive him down to the river where the Bobcat was sitting.

"We're not allowed to affect the river's natural flow, but where there's been washout of the bank from spring rains, we can rebuild that," Brother Abram stated. He made Felipe show his proficiency with the Bobcat before leaving Felipe to the work.

Alone in the high valley with the morning sun starting to peek over the eastern cliff face, Felipe sat down on one of the boulders and surveyed the scene. The morning air was chilly, but Brother Abram gave him a windbreaker. He also knew that the morning would increasingly heat up, and the spring afternoon would be even hotter.

He was glad to have the time alone, with Brother Abram not expected back until noon. The work was never hard, and he felt himself letting more of his guard down. Even Father Fortis, after asking how his injuries were the previous morning, commented on his more relaxed expression.

This was not to say that he'd given up the idea of escape. He pictured himself running away and somehow making it out to the highway. He might be able to hitch a ride, but he wondered what he'd say to a driver other than "Take me as far as you're going."And then what? If he was dropped in southern Colorado, eastern Arizona or western Texas, what would he do next? Wouldn't his life be one ride after another with no destination in mind?

As he studied a canyon on the other side of the river, he felt a pang of sorrow. The canyon was the kind of place Freddie took his mom and him for a weekend of camping. Freddie never told them ahead of time where they were going, so there was always a sense of adventure. Yet, Felipe knew that they'd always be near a stretch of a river to fish and, then, at night, they'd build a campfire. It was always just the three of them, Freddie pointing out constellations and planets until the fire died out.

Felipe hated how much he longed to turn the clock back. If he could, he'd somehow stop Freddie from going to Afghanistan that last time, when something happened that no one was telling him about. But no clock runs backwards.

He envied the monks, living with all this beauty around them. His envy didn't extend to their life; no, that wasn't for him. But how could a person not come to love this place—the cliffs in shades of Neapolitan ice cream, the river flowing over the rocks, the cry of the hawks overhead, and the cumulus clouds floating over everything?

But don't forget, he told himself, *that when you've served out your time at St. Mary's, the court is going to throw you back on the streets.* And then what? Even if he got his GED, wouldn't he end up, with his record, working a factory job or in a car repair place, coming home filthy and exhausted from work he hated?

In his first year of high school, for a book report, he'd chosen John Updike's *Rabbit Run.* He hadn't thought much of "Rabbit" Angstrom at the time, but now felt he understood the man's need to run away and keep running. *There are probably a whole bunch of rabbits stuck in shit jobs in Santa Fe,* he thought, *guys like me looking out to the desert and the mountains every day, knowing that open spaces don't always translate into freedom.*

He crawled into the Bobcat and started the motor. The throb of the engine beneath his seat gave him a strange sense of authority. He thought of what Abbot Peter said, that no one would be watching him except God.

Do I believe in God? he wondered. He thought of his great-grandfather who died two years before, of how he was taken by that great-grandfather to the Penitentes' morada during Holy Week when he was just twelve. He'd felt something in the airless morada from the men around him besides the heat. He saw them whip themselves as they sang sad ballads and, on Good Friday, crawl until their knees were bloody.

Even though only twelve, he wasn't scared by what he witnessed in the morada. In the dark, he heard his great-grandfather cry along with the other men, most as old as him, and even though Felipe didn't cry, he felt there was something fitting about the moans and tears. From his mother, he knew enough of his great-grandfather's story to know that the Penitente brotherhood, years before he was born, saved his great-grandfather from descending into alcoholism. Felipe wasn't sure about God, but he understood that believing in God and suffering for this God had somehow saved his family.

He tried to picture Abbot Peter or Brother Abram whipping themselves or carrying the heavy beam of a cross. Maybe the monks of St. Mary's do the same during Holy Week, though he doubted it. From the Penitentes, Felipe understood that God desired the whip marks and the bloody knees and feet. What he'd observed so far at St. Mary's suggested the monks held a different view of God.

He worked the levers in the Bobcat to dip down and scoop up a load of rocks that were deposited higher up the bank by the spring rains. He lifted the load high enough to see below it so he could deposit the load where the shore was washed out. He edged the Bobcat to the spot and, flipping a lever, dropped the load with a sound of rock on rock loud enough to create an echo from the other side of the river. Lowering the empty scoop, he dragged its bottom edge like a rake across the mound of rocks.

For a reason Felipe couldn't explain, he smiled when he saw the neat row of rocks he created. And, in doing so, he realized that it was a long time since he felt such lightness in his chest.

About the same time Brother Abram arrived at Felipe's work site, Worthy sat at a table in front of a bookstore in the old center of Santa Fe to review the notes from the interviews with Freddie's fellow soldiers and Burgess' wife. He drew a line half-way down the middle of a blank page and then another line dividing the page. The top two squares compared the unit's impressions and the wife's impressions of Burgess. In the top left-hand box, he listed the name Durbin, who saw Burgess as a pal, as someone respected. In the top right-hand box, he listed the name Rosario, who saw Burgess in a darker light. On the dividing line, he wrote the name Padilla, the Laguna Pueblo private who had no feeling for Burgess either way.

In the bottom space, he listed how the same people saw Freddie Contreras, their sergeant, both in Afghanistan and in the Milky Way Bar. "Aloof," "professional," "a solid guy" and even "standoffish" were how the unit saw Freddie in Afghanistan; "wounded," "out of it," and "zombie" were how they saw him at the bar. He wondered if it was significant that the unit was divided in its view of Burgess and more united in its view of their sergeant.

Worthy looked at his watch. In twenty minutes, he would meet with Corporal Gabby Sanchez and Pvt. Ray Gregory, the two remaining members from the unit who were at the Milky Way Bar the night of the murder. Sanchez was in Santa Fe for the upcoming three days on Army business, while Ray Gregory was driving in from Los Alamos, where he lived with his parents.

The flow of foot traffic on the main street was heavy, giving Worthy a chance to guess which of the pedestrians could be Gabby Sanchez and Ray Gregory. Shortly, the game ended as two soldiers in uniform approached the table. He rose to shake their hands and ask if the two wanted coffee or a soft drink.

Gabby Sanchez stood no taller than five feet two inches, her hair cut short, military-style. As she sat down, she asked for water with lemon and ice, and Gregory nodded that he'd take the same. Gregory spoke in a quiet voice, and Worthy sensed the guy would let Sanchez take the lead. As Worthy walked into the bookstore to order the drinks, he noted an engagement ring on Gabby Sanchez's left hand.

When he returned with the drinks, Gabby Sanchez asked, looking directly into Worthy's eyes, "You're working with Sgt. Contreras' family, right? How's he doing?"

"He's better than he was two weeks ago," Worthy said.

"I heard he was mute. That's tough with the trial coming up."

Worthy noted that she spoke rapidly in short bursts.

"He's not speaking yet, but there's a chance he will by the time of the trial."

Sanchez took a sip of her water, then wiped her lips with a napkin. Gregory cleared his throat and said, "I heard the cops have his confession on tape. Looks bad, then."

Worthy nodded but felt he gave them enough information about Freddie's present condition. Both would undoubtedly be called as witnesses, so now it was time for him to ask the questions.

"Tell me about the firefight in Afghanistan."

Sanchez frowned and waited a moment before speaking. "It was touch and go. We didn't know how many Taliban we were up against. Bam, someone broke down the door to our interrogation room, and then dust was flying all around us and so were the rounds."

"Was either of you near Sgt. Contreras during that exchange?"

"We all were at the beginning," she answered, looking at Gregory for confirmation. "What we were told later was that at some point he took off to the other side of the compound. You see, there were two scenes of action."

"Who told you about Sgt. Contreras going to the other exchange of fire?" Worthy asked.

Sanchez gazed down the street, leaving it to Gregory to answer. "Burgess."

"How did Burgess know?"

"He took off after Sarge," Sanchez explained.

"Anyone else with Sgt. Contreras and Burgess at that time?"

"As far as I can recall, it was just Sarge and Burgess from our group," Sanchez replied. "You have to understand, it was total chaos for a couple of minutes, at least five, maybe more. Seemed like five hours, and after that, we discovered that Sarge was missing."

"Who was the first person to tell you Sgt. Contreras was captured?"

After a moment, Gregory replied. "Again, it was Burgess. He saw Sarge dragged away by several Taliban."

"Did that surprise you?"

"What do you mean?" Gregory asked.

"Were you surprised the Taliban took him rather than kill him immediately?"

Sanchez shook her head. "Taliban do both, so no, not surprised."

"How many were killed in the assault?"

"I sent in that report, so I know exactly," she said. "Fifteen Taliban, four of ours, and six Afghans. It was hell."

Worthy tried to picture the scene. "So, Sgt. Contreras and Burgess are together in a fire fight, and the Taliban manage to pull your sergeant away but leave Burgess. Why didn't they take Burgess as well?"

Gregory looked at Sanchez to answer, who remained quiet for a moment. "Don't mean to be rude, Lieutenant, but it's pretty clear you never served in combat. Look, the two obviously got separated in the chaos. Or the Taliban saw Sarge's extra stripes and thought they'd get some ransom money for him."

"Even though we don't officially pay ransom?"

A slight smile formed at the corner of Cpl. Sanchez's mouth. "Remember, you said that, not me."She paused before adding, "Here's something you need to understand. Burgess was one lucky son of a bitch. That is, until that night at the bar."

"What do you mean?"

"Okay, here's an example. About a month earlier, we were up in the same province at another forward position and were getting shelled pretty heavily one day. Anyway, a mortar round landed not more than two feet from Burgess. Remember this, Ray?"

Gregory nodded, but didn't smile.

"If the damn thing exploded, we would have been picking up his body parts with a kitchen spoon. But it was a dud. So what does Burgess do? He laughs and goes over and writes his name on the shell. He was one cocky bastard, and, if he could hear me say it, he'd just smile and say, 'damn straight.'"

"I heard he sometimes took the teasing too far," Worthy said.

"I see his kind all the time. I told him one time he had a nasty mouth. Know what he said?" Sanchez asked.

Worthy shook his head.

"He said, 'au contraire, I'm loquacious.'I never heard the expression before and, God damn it, he knew I hadn't. Gave me that shit-eating sneer of his.

Like I said, one cocky bastard."

"Was he in that mood that night in the Milky Way Bar?"

"He was never not in that mood, but with Sarge there, the night was kind of a downer," Gregory said.

"Shit, the man looked like he'd lost fifty pounds, and I'm not sure he said a word until Burgess took him outside," Sanchez added.

"Why do you think Burgess did that?"

"I thought he was taking him home. Like I said, we were supposed to be celebrating that night, but Sarge was out of it," Sanchez said.

"And neither Burgess nor Sgt. Contreras was there with anyone? Whereas most of you were with somebody, right?" Worthy asked.

Gabby Sanchez thought for a moment. "I hadn't put that together, but you're right. My fiancé, Hector, was there with me, and your girlfriend was with you, Ray, right?"

Ray Gregory nodded. "Yeah, Audrey was there."

"Did you have any idea that they were fighting out in the parking lot?"

Sanchez shook her head and took another sip. "None of us did until someone ran in and told the bartender to call the cops. Sarge already killed Burgess by then."

Worthy ignored the supposition, knowing that Freddie's lawyer would object to it in the trial.

"And nobody left your group during all that time?"

Cpl. Sanchez closed her eyes as if she were trying to remember. Gregory shook his head but didn't say anything.

"I think Durbin may have gone to the can. I think I did, too," she said, "but the heads are at the opposite end of the bar, at the back."

This was news to Worthy. No one else had mentioned that, but then again going to the restroom in a bar is nothing out of the ordinary. He made a note and looked up to see both looking down at his pad.

Worthy waited a moment to give his last question. "Do you think it's possible someone else killed Pvt. Burgess in the parking lot?"

Gregory stared at the table, but Sanchez's head bounced back. "What? Sarge confessed."

"Just a question."

"No, no. Wait. Is that what Sarge is saying?" she asked.

"Like I said earlier, Sgt. Contreras isn't saying anything yet."

Sanchez sat silently for a moment, studying her glass. Gregory was now looking down the street.

"Look, I know you're trying to help Sarge's family out, but hell, he did it. He had to have done it. God, there's his blood and...and the confession. He's going to get off with a medical plea, right?" she asked.

Worthy didn't answer. Everyone in Freddie's unit seemed relieved that he'd "get off" with an insanity plea. Even Burgess' ex-wife was happy with that. Was it just his own training that made him suspicious of their willingness to write Freddie off, their inability to even imagine that someone else came upon Burgess unconscious in the parking lot and knifed him?

Chapter Twenty-Four

That evening, Father Fortis once again knelt in St. Mary's chapel and thought about the seemingly impossible task Lt. Col. Bratton gave him—to determine what Freddie, still mute, was trying to say. Yet, Father Fortis knew, as a priest who heard confessions, that he often listened for the unspoken as well as the spoken. Could he do that in Freddie's case?

He would have liked to have his abbot from Ohio kneeling beside him. His abbot viewed his detective and priestly roles as being in conflict, if not in contradiction. What would his abbot say to him tonight, knowing his detective work led him to hear what could be the most important confession he'd ever hear?

He pushed his abbot out of his mind and concentrated on Freddie. From their last two sessions together, Father Fortis knew Freddie was desperate to communicate something about Felipe. Why didn't he want to say something about Sera, he wondered? And then earlier that afternoon after he'd talked with the last of Freddie's unit, Worthy shared the nagging question he was left with—why was Freddie captured, rather than killed, in the firefight? Was it possible that Freddie was also trying to find the words to explain that?

Father Fortis reasoned that both these issues could be weighing on Freddie's fragile mind. Would there be some point in the days ahead when the words would explode from Freddie like an erupting volcano?

Catharsis—that was Dr. Bratton's term that kept coming to mind. Freddie was nearing the moment of cathartic release. As he thought again of the word "catharsis," another word, "confession," came to mind. He paused again in his prayers to ask, could that be it? Was that why Freddie latched onto him instead of Sera or Dr. Bratton? Was Freddie trying to offer his confession?

The feeling that he rounded some corner excited Father Fortis. Yes, he was sure Freddie had something he needed to tell a priest. But Freddie offering his confession also worried Father Fortis. What if Freddie's first words were, "Father, I have sinned. I killed Ash Burgess?" Father Fortis knew that he'd be exempt from testifying to that in court, and maybe Bratton, as his doctor, would be protected by confidentiality, but the soldiers standing guard in the room where Freddie might utter those words would be only too happy to let the prosecution know.

Yet once again, he felt that those trying to help Freddie kept returning to the same question: is it in Freddie's best interests to bring him back to life?

Father Fortis looked up at the crucified Christ suspended over St. Mary's altar. For some reason, the New Testament story of Jesus encountering a man paralyzed for thirty-eight years came to mind. Jesus' words to the man were not "how sad you're in this state," but "do you want to be healed?"

He remembered Freddie's pleading eyes and a mouth that kept opening and closing, with only moans coming out. Yes, this was a man who was saying with every part of his being except his vocal cords, "yes, I want to be healed." And that, Father Fortis saw again, was the only thing that mattered.

April 12

The next afternoon, Freddie was escorted into the room, but appeared again not to need the guard to steady him. His eyes, too, seemed more focused. As he sat in the chair, he watched his handcuffs being attached to the ring on the table. Father Fortis thought that if he hadn't seen Freddie previously, he would assume the man was normal.

But with Freddie still not uttering a recognizable word, Father Fortis knew that the man was far from normal. When Father Fortis shared his conviction with Dr. Bratton, that Freddie was trying to make a confession, she encouraged him to act on his hunch. Father Fortis felt his heart race as he realized the future of the man in front of him could be settled in the next fifteen minutes.

He sat forward and saw that he caught Freddie's attention. Then, he slowly reached into his briefcase and brought out an *epitracheleon*, the vestment piece that he was required to drape around his shoulders when hearing a confession. Knowing that a Catholic priest would don something similar, he watched to see how Freddie would react.

Initially, Freddie's facial affect remained flat, but then Father Fortis heard a guttural sound coming from Freddie. Again, very slowly, Father Fortis made the sign of the cross, first on himself and then again on Freddie. More sounds, now the moans Freddie had uttered last time, filled the room, even as beads of sweat formed on the prisoner's brow.

For a moment, the three remained as they were, Dr. Bratton sitting next to Father Fortis, with Freddie's face growing redder and redder. *He's going to explode,* Father Fortis thought.

But it was the psychiatrist who broke the spell. Dr. Bratton pushed her legal pad along with a pen across the table toward Freddie as she had the previous session. When the guard by the door coughed and shook his head at the pen, a potential weapon, being given to the prisoner, the psychiatrist waved him off. Nevertheless, the guard took two steps closer to the table.

Freddie looked at the paper and pen for a moment before bringing both closer to him. The pen hovered over the paper for a moment like a hawk waiting to pounce, before his hand descended slowly. At first, with groans and moans accompanying it, Freddie made a long line on the paper and stopped to look at it.

He's frustrated, Father Fortis thought. *He's as mute on paper as he with speech.*

But then Freddie took up the pen again and laboriously began drawing smaller lines on the paper. After a moment of trying to decipher the scribbles upside down, Father Fortis realized the marks were beginning to resemble how a kindergartner would draw letters.

Freddie looked up, and Father Fortis nodded that he understood. The groaning stopped, and the only sound in the room for a few moments was the scratching of the pen on paper. Father Fortis thought if the process seemed agonizingly slow to him, it must be even more so to Freddie. At one point, Freddie scratched out some of the lines he'd made, and a groan followed.

"Keep going, Freddie, there's no hurry," Father Fortis said.

After what seemed like ten minutes, Freddie put down the pen and leaned as far back in his chair as his shackled hands would let him. Father Fortis leaned forward and rested his hand on the pad of paper before looking up to see Freddie's expression.

Freddie sat forward again and, with a trembling hand, manage to wipe the sweat from his brow as he stared down at the pad of paper. Father Fortis turned the pad and looked down at the marks. Though crudely drawn, he could make out four words. The message read, "Felipe dead fault my."

Now it was Father Fortis who reeled back in his chair. Dr. Bratton also reacted by gasping when she read the note. What did this mean? Was Freddie still psychotic? In his confusion, Father Fortis remembered something Sera shared at the airport, about how Freddie would come into Felipe's room in the middle of the night and ask, "Is that you?"He also remembered Sera describing how Freddie would often exit the TV room when Felipe came home from school.

Pieces of the puzzle of the case began to shift in Father Fortis' mind. What if Freddie didn't respond to his son, not because he no longer cared about Felipe but because he, for some reason, couldn't believe Felipe was alive? No, this wasn't just Freddie's brain being scrambled from the torture. With a groan of his own, Father Fortis realized that all of Freddie's actions upon his return to the States made a kind of sense if Freddie thought, when he saw Felipe, that he was seeing a ghost.

✝

The same day, Noah Frost's photo appeared in the local newspaper, asking anyone who saw Noah to contact the police. The photo had brought six phone calls, with one sighting reported in the railyards south of Santa Fe and another on the Turquoise Trail. It was while Sera was walking through the railyards, looking into the open cars, that she received a call from Rev. Frost.

"Who gave you permission to plaster Noah's picture in the paper? Do you have any idea how hurtful this is to our family?"

Sera pulled the phone away from her ear and stared at it for a moment before speaking into it. "My job is to find your son, not to avoid hurting your reputation, Reverend," she replied. "Besides, the public often gives us the whereabouts of runaways—like Noah."

"Noah is not...he is not your typical runaway."

Sera was tempted to remind Rev. Frost of something she thought any decent minister should understand, that no runaway is typical. Instead, she let the awkward silence continue.

"At least tell us if you're making progress," he said.

With a pang of guilt, Sera realized how legitimate was the father's request. With everything happening and then not happening with Freddie and Felipe, along with her anger at Rev. Frost, she neglected to report daily to them as she normally would have. "Right now, I'm in the railyards outside of the city."

"What? You think Noah hopped a train?"

"If Noah did that, I won't find him here. He'll be long gone. I'm checking to see if he's holed up in one of the old cars, the ones they keep for spare parts."

"Oh, I see. We didn't consider that Noah might not be in Santa Fe."

"I'm not saying he left the area. But that photo you're so concerned about—we've sent it to all the surrounding states."

There was silence again. "Is there anything else, Rev. Frost, or can I get back to looking for your son?"

Sera heard a click on the other end of the line. She admitted to herself that she could have been more understanding, but she couldn't believe any father, now over two weeks after his child ran away, would still be trying to save his reputation.

What she didn't share was that she considered jumping a train to be something that hadn't crossed Noah's mind. Yet, with every old car in the yard covered with gang graffiti, she found herself thinking for the first time that her son, Felipe, and those he began hanging out with might be quite familiar with the place. Had Felipe thought of escaping that way?

I need to stay busy and focused on Noah, she thought, as she left the yard. On an impulse, she called Worthy to invite him to accompany her to Los Cerrillos, the town on the Turquoise Trail where a second sighting of Noah had been reported. She thought the ride down would also give her a chance to hear what Worthy discovered in his interview with the last two members of Freddie's unit. Worthy had noticeably pulled away from her over the past few days, and she hoped Nick hadn't shared her earlier confession about Worthy.

She looked at her watch. One-thirty. Was Father Fortis' session with Freddie over? She felt that Father Fortis was also holding something back when he told her of the upcoming session, which only set her mind racing even faster. How could she not take offense at the "request" from Lt. Col. Bratton that only Father Fortis attend the sessions with Freddie? Being left in the dark was like being locked in her own prison, making her feel she was somehow leprous. *Is that how Nick and Worthy see me? Am I the problem for both my husband and son?*

After a hesitation that made Sera's stomach tighten, Worthy agreed to accompany her, and, when she picked him up, he seemed to be unguarded with her. He shared without prompting what he learned from Cpl. Sanchez and Pvt. Gregory about the firefight in Afghanistan and what transpired at the Milky Way Bar. She relaxed as he talked, grateful that Worthy, with all his faults, was unable to be duplicitous. He could be stubborn, arrogant, withdrawn, his instincts maddeningly right for the most part, but donning a mask? No, that wasn't Worthy.

Sera turned off at the Los Cerrillos exit and drove toward the little town set in a valley. In a moment, they came to an intersection, and Sera turned right to park in front of one of the shops.

Exiting the car, Sera pointed to a shop farther down the block. As they walked toward the it, she asked, "Did you ever see the film *Young Guns*?"

"Emilio Estevez and Kiefer Sutherland. Something about Billy the Kid, isn't it?"

"That's the one. They shot some of the scenes here in Los Cerrillos."

"That explains why the whole street looks like an old movie set," Worthy said, gazing down the street in the other direction.

They stopped in front of the shop with a "General Store" sign swinging gently in the breeze. Sera was in Los Cerrillos more than two years ago, with

Freddie and Felipe, and what she saw in the window now seemed to be the same collection of old signs, rocks, and cracked-leather cowboy boots.

Their entering the store set off a bell. From a back room came a woman somewhere in her seventies, in a faded housecoat, her frizzy hair pulled up poorly in a bun. Sera showed her I. D. and said, "You called our office and said you recognized the photo of a missing boy."

"That's me. Don't usually watch the news, but the picture came on right before *Wheel of Fortune*."

"When was this?"

"What's today? April twelve? Must have been two days ago when I think I saw him."

Sera placed Noah's photo on the counter.

"Is this the boy who came into your shop?"

The woman looked over her glasses at the photo. "Not sure; could be. Only tourists come in. *Young Guns*, you know. Used to be about a hundred visitors a day, but the movie's getting old now. We're lucky to have one visitor a day, more's the pity. That's why I remember the boy."

"Did you talk to him?"

"Of course. He was interested in arrowheads. Stood right over there looking in that there case."

Worthy stood by the case. "He didn't buy any food? Chips, maybe, or candy bars?"

"Didn't have time, did he?"

"What do mean?"

"His parents and a really snotty little girl came in. Whiny one, told him it was time to go. So off he goes. Thought I had a sale."She looked at Worthy. "You want a candy bar or chips?"

Worthy looked at Sera and shook his head. "Sure," he said to the owner. "We'll both have some candy. Show me what you got."

Back in the car, Sera drove out of Los Cerrillos. They seemed to be the only moving car in the town. "Well, that was a waste of time," she said, wondering if she should apologize.

"Looks like it. But we both know that most so-called sightings turn out to be false."

"We need some good luck," she said, pounding on the steering wheel. "Unless Noah Frost is dead, someone must have seen him. It's like he's invisible."

Worthy unwrapped the candy bar and took a bite. He grimaced. "I'd say this candy bar is as old as everything else in that shop. Just a warning in case you're tempted to try yours."

"No, I'm not very hungry these days."After a moment of silence, she added,

"You're not satisfied with the Army's story about Freddie's capture, are you?"

"Are you?" he asked.

"No, I don't think I've ever been, but what choice do we have? His entire unit describes the same thing."

"But remember, what they all told me was what Ash Burgess told them. And Burgess is dead."

Sera considered what Worthy was saying. "Okay, forget what Burgess told the Army. What do you think happened?"

Worthy gazed out at the mountains to the south and west. "As I was reminded the other day by someone in Freddie's unit, I never served in the military. So what do I know?"

"I don't care about that, Chris. I asked you to help me because you can... you can put things together that others can't."

"Sera," Worthy said, turning toward her, "I'm wrong on cases at least as much as I'm right. Even four years ago, remember?"

"And yet, four years ago, even by being wrong, you were—"

Sera's phone rang. She pressed a button on the steering wheel and said, "Yes?"

Father Fortis' booming voice filled the car. "It's Father Nick, Sera. I'm at the prison. There's to be a meeting."

"A meeting? Who with?"

"Everyone."

Sera pulled the car off to the side of the road. "What do you mean, 'everyone,' Nick?"

"Sera, all I can say is that Freddie's lawyer called it. How soon can you get here?"

"Nick," Worthy said. "What's this about?"

"Please, Christopher, just get here as fast as you can."

Chapter Twenty-Five

April 12

Brother Abram looked over the banks of the river rebuilt by Felipe. "Nice work, especially considering your injuries. And in only a day and a half. You might have a future in landscaping."

The comment took Felipe by surprise. He'd gathered quickly that Brother Abram was easy-going and positive by nature—or maybe by vocation. While Brother Abram offered suggestions to Felipe on his work, Felipe never felt the man was judging him. So it wasn't the compliment from Brother Abram that surprised him, but rather the idea that someone believed he had a future.

"It's not hard with the Bobcat," Felipe said.

"It would be for most of the brothers," Brother Abram said with a laugh. "No, you did good work here. I hope you feel it."

Brother Abram looked at Felipe, as if to see if Felipe felt pleased with the outcome of his work, but Felipe said nothing for a moment. "Can I ask you a question?" Felipe said.

"Sure."

"How'd you know you wanted to be a monk?"

"Ah, the 'big question,'" Abram said as he sat on a boulder overlooking the river. "What I mean is, I've had to answer that question more than any other except maybe my Mom's 'Jerry, are you hungry?'"

"Jerry?"

"Yeah, that's my secular name. Abram is my monastic name." Brother Abram picked up a rock and threw it out across the river. Felipe realized with the toss that Jerry—Brother Abram—was once an athlete.

"Anyway, every one of us here has a different answer to the big question. Mine has some pain in it."

Felipe sat on another boulder and waited. Did the monk know that he wanted—no, he needed—to hear about someone else's pain?

"I'm from Long Beach, California, originally. I played a lot of baseball growing up. One of my coaches said if I focused on it, I might get a college scholarship or maybe even a tryout. But when I got to high school, my Mom moved us to Compton. My new buddies were potheads—recreational druggies, I guess you'd say—and that's what I became. When I was in high school, I didn't even try out for the baseball team. I was too busy getting a good laugh and a lid whenever I wanted.

"So, when we had to write an essay on that classic theme of 'what do you want to be when you grow up,' the only thing I could think to write was a drug enforcement officer. My buddies thought that was hysterical. The truth was that I never thought about the future, Felipe. I don't think many of my friends did, either. One's a lawyer, though, but my closest friend died of an overdose a couple of years later."

Brother Abram threw another rock, this one far enough to hit the other bank. "But I had this English teacher, Mr. Strickland, who was the only one to reach out to me. He knew my reputation, but in spite of that, or maybe because of that, he gave me a book on Buddhist meditation."

"You're not a Christian?"

"Now I am, but I was a nothing back then. I started reading the book, and something clicked for me. I could see how my thoughts and feelings were all over the place, which meant that my life was all over the place as well. I realized that I didn't know myself at all. All I knew is what people expected a Compton kid like me to be—a druggie or gang guy. When I finished the book, I read it again, cover to cover, and by that time, I was no longer using."

A bird circled overhead, and both of them looked up as it shrieked. "I think that vulture hopes we're a couple of dead bodies," Brother Abram said.

"So, how'd you end up here?" Felipe asked.

Brother Abram picked up a stone the size of a baseball and studied it. "After high school, I took some courses on world religions at a junior college not far from Compton. I also began to do what Buddhists call 'sitting mediation' at a Zen center. Then I met a girl who was also interested in that kind of stuff and, long story short, we got married."He paused before continuing. "This is the painful part. I was a poor excuse for a husband. I mean, I didn't play around, but I wasn't a very open guy. Anyway, about a year later, she asked for a divorce."

"Did you go back to the drugs?" Felipe asked.

"No, I didn't. I was working at one of those quick-print stores, not because

I liked the work, but because the work kept me busy. I still had no clue about my future, but I knew this other guy at work who'd taken a couple of retreats out here at St. Mary's. He was more chill than I was, despite my Buddhist practice, so when he heard I meditated, he invited me to come here for a weekend. I'd never been out of California, so I thought, 'why not?'And something clicked for me here."

"But you had to be a Christian, didn't you?"

Brother Abram laughed. "I didn't have a dramatic conversion, Felipe. It was a slow kind of waking up for me. In the end, I let my guard down and realized I needed to let something in that I've fought off most of my life. That something is more of a realization, I guess. It's this—there's a center to everything in this world—everything in these canyons, everything in the city, everybody here at St. Mary's. Really, it's in everybody we get to know and never get to know, every stupid and every wonderful thing that happens to us. I don't like to put a name on it; I let others who are a lot wiser than me do that. But I think I know what that center is about. It's a force, a powerful force that works every minute to heal what's broken in our messed-up world. This power is in me and it's in you, whether we know it or not."

Felipe glanced away, not wanting to meet Brother Abram's eye. Better, he thought, to change the subject. "I don't understand you guys," he said. "I mean, no sex. Shit, man, how do you do that?"

Brother Abram threw the rock well beyond the other bank as if he were throwing a ball to home plate from deep centerfield. "It might surprise you to know that obedience to the abbot is much harder than the celibate thing. I'm not in charge of my own life here, Felipe. Sometimes that's so frustrating I could scream, but then I remember that my life wasn't going so well when I was running it. Here at St. Mary's, I'm encouraged to believe that God knows what's good for me better than I do."

"I'm not sure I believe in God."

"I don't mean to shock you, but I've gone through periods at St. Mary's—sometimes months long—when I'm not sure I believe in God either."

"So why do you stay?"

"In what I call my dark days, I lean on the faith of the other monks and the guests who come here to be with God. Then, a couple of months later, my faith is back and it's my turn to help somebody else out. The bottom line is that we're not meant to get through this life on our own."

"Sometimes, you have to," Felipe said, standing up.

Brother Abram sat down again and was silent for a few moments. The vulture was gone, having given up hope of finding something dead. What was left in the canyon was the sound of the water rippling over the rocks in the river.

"Maybe you're right, Felipe, but I hope not. I'll even go so far as to say, 'I'll pray you're wrong.' Life's just too damn hard when you're all alone."

As Worthy practically jogged with Sera toward the prison hospital, he noted the whiteness and shape of the clouds hovering over the Sangre de Christo Mountains. Many times before, when he faced a critical interrogation or a problematic arrest, he experienced the same, an intensification of color, smell, or sound. His eyes now also found several large birds, hawks circling in the air, which reminded him of four years before when circling vultures led to a gruesome discovery.

Worthy chose to let Sera drive in silence from Los Cerrillos back to Santa Fe. He needed the silence himself, and he knew if he tried to console her, she'd rightfully bite his head off. He knew no more about the upcoming meeting than she did.

In the building, Worthy and Sera were escorted to a different room, a conference room, its old window-unit air-conditioner struggling. Seated on one side of the long table were Father Fortis and Lt. Col. Bratton. Neither looked happy. On the other side of the table, standing, was Captain Mills, Freddie's defense attorney. The lawyer's gaze remained on the papers he was shuffling, even as Sera and Worthy entered. The silence of the room seemed brittle to Worthy, as if an argument had preceded their arrival.

Sera chose to sit next to Dr. Bratton, while Worthy look a seat at the end of the table. Four against one, Worthy thought. But the one, the defense attorney, was clearly in charge.

After a moment of fanning the papers out in front of him, Captain Mills spoke. "This is to inform you that we are going to trial in three days." The attorney immediately put up his hand to silence any response and continued. "This change took place at my request as Sgt. Contreras' appointed counsel and was agreed upon by the prosecution."

Worthy glanced over at Sera and Dr. Bratton. It was difficult to decide whose face was more ashen.

"You can't...you can't do that," Sera sputtered. "We still have ten days."

"What's the rationale for the change?" Worthy asked, knowing that even though a military court probably was within its rights to make such a change, the court would also have to provide a reason.

The lawyer remained standing, a soldier used to giving orders, but not so used to having to explain them. "Moving the trial date is, in my legal opinion, in the best interests of my client."

Something prompted this move, Worthy thought. The papers on the table, already printed out in duplicate, suggested a speeded-up trial date was thought out previously, but Worthy still sensed that something specific triggered it.

The lawyer continued, reading off one of the papers. "The defense has received the agreement of the prosecution that it's in the best interests of my client and the court to submit an innocent plea, on the basis of mental incapacitation."

Worthy's gaze moved to Dr. Bratton, Freddie's psychiatrist. Her expression hadn't changed since Worthy entered the room, but he could see that she was holding her tongue with difficulty.

"You're afraid Freddie's getting better, aren't you?" Father Fortis asked, his voice quivering with emotion. "You're afraid that in ten days, Freddie could be better...too much better."

"I have weighed the only two options and have decided it's in Sgt. Contreras' best interest as well as his long-term recovery that he be sent to a psychiatric ward in a military prison rather than stand trial for willful murder or manslaughter. With proper treatment, Sgt. Contreras could be released in ten years; otherwise, we're talking about life or even the death penalty."

Sera stood and leaned over the table at Captain Mills. "You've never even considered that Freddie is innocent, have you, you bastard?"

"And you, Mrs. Contreras...Mrs. Lacey, in all our meetings, have never considered that the evidence against your husband is damning and conclusive. My job is to give my client the best defense in light of the evidence that will be presented."He gathered the papers and returned them to a folder. "Frankly, I wonder if you have your husband's best interests at heart."

Captain Miles exited the room, and Sera sat down wearily in her chair. With a hand, she shielded her eyes, and no one said a word for a moment.

"Why today?" Worthy asked, looking at Dr. Bratton and Father Fortis. "Is this just a coincidence, or did something happen with Freddie?"

Dr. Bratton looked up from her lap and nodded to Father Fortis.

"Freddie started to communicate today. By writing, not by speaking."

"But I think it's possible Sgt. Contreras could be speaking in a matter of days. Of course, it could be months," Dr. Bratton said.

"I think I'm beginning to get the picture," Worthy said. "One of the guards communicated with Mills as soon as Freddie was escorted back to his cell."

"Everyone stop!" Sera yelled. "You say that my husband wrote something. WHAT DID HE WRITE?"

"My dear, what he wrote makes no sense," Father Fortis said.

"WHAT DID HE WRITE? Damn it all, will someone tell me what my husband wrote?"

After a moment, Dr. Bratton said, "Freddie wrote 'Felipe dead fault my.'"

"Oh, God," Sera sobbed. "Oh, God. I can't take this anymore."

"Wait, Sera," Father Fortis said. "What happened isn't as bizarre as it sounds." He reminded Sera of what she told both Worthy and him at the airport about Freddie peering into her son's room at night and asking if the boy were Felipe. He also reminded her how anxious Freddie was when Felipe came home from school.

"So you see, Sera, I don't think what Freddie wrote is as random as it seems. I think he imagines that Felipe, for some reason, is a ghost."

Sera pulled at her hair with both hands. "And that's not crazy?"

Dr. Bratton gently brought Sera's arms down to rest on the table. "It's delusional, but not necessarily psychotic, Sera. For some reason, your husband has twisted reality, but every manifestation he's presented fits with what Father Fortis is saying. We need to take Freddie's delusion seriously and try to figure out why he holds on to it, despite all the evidence to the contrary."

The psychiatrist's words echoed in Worthy's head: *We need to take Freddie's delusion seriously.* "Hang on a second," he said, pulling his notepad from his coat's inner pocket. His heart racing and his breath coming in short bursts as if he were running, Worthy flipped the pages hurriedly until he came to the one he was looking for.

He glanced over at Father Fortis and saw his friend was staring at him. *He understands,* Worthy thought as heat radiated from his neck into his cheeks. *In that same moment, he realized Sera had stopped crying. She saw this same thing four years ago, he thought. She knows I've figured out something.*

Chapter Twenty-Six

After eating their sack lunches and Brother Abram throwing one last stone, Felipe and the monk got into the jeep and headed down a gravel road. At an intersection with another gravel road, Brother Abram turned right, not left as Felipe expected.

"Where're we going?"

"For the afternoon and next couple of days, you'll be doing some repairs at our retreat house. I hope you don't mind mopping floors and whitewashing walls."

Something jogged in the back of Felipe's mind. "Is that the place where they found the nun, the one who was murdered?"

Brother Abram glanced over at Felipe. "Yeah, the same place. Does that bother you?"

For a moment, Felipe wondered if the place could be haunted, but said, "Nope, I'm not superstitious. It's been used since then, right?"

"Sure. People who want what we call a solo retreat, lots of privacy, ask for it. I wouldn't say it's used a lot, but someone signed up for next week. Before the person comes, the place needs a good sprucing up."

Felipe knew that his mom saw corpses in her job in homicide and that Freddie witnessed people dying in Afghanistan. He also had a faint memory of his real father's funeral, although he was only five years old at the time. His real dad's body looked like a statue, the skin on his face looking frozen, and the smell of flowers in the air-tight funeral home made him feel sick to his stomach. But the retreat house would be the first place he would be where a murder took place.

The farther they drove away from St. Mary's, the more Felipe realized the retreat house had to be close to the monastery's outer boundaries. But clearer every day was the realization that being on the run from St. Mary's would solve nothing, even as he wasn't sure what would.

He thought back on Brother Abram's belief, that in the center of everything broken, there lives a force, a power, intent on healing. He thought about the nun murdered four years before at the retreat house and realized what he wished he'd said back at the river. What the last three weeks had taught him was that there *is* a force at center of everything, but it isn't a force intent on healing. The force at the center of everything is intent on destroying all hope.

Thirty-five minutes of bone-jarring travel later, Felipe and Brother Abram pulled up to a building that seemed oddly familiar to Felipe. It took him a few seconds to realize that the building was almost identical to the Penitente morada his great-grandfather took him to as a boy. Following Brother Abram inside, Felipe wasn't surprised to see the simple altar, so much like the one in the morada.

Brother Abram's instructions for the afternoon began with explaining to Felipe how the manual pump to the well outside worked.

"It hasn't been used for almost a month, so it's going to need a lot of priming," the monk explained as he poured a bucket of water he brought from the river.

Brother Abram began to pump hard, his forearm muscles bulging like tight cords. Suddenly, the water gushed out, falling on the monk's sandals.

"Huh, that's strange," Brother Abram said. "I thought it'd take a lot longer to bring the water up. Lucky us."

Inside, Brother Abram opened a door to a back room where tools and life-size wooden crosses were kept. He pulled out the mop and bucket and returned to the main room.

"There's bound to be a lot of dust, so don't be stingy with the soap and water," he said as he opened a squeaky window. "Other than that, I'll be back about five-thirty. Take breaks when you need to, okay? Tomorrow, you can start whitewashing the walls."

With that, the monk drove off in a hurry. Felipe wondered if Brother Abram was required to pray on the schedule of St. Mary's, even when he was away from the monastery. An unexpected thought came to mind. *How do I know he wasn't praying while he was throwing rocks and talking about healing?*

No, he reasoned, *Brother Abram probably enjoys playing hooky.* Yet the thought that Brother Abram was praying, and praying for him, nagged at him.

He started on the floor in the room with the altar. As Brother Abram had predicted, there was considerable dust in the corners and around the edges of the altar, but there was a noticeable space without dust in front of the altar. The ghost of the nun, he wondered?

The other rooms, a bedroom, a basic kitchen, and the storage room, completed the building. The kitchen and the bedroom also seemed to have parts of the floor that showed no dust.

By four-thirty, Felipe had finished the mopping and took the pail of dirty water one last time outside to dump. It was when he flung the dirty water away from him that he noticed a mass of ants in the shadow of a boulder. On closer inspection, he saw where a rodent had dug a hole in the same area.

With an hour to relax before Brother Abram returned, he retrieved a shovel from the storage room and returned to the site. He dug down and immediately hit something, sending the ants immediately into a panic. He tried another spot inches away and again hit something metallic.

On his knees, Felipe used his hands to remove the loose dirt. A shot of pain ran through one finger and he swore. Seeing he was bleeding, he used his other hand to more carefully remove the dirt and expose the empty tins of tuna fish. A smell of rotten fish wafted up, causing his head to turn away.

Yet, in the same instance, he understood what he discovered. Someone had buried the tins recently, in the last few days at most. That meant that someone broke into the retreat house and ate canned food from the kitchen.

He remembered the dustless space in front of the altar, which now took on new meaning. *Someone has been praying in this retreat house. Is someone also staying here?*

✝

"Dr. Bratton, how much clout do you have here at the base?" Worthy asked.

The psychiatrist shook her head. "You just saw how much respect I have from Freddie's attorney. The fact that I was given no warning about what we just heard means he'll be calling a different psychiatrist to testify. I'm being pushed out. Please believe me," she said, turning toward Sera, "this isn't my wish."

But Worthy knew that Sera's attention was fully on him. *I hope I'm right about this,* he thought.

"What we need is a list of the Afghans killed in the firefight. We especially need the ages of those killed. Is that possible?"

The room was silent, and the three looked at him quizzically. Father Fortis and maybe even Sera would be patient, he thought, but he wasn't sure about the psychiatrist.

"I don't follow, Lieutenant," Dr. Bratton said.

"I'll explain in a minute, but can you get us that information?"

"I can try. Names of those killed, as far as we know them, should be in some database. But other than US personnel, the age of those killed in action isn't usually listed."

Worthy frowned. That would make it difficult to prove his theory.

Sera sat up and wiped the tears from her cheeks. "What's this about, Chris?"

He thought he heard a whisper of hope in her question. "Dr. Bratton, you said we need to take Freddie's delusion seriously. And that delusion is that Felipe died somehow. From what Sera has told us, Freddie came back from Afghanistan already losing contact with reality. So, what I'm thinking is that his delusion began in Afghanistan."

Father Fortis pulled on his beard. "Are you saying that when he was captured in Afghanistan, he thought he would die? And that fear somehow got transferred to Felipe?"

"Transference is possible," Dr. Bratton said, "but there'd be no reason to need to know the names and ages of those killed in the firefight."

"That's right. What I'm thinking is far simpler, Nick. I think Freddie saw a young person about Felipe's age, maybe even someone who reminded him of Felipe, die in that firefight. For some reason, Freddie believes he should have saved the boy."

He waited to see if the psychiatrist was following him. When she nodded, he continued. "Doctor, could Freddie's guilt for the boy's death, if I'm right about that, drive him to his delusion?"

The psychiatrist slowly nodded. "I think it's definitely possible, especially when you factor in the torture that began almost immediately after the firefight."

"Oh, my God," Sera uttered. "Freddie isn't crazy. Okay, delusional; yes, I get that, but that's the Freddie I know, the man with the big heart. Isn't that what he's trying to tell us?"

Dr. Bratton raised a hand. "Let's not go too fast. We have to be very careful about confronting Freddie with what we think we know. To spring this on him might bring back more memories from those days than he can handle. We could drive him back into himself."

"But if we can't ask Freddie and the Army doesn't keep this information, how will we ever prove it?" Sera asked. "Shit, shit, shit—"

Father Fortis interrupted. "Wait a minute, Sera. Isn't there an easier way to get that information? Can't we just ask members of Freddie's unit about the boy?"

Worthy shook his head slowly. "If what I'm thinking happened, members of his unit witnessed what happened, maybe even participated in the slaughter. The fact that all of them are telling a far different story means either that my theory is way off base or they're deliberately covering the matter up. I'm betting on the latter."

Chapter Twenty-Seven

April 13

The next morning when Brother Abram drove Felipe back to the retreat house, he decided not to say anything about his discovery of the mystery intruder. He felt a kinship with whoever it was, one lost person to another. Since he awakened, he tried to work out what type of person she or he might be. The intruder was neat, not trashing the retreat house or even leaving much evidence of his or her presence. He or she was also religious, judging by the evidence of the floorboards in front of the altar. He or she was careful about disposing of the empty tins, but obviously didn't know that he or she had to bury foodstuffs a lot deeper to avoid animals discovering them. And finally, even with the mystery person's care, Felipe suspected he'd find evidence that the bed was recently slept in.

By the time Brother Abram parked in front of the retreat house, Felipe had a plan to flush the mystery person out. He looked back to the road on which they arrived. The cloud of dust from the jeep was still floating in the air, which meant the intruder, if still there, easily saw them coming.

He listened with half an ear as Brother Abram showed him how to whitewash the adobe walls. It was only eight o'clock in the morning, which meant Felipe had four hours before Brother Abram returned with lunch, and then another four hours in the afternoon before Brother Abram came back to pick him up.

Felipe's plan was to speed through the painting from eight until ten in the morning, finishing enough of the overall project for Brother Abram to believe he painted the whole morning. But from ten until noon, he'd devise a trap to lure the person out. Before Brother Abram returned at noon, Felipe would assure the intruder that he wouldn't turn him in, and then after Brother Abram left after lunch, the two of them could talk.

By ten o'clock, he'd finished the chapel and the walls in the kitchen, a respectable amount. He made a point of soaking the brushes outside at the well, in full view of anyone who might be watching, before reentering the retreat house.

He looked at his watch, one of Freddie's military ones given him two years before, when life still made sense. He waited five minutes, then ten, before hiding behind the door.

He took a deep breath and screamed, "Oh, God, it bit me! The snake bit me."He moaned loudly and after a few minutes repeated the words. "My leg's on fire. I'm going to die!" he screamed as loud as he could. "Anybody, anybody," he added, making sure that his voice lost volume as he did so. "God, if you can...if you can hear me, please send someone. Oh, God, I don't want to die."

With that, he tipped over a chair, imitating the sound of a body crashing to the floor. He waited in silence for one minute, then two, then five. Was his charade for nothing? He moaned louder and then made the sound of choking.

Again, he waited in silence for what seemed an hour instead of just minutes before hearing what he hoped to hear, the sound of someone approaching the retreat house. He lay on his side and closed his eyes. He heard the door squeak on its hinges, then footsteps in the room. Was it an old man whom he'd tricked or a woman on the run? Then a more alarming thought crossed his mind. *What if the person is carrying a weapon?*

The person knelt beside Felipe. The person's breathing was short, and Felipe realized whoever it was, was scared. Did the mystery person sense he'd been fooled?

In a quick movement, Felipe rolled over, catching the ankle of the person and pulling it as Freddie taught him. The person fell on his back with a groan, and Felipe shot to his feet to stand over the intruder.

It was a boy, smaller than Felipe and not more than fourteen or fifteen, with eyes filled with fear.

MOMENTS LATER, THE TWO TEENAGE BOYS sat at the kitchen table in the retreat house. The smaller boy's clothes were dirty and ragged, his face also dirty, his sandy-colored hair stringy, while his eyes still looked frightened. Felipe's eyes were filled with curiosity.

"We've got almost two hours before Brother Abram could be back with my lunch. But I suspect you already know that," Felipe said.

The boy looked up. Now his was the curious expression. "You're not going to turn me in?"

Felipe shook his head. "I don't see why I should. At least until I hear your story."

"Don't you work for the monastery?"

With a laugh, Felipe said, "Not exactly, but I'll explain that later. You need anything?"

The boy shrugged. "I'm getting a little tired of tuna fish and baked beans."

"Yeah, I bet. I can't do anything about that today, except to save you some of my lunch. I'll bring some better food tomorrow from the monastery."

"I can stay here?"

"You can for a couple of days. I'm cleaning things up because the place is reserved after the weekend."

The boy moaned. "So three days."

"Maybe four. Why the hell would you want to stay here?"

The boy looked down at his hands. "I'm...I'm not used to people swearing."

"What? What'd I say?"

"You said 'hell.'"

"That's not swearing," Felipe said with a laugh. "If you want to hear swearing..."

The boy raised his hand. "No, please."

Felipe stood and looked around, trying to spot evidence of the boy's presence. He figured his mom could find some, but Brother Abram wasn't his mom, nor would the monk expect anything out of the ordinary.

"Before Abram comes back, you need to hide. By the way, where were you hiding yesterday?"

The boy gave a sheepish smile. "Behind the outhouse. I'm sure glad you didn't need to use it."

Felipe smiled back. "Okay. If Brother Abram says he needs to use it, I'll tell him I saw a rattler over by it."

"You'll lie for me?"

Felipe shook his head. "You're really something, you know that? You don't swear, and you don't lie. So what the hell...what do you do?"

The boy looked down again at his hands. "I disappoint."

Chapter Twenty-Eight

At the same moment, Sera, Worthy, and Father Fortis huddled in Lt. Col. Bratton's office as she reported on the information Worthy had requested. Father Fortis glanced at Sera, whose gaze was focused on Worthy as much as on the psychiatrist. *Sera's about one more disappointment away from total collapse,* he thought.

"Thank God they didn't shut me out of Freddie's file—at least not yet," Dr. Bratton said. Father Fortis noted it was the first time she hadn't called her patient Sgt. Contreras. *She's with us,* he thought.

"Here's the Army's official incident report on the firefight."

On February 20, 2017, an advance Army emplacement was the site of an interrogation, with Sgt. Contreras' unit in charge. The Army believed the meeting with a key Afghan warlord had the potential of gaining intel on recent Taliban activity in the region. At 13:00 hours, the compound was overrun by what is estimated to be twenty-five to thirty Taliban. The assault occurred on the NE and SW flanks of the camp. Army personnel immediately returned fire at both locations. The assault on the NE flank was repelled first, with the assault on the SW flank repelled only after unit members dealing with the first assault joined forces with those on the SW flank.

The greater number of US Army and Allied Afghan casualties occurred at the SW location.

Following that, Dr. Bratton read off the names, ranks, and ages of the U. S. Army dead, followed by the Allied Afghan killed, the US Army wounded, the Allied Afghan wounded, the Taliban killed, and ending with the last line: *US Army missing in action: Sgt. Frederick Contreras.*

"Read again the names of the Afghan killed," Worthy asked.

Dr. Bratton obliged, struggling to pronounce some of the names.

"Two of those have the same last name. I'm guessing a family connection," Worthy said.

"I've not served in Afghanistan, but I'd guess there's at least a tribal connection."

Father Fortis tried to imagine the scene, the chaos, the carnage. "What does it mean that none of those listed as Allied Afghan survived the attack?"

The psychiatrist shook her head. "Maybe they were the prime targets of the Taliban. If the Taliban saw them as collaborators, that'd mean no mercy. The slaughter was probably meant to send a message to other warlords who were tempted to cooperate. Any US forces killed or wounded would have been a bonus."

Worthy stood by the window, his back to the other three. "Dr. Bratton, you told us to take Freddie's delusion seriously. Doesn't that mean what Freddie experienced that day wasn't what you just read?"

"I'm with you, Christopher," Father Fortis said. "Freddie experienced something in the firefight that he can't live with."

"Wasn't it the attack by the Taliban?" Sera asked.

"I don't think so, Sera," Dr. Bratton said. "Freddie's unit wouldn't have been responsible for perimeter security. His unit was all in the interrogation room—someplace in a more protected part of the compound. But everything no doubt changed with the firefight."

"So let's start there, before the firefight," Worthy said, turning around and facing the other three. "Freddie and his unit are in a room with the warlord and those with him. I'm thinking one of them had to have been a boy—maybe even a teenager."

"Before the firefight, I think we can assume Freddie was getting intel, giving intel, or maybe both," Dr. Bratton added. "But then they had to hear the exchange of fire."

"Let's stop at that point. What would Freddie's unit in the interrogation room have thought?" Worthy asked.

"I'd say they went into crisis mode immediately. They must have feared the compound's perimeter was being breached," Dr. Bratton replied.

"From his training, what would Freddie have done at that point?" Father Fortis asked.

"I don't know about his training, but I know my husband. He would do all could to protect his sources—the warlord and his people."

"I agree," Worthy said. "So let's say that's what he did. Despite what the Army believes, Freddie didn't run out of the room to join in the shootout. Somehow, all the Afghans Freddie was interrogating in the room ended up dead."

Father Fortis saw the scene as Worthy was describing it. "What kind of weapons did Freddie and his unit have?" he asked.

Dr. Bratton sat forward. "Just a guess, but Freddie, as the key negotiator, probably had nothing but a pistol."

"What about the other members of the unit?" Worthy asked.

Father Fortis could see that Dr. Bratton was at least playing along with Worthy's theory. "The ones recording the session would have been lightly armed. But at least two of the others would have had automatic weapons."

"And the Taliban?"

"From what I've read, they use whatever they can get their hands on. They especially like to use our weapons, those they stole or took in raids, on our troops."

"So...," Worthy said slowly, "bullets taken from the bodies of the Afghans in the room could be indistinguishable from the Army's."

"I wouldn't doubt it. That means the Army report is based on nothing but the word of the members of the unit."

After a moment of silence, Worthy said in a low voice, "I bet Burgess was one of those with an automatic weapon."

The room was deathly quiet until Father Fortis spoke. "Good heavens, Christopher, you're saying Burgess was the one who shot the Afghans."

"Or was at least the first to open fire on them," Worthy said.

"But why?" Sera asked.

"Dr. Bratton?" Worthy posed.

The psychiatrist shrugged, but then nodded. "Ah, I think I see what you're getting at. If Burgess or whoever else providing internal security thought the warlord and his people were pro-Taliban, he or they would assume the meeting was a set-up, a trap."

Sera bowed her head. "Chris, you said you thought a teenage boy was in the room. If that's true, I know what Freddie did—he tried to save him."

"But if I'm right, he wasn't able to," Worthy said. "With automatic weapons in play, the Afghans died in a matter of seconds."

After a pause, Dr. Bratton added, "If you are right and this is what happened, that would be the moment his mind first shut down. He couldn't process what occurred. Especially, as he was the commanding soldier, the one responsible for the safety of everyone in the room."

Worthy gazed up at the ceiling. "So he ran. He had only a pistol, and he ran. So what did Freddie see once he was outside the interrogation room?"

Father Fortis could feel the tension in the room. The four of them were either constructing a complete fiction, or they were putting together what actually happened that day.

"What if—," Father Fortis began.

"No, don't say it," Sera interrupted, her voice unsteady. "You're going to say Freddie ran into the firefight hoping he'd be killed."

"No, Sera, I don't see it that way."

"Nor do I," Dr. Bratton added. "If he wanted to kill himself, he would have turned his pistol on himself."

"So what happened to him?" Sera asked.

Worthy returned to the window and stared out of it. "When I was a teenager about Felipe's age, I was riding my bike home from basketball practice. It was a Saturday practice, in the afternoon. I was a couple of blocks from my house, and this four-year-old kid in the neighborhood ran out into traffic. I saw the car hit him, and I saw the kid, like he was in slow motion, flying through the air. I was frozen for a couple of seconds, and then his mother came screaming out of their house. She picked up her son and threw him in a car before racing off to the hospital. Can you guess what I did?"

Dr. Bratton sighed. "You ran as far away from the scene as you could."

"That's exactly what I did," Worthy said, his back still to the others. "There was this overwhelming urge to get away, not just from the accident, but from a question torturing me—if I'd seen the kid get hit, could I have done something to prevent it?"

The room was quiet for a moment before Worthy continued. "I think something like that happened to Freddie. He was in combat many times before, but I think this might have been the first time he saw a kid, a child, killed right in front of him by one of his own soldiers. This was his nightmare, and Freddie tried to run as far away from the scene as he could."

"If we're right, Freddie might not have known where he was headed," Father Fortis said. "Unfortunately, he ran right into the hands of the Taliban."

Hearing Sera sob, Father Fortis put his hand on her arm. "This could explain a lot, Sera, including why Burgess followed Freddie out of the interrogation room. Burgess was probably the one who did the killing."

But when Sera looked up, Father Fortis could see terror on her face. "Don't you see? If Freddie saw Burgess kill a teenage boy, wouldn't Freddie have all the more reason to kill Burgess when they met up again back in the States?"

Father Fortis glanced over at Worthy, who was still facing the window. *Yes, that's why Christopher has said nothing to comfort Sera. He knew where all of this would lead, the slaughter in Afghanistan leading directly to Burgess' death outside the Milky Way Bar. Freddie doesn't look less guilty but more so.*

✝

After lunch, when Brother Abram drove back toward the monastery, the boy came out from behind the outhouse. Felipe thought the boy looked even smaller and younger than he had that morning. *He's the kind of kid we picked on,* Felipe thought. But after getting beaten up himself in juvenile detention, he felt protective toward the boy, as if the visitor were now his responsibility.

"I saved you half of my ham sandwich," Felipe said as the two returned to the kitchen in the retreat house.

They sat as they did in the morning, across the table from one another. It took the boy four big bites to devour the sandwich which he followed by gulping the glass of water Felipe set before him.

"Why do you trust me?" the boy asked. "I mean, you don't know who I am, what kind of person I could be. What if I have a gun?"

Felipe shrugged. "Maybe I'm just stupid. I didn't think about you being armed until I heard you come through the door. But there's another reason. When I washed the floors, I noticed that someone had knelt in front of the altar. I figured anyone who broke into this place to pray wasn't going to hurt me."

Felipe thought he detected a look of pain on the boy's face. "Praying? No, I wasn't praying."

"What were you doing, then?"

Tears formed in the boy's eyes. "Trying to pray."

Felipe waited for the boy to gain control. "How can you try to pray and not pray?"

The boy shook his head and looked down at the empty plate on the table. "All the prayers in my head are in someone else's voice. So, I just knelt in that room, not saying anything, and somehow that felt right."

"I'm pretty sure I've never heard of anyone running away so they could try to pray," Felipe said.

The boy tried to smile even as he sniffled. "You've heard of one now." After a moment, he added, "I'm not sorry I did it, at least, not completely."

"You mean running away from home?"

The boy nodded. "Not just from home. In my father's opinion, I ran away from my vocation."

"You call your dad 'father?'"

The boy nodded again. "You have a dad; I have a father."

Felipe thought about that for a moment before asking, "What's a vocation?"

"It's what God calls a person to do. My father thinks my vocation is to be a minister like my brother and him."

"Well, I guess I can see that. You're obviously pretty religious."

"You don't get it. My father's job is coaxing people to give money and join new programs at his church, Bountiful Blessings Bible."

"I've seen commercials for that church on TV. Is that guy your dad...your father? What's his name? Isn't it Frost?"

"I'm Noah Frost."

"Damn, your dad's intense—sorry, I forgot. But the way he stares into the camera and does that 'you might die tonight' shtick."

"I guess some people need that, but that's not me. I can't do that."

Felipe could see that Noah Frost was again near to tears. "Yeah, I can see you're not the type. So, you're not like your old man, but you came here to try to pray. You want this monastic thing, right?"

The boy shook his head. "I don't know what I want. But I know what I don't want. A couple of months ago, I found myself in the back of a Catholic church near my paper route. I just sat there in the silence. It was like being here. But the day before I ran away, I was supposed to do a TV interview with my brother. It was about a Bible contest that my father made me enter. The closer we got to that interview, the more I knew I couldn't do it. It was like I couldn't breathe."

"How the hell—how did you end up here, miles from nowhere?" Felipe asked.

Noah shook his head. "In the back of the Catholic Church, I found a brochure for this place. It said the retreat house was for those who wanted to be alone with...with God. There was a map, and it seemed like an answer. I hitched a couple of rides and walked in from the highway."

The boy pulled out a compass from his pocket. "Triple B has a scout troop. Not a real one, a Boy Scout troop, I mean. I guess I'm pretty good at orienteering."

"What now?" Felipe asked.

Noah sank further down in the chair. "I've been trying not to think about tomorrow or the day after that, but you're right. I have to leave. I suppose that means I go back."

"What will your dad...your father do?"

The boy shrugged. "I have no idea. I've never run away before. But I know he won't listen."

"What about your mom?"

Noah sniffled and wiped a tear away from his cheek. "I tried to think of a way to call her, to tell her I'm okay. I know she's worried sick, and yes, she listens to me, but she can't stand up to my father. She never has."He looked up at Felipe and added, "I wish I could trade places with you, find a way to stay here and work at the monastery."

Felipe laughed. "You don't want to change places with me. A judge sent me here instead of being locked up in juvenile hall. That's where I got these bruises around my eye."

Noah looked up briefly, a worried look on his face. "I don't fight."

"You would if four guys started kicking your ass in a shower."

The boy shivered at the thought. "What were you in detention for?"

Felipe felt ashamed at what he'd done, but thought he owed Noah the same honesty that Noah showed him. "You told me your tale of woe; well, here's mine. It started when my dad came back from Afghanistan all messed up. And a couple of weeks after he got home, he stabbed an Army buddy to death outside a bar. He's psycho, I guess. But I was already in trouble. Anyway, I'm none too proud of what I did, but I beat up this homeless guy who got in my way."

In a weak voice, Noah asked "Oh" and then "why?"

"Relax, I'm not going to hit you. Honestly, I don't know why I picked on the guy. I'm not...or I wasn't the type to do that. Beat up on somebody down and out, I mean. But my dad's in jail, my mom's a cop, and she's falling apart herself. Are those good enough reasons?"

Noah looked down at his hands. "I guess you're like me, in a way. You were just trying to get away from everything."

Felipe nodded. "And one of these days, just like you, I'm going to have to go back."

Chapter Twenty-Nine

April 14

Worthy lay in bed the next morning, remembering what he'd said to Father Fortis on the plane trip out. *Sera wants us to find Freddie innocent.* Our task is to find the truth, no matter where it leads. He thought about that last part. He awoke even more confident than ever that they uncovered the truth of what happened in Afghanistan. But in the process, it also looked like they confirmed what the Army believed happened at the Milky Way Bar.

The evening before, as the four of them went their separate ways, Sera kept repeating that Freddie must have stabbed Burgess in self-defense. Worthy could hear the unspoken—Sera too accepted that Freddie was the one who'd silenced Burgess for good.

But where's the damned knife? If Sera is right, that Freddie stabbed Burgess in self-defense, how did a man so delusional manage to dispose of the knife?

What nagged at Worthy was the testimonies of those in Freddie's unit. If his theory was correct, they all lied about what happened in the firefight that led to the death of the Afghan boy. And if they lied about that, couldn't they have lied about what happened outside the bar?

But as Worthy sat up and started to rise from the bed, another thought struck him. If the other members of the unit lied to cover up the bloodshed back in Afghanistan, why would they gather for a reunion five weeks later? What was there to celebrate?

Worthy realized how everything rested on Dr. Bratton's conviction that they needed to take Freddie's delusion seriously. From that, he made the leap that in his delusional state upon his return to the States, Freddie confused Felipe with the dead Afghan boy. And that premise led them to question the other soldiers' account of both the firefight and the meeting at the bar back in the States.

So, if the gathering at the Milky Way Bar wasn't a reunion, what was the real reason the unit met with Freddie that night?

As Worthy stood in front of the bathroom mirror, he tried to picture himself as a member of Freddie's unit, blood on their hands and consciences for what occurred in Afghanistan. The last thing he'd want in their place would be to see one another again. But as he washed his face, a possible reason for the false reunion dawned on him. If Freddie had been killed by the Taliban, the unit wouldn't have met up again. But Freddie's release by the Taliban changed everything. The unit had to gather again, to see if their Sarge posed a threat by remembering what happened back in Afghanistan. Worthy realized that the rest of the unit must have sat there that night, pretending to enjoy each other's company, the whole time trying to determine with their own eyes if their Sarge was as far gone as they heard—and as they hoped.

As he showered, Worthy tried to play out what happened next at the bar. If Freddie revealed that he remembered what happened in the firefight, what was the plan? Wouldn't it be for Burgess, who as the instigator had brought on all their troubles, to take Freddie outside for a fight that would end with their Sarge stabbed to death? And the role of the rest of the unit there that night, wasn't it to testify to the police that their Sarge was clearly out of his mind in the bar? But still, in the end, Worthy thought, wasn't the most likely ending to the evening what Sera feared—that Freddie *had* killed Burgess in self-defense?

But where's the damned knife? he asked himself again. *Didn't everything point to the knife being removed and made to disappear? And where does that leave us?*

As he toweled off, Worthy pushed back on the most obvious conclusion, that Freddie killed Burgess and then disposed of the knife. If Freddie wasn't Burgess' killer, wasn't the most likely suspect one or more of the others in the unit? But what was the motive? What threat did Burgess pose to the rest of the unit?

A mystery within a mystery within a mystery, Worthy thought as he dressed. The day ahead, with his joining Father Fortis and Sera in their interview with Freddie, might give Freddie the opportunity to break his silence. At best, Freddie would tell them what really happened back in Afghanistan. He might also shed light on why he and Burgess fought outside the bar. At worst, however, Freddie would explain where he stashed the murder weapon.

When Father Fortis and Worthy arrived at the military prison, they found

Sera and Dr. Bratton waiting for them. They both looked sad and determined. It was as if all knew that this day, just one day before the trial, was the make-or-break day.

Worthy sat off to the side in the hospital's interrogation room to be out of Freddie's line of vision. Directly across the table from Freddie's chair sat Father Fortis. On his left was Dr. Bratton, and on his right was Sera. The expression on the faces of the three was so sober that Worthy feared Freddie would sense something was wrong.

When Freddie was brought in by the guards, Worthy saw a man quite different from the one he remembered. Freddie looked like he gained a bit of weight and a couple inches in height, but more telling was the way his eyes moved from one of them to the other as he was handcuffed to the ring on the table. Worthy almost expected this new Freddie to say something.

But Freddie sat in silence as his gaze centered on Father Fortis. The strategy was for Father Fortis to encourage Freddie to once again attempt to write responses to the questions Father Fortis would ask.

"You look so much better, Freddie," Sera said tearfully. Her words violated the strategy, but Worthy knew no one would object.

Freddie glanced briefly at Sera, then looked back at Father Fortis.

"Freddie, I promised you that I'd always tell you the truth about Felipe. He's doing well at the monastery, so well that he's working on his own at the retreat house out at St. Mary's. The monk who drops by to see him says Felipe is a very good worker, someone they believe they can trust. And Freddie, I've also seen your son. Felipe is getting better; I'm sure of it."

Although Freddie's only reaction during the update on Felipe was to keep his eyes on Father Fortis, there was none of the strain or fear that they'd observed in Freddie when Felipe's name came up in the past.

Father Fortis nodded and, as he passed a legal pad and pen across the table, said, "Good, I can see that you understand. Freddie, I have a few questions to ask you. You can use the paper and pen anytime you wish, or, if you would prefer, you can speak to me."

Freddie didn't say anything, but glanced up from the pad to look in Worthy's direction.

"Ah, yes," Father Fortis said. "That's Christopher Worthy, a friend of Sera and me. He came to see you several weeks ago, but it's okay if you don't remember."

Freddie looked back at Father Fortis as if the explanation satisfied him.

Father Fortis pointed to the paper on which he had written a big Y and N at the top. "Do you know what month this is, Freddie? If it's November, you can point to the Y for yes. If not, point to the N for no."

Freddie studied the pen as if he had never seen one before, but after a moment picked it up awkwardly and pointed to the N on the paper.

"Is it April?"

Freddie frowned for a moment, but then with great effort pointed to the Y. "That's right, Freddie. Today is April 14. Another question, Freddie. Where are we meeting? Are we in Afghanistan?"

Freddie's hand froze over the page. After a moment, Father Fortis said, "We're meeting in Albuquerque, Freddie. You're not in Afghanistan. You're home. That's why Sera is here. Do you understand?"

A different sound emanated from Freddie, almost, to Worthy's ears, as a "huh."Once again, he pointed with difficulty at the Y.

Worthy saw Dr. Bratton pat Father Fortis' arm. Time for the big questions. "Good, Freddie," Father Fortis said. "I have some names of people you met in Afghanistan. I will read them slowly. Just tap the paper with the pen if you recognize the name I say."Father Fortis waited for a moment for Freddie before beginning with the name Sadar Rakmani.

There was no change of expression on Freddie's face. *Good,* Worthy thought, *that's a fictitious name.*

"Okay, what about DeShan Durbin?" Father Fortis asked. Worthy understood that this was a member of Freddie's unit.

Freddie tapped the Y on the page.

Father Fortis again approved of Freddie's answer, before proceeding through a list of other names, some fictitious, others from the list of Afghans with whom Freddie was negotiating when the firefight began, and others from Freddie's unit. In each case, Freddie tapped correct answers.

Worthy wondered if it was just his imagination or if Freddie's responses were coming more quickly. He saw that Sera's expression had changed as well. There was a light in her eyes that he hadn't seen since they'd worked together four years before.

There was a pause, and Freddie sat forward in his chair, the shackles clanging on the table. *He doesn't want this to end,* Worthy thought.

"Did you remember Mustaffah Ahmad?" Father Fortis asked.

Freddie's eyes grew wide. He began moaning, his mouth opening and closing, but the pen hit the table hard.

"Freddie, I think you saw Ibrahim Ahmad, his son, killed, didn't you?"

Freddie closed his eyes and took a deep breath. A low, animal sound came from his lips, escalating into screams that seemed to last for Worthy for five minutes. The screams morphed into sobs and Freddie lowered his head to the table.

"Freddie, we think we know what happened. We know you saw the Afghans killed, including the boy Ibrahim. And we know it wasn't what you wanted to happen."

Worthy wondered how long Dr. Bratton would allow Freddie's pain to go on, but she tapped Father Fortis' arm again and nodded for him to proceed.

Freddie sat up, the tears streaming down his face. He took the pen and looked at it for a long moment, leading Worthy to wonder if Freddie was considering blinding himself with it. But slowly, his arm moved down to the pad of paper and he painstakingly began to make letters. It took Freddie over three minutes before he pushed the paper across the table to Father Fortis.

As Father Fortis and Sera read the note, Father Fortis' lower lip began to tremble. Sera read it and dissolved into tears.

"Freddie has written 'died in my arms,'" Father Fortis read aloud.

Worthy bent down and whispered in Father Fortis' ear. "Nick, ask him if Burgess killed the boy."

Dr. Bratton overhead the message and nodded. Father Fortis did as Worthy had requested.

Freddie looked up at the ceiling, his breathing coming in short gasps. "They all...did," he said barely above a whisper.

Out of the corner of his eye, Worthy noticed one of the guards by the door stepping out of the room and shutting the door behind him. *Probably to report to defense counsel,* he speculated.

Sera reached over and clasped Freddie's hands. "Oh, Freddie, oh, Freddie. It's all right. We know, we know."

Dr. Bratton must have seen the guard depart as well, for Worthy heard her whisper to Father Fortis, "We won't have much time. Ask Freddie about the fight outside the bar."

"Freddie, we know that you had a fight with Ashton Burgess outside a bar in Santa Fe. Do you remember the fight?"

Freddie nodding was exaggerated. *He wants this as much as we do,* Worthy thought.

"When you were fighting with Burgess, did you see a knife?" Father Fortis asked.

The room was quiet for a moment before Freddie pointed to the large N on the pad of paper.

"Did you knock Burgess out in the fight, Freddie?"

Freddie pointed to the large Y.

"Is that when you ran away?" Father Fortis asked.

Freddie pointed again to the second Y.

"You didn't have a knife?" Dr. Bratton repeated the question.

Freddie looked over at his psychiatrist as if noticing her for the first time before shaking his head.

The door burst open, and Captain Mills rushed in. "God damn it, who gave you permission to talk with my client?"

The effect on Freddie was instantaneous. He began trembling and moaning.

"I did," Dr. Bratton said. "He's told us what happened both in Afghanistan and at the bar."

"I don't believe you," Mills said, grimacing. He turned to the one guard remaining by the door. "Corporal, did Sergeant Contreras say anything?"

"Just two words, sir. I couldn't make them out."

Mills spun around to face the four of them. "Just as I thought. You told Freddie what you wanted to hear and he, what?" He jabbed at the pad of paper. "Lines and letters, which could mean anything."

"What they mean—" Dr. Bratton tried to speak, but Mills cut her off.

"You may outrank me, Lt. Col. Bratton, but in this situation, I make the decisions. None of you will have contact with my client until after the trial. Clearly, you upset and confused him. I order you all to leave. Soldier, escort Sergeant Contreras back to his cell."

Sera kept her hands on her husband's. "Freddie, we believe you. You didn't kill Burgess. Somehow, we'll get you out of here."

The defense attorney took out his phone. "I want three men in interrogation room number two stat. Sergeant Contreras' visitors are to be escorted from the premises immediately and are not to be allowed to return. That goes for Lt. Col. Bratton as well."

As Freddie was unshackled and pulled away from the table, he turned and said one word in Sera's direction. "Felipe?"

Sobbing, Sera shouted to Freddie as he was taken from the room. "Felipe is fine, Freddie. Your son is fine."

April 15

The next day, Sera awoke after a fitful sleep despite help from a sleeping pill. Lately, she awoke and for a few seconds experienced a feeling of lightness, a remembered feeling from before the nightmare she was living in returned to mind. But this morning, the morning of Freddie's trial, she awoke with despair burning like acid in her throat. There was no mystery to this for her, but an inner acknowledgement that despair had, at last, eaten through her final layer of hope.

Sera knew that she, Worthy, Father Fortis, and Dr. Bratton would spend every moment of the day knowing that Freddie was isolated by the Army beyond their reach.

On the way back to Sera's house the evening before, Father Fortis tried to comfort her that whatever happened at the trial, a recovered Freddie could appeal for a new trial in light of what he remembered.

Worthy, on the other hand, was quiet both in the car and in her living room. He listened to Father Fortis and would occasionally nod, but he avoided eye contact with her. It took her a few minutes to understand Worthy's reticence, but then it dawned on her. A recovered Freddie with an unprovable story would be dismissed by a later court as just another convict with a fiction to sell.

The only hope left was that Freddie could somehow convince the court that he was neither insane nor guilty of murder. But Freddie in his current state was barely able to scratch childish letters on paper. And Sera knew that there would be no paper and pen in front of Freddie at the trial.

Her cellphone rang, and she looked down to see it was a call from the station. She wanted to ignore it, to call in later to say that she'd be off-duty until the trial was over, but something prompted her to answer it.

"Sera, it's Cam from the station. You got a hit on the photo of Noah Frost. It's from a Catholic priest. He says he's pretty sure he saw the boy stop into his church on occasion."

Sera looked down at her phone as if someone were playing a gag on her. Noah, son of Rev. Daniel Frost, frequenting a Catholic church?

"That's got to be false," she said in a tired voice.

"He's pretty adamant," Cam countered.

"Then why didn't he come forward earlier?"

"I asked him that. For the past two weeks, he's been leading a pilgrimage with some parishioners to Rome. He just got back yesterday. Look, given everything you're dealing with, especially today, Sera, do you want me to handle it?"

Out of her mouth, as if against her will, she heard herself say, "No. Give me the address."

Cam did so, and it took Sera only a moment to realize St. Jude's Catholic Church was located two blocks off Noah's paper route, a site that Worthy and she passed on. She comforted herself with the thought that with the priest being on pilgrimage, they would have struck out even if they bothered to check.

She called Worthy's number and then remembered Worthy tended to ignore his cellphone. She next called Father Fortis, who answered on the second ring.

"Is Chris with you, Nick?"

"Not at the moment. We're both in town, but he's running down some things about the soldiers in Freddie's unit. Christopher is in one of his quiet moods, Sera. He needs the morning to be with himself."

Her heart sank. Today was the day more than any other that she needed

Worthy to open up her and give her hope.

"Sera, is there something I can do?" Father Fortis asked.

She thought of a morning spent in Father Fortis' comforting presence and wasn't sure she could stand that. But more than anything, she wanted to avoid being alone today. "Nick, I got a tip about my missing teenager. Could you come with me to check it out?"

"I'm at your disposal, my dear. I'm at the central library."

"Why are you there?"

"I wanted to read about Burgess and Freddie, from beginning to...to where we are now. Just in case we missed something."

Sera didn't have the heart to tell him that she had a complete file of clippings at her house. "I get it, Nick. I can be there in fifteen minutes."

On the way to St. Jude's, Sera filled Father Fortis in on the tip from Father Corcoran. "I'm fifty percent sure that this lead goes nowhere, but the church is close to Noah's paper route."

"Huh," Father Fortis uttered.

"What?"

"I'm about ninety percent sure that this is going to be our first break, Sera."

At St. Jude's, Father Corcoran met them at the door and led them into the sanctuary. Both priests made the sign of the cross and bowed toward the altar, and Sera hastily did as well. *When in all this mess did I stop going to church,* she thought? *About the same time I stopped bothering God with my woes.*

After showing the priest several family photos of Noah, Father Corcoran nodded and pointed to the back pew.

"I first saw him sitting there about six weeks ago, maybe seven," Father Corcoran said. "On his third or fourth visit, I walked toward him to see if there was anything I could do to help. He took off before I could get near him."

"But he continued to come back?" Sera asked.

"Yes, and I realized he didn't want to talk, at least not talk with me. Once I read in the newspaper who his father is, I began to understand why."

"About how long did he stay, Father Corcoran?" Father Fortis asked.

"Please, it's Father Bill."

"That's fine. I'm Father Nick or just Nick."

The Catholic priest nodded. "To answer your question, he came two or three afternoons a week. He wasn't doing any harm, and he seemed to need to sit here in the quiet."

"Week after week?" Sera asked. The frequency matched quite closely what Noah's sister had maintained.

"Yes. I found his presence quite moving. I never worried that he was up to something. I had a sense he had his reasons."

Sera asked a few more questions, hoping Father Bill would recall something more helpful. She could accept that this was where Noah had spent the extra thirty minutes noted by his sister, but the priest obviously was as clueless about where Noah could be now as she was.

On their way out, she stepped outside into the morning sun, only to realize that Father Fortis had lagged behind. *Maybe it's a priest thing,* she considered. But when Father Fortis emerged from St. Jude's, she noticed he carried a pamphlet.

In the car, as they drove away from the church, Sera asked, "Why were you so certain this tip would pay off?"

Father Fortis shrugged as he reached up and held his pectoral cross. "Because I think God has a sense of humor."

"What's that supposed to mean?"

"What would God give one of those fiery TV preachers but a son who has a contemplative nature? I think Noah sat in that church because the quiet gave him something his soul was missing—silence with God."

"Then he got that from his mother's side of the family," Sera said. "Noah's brother, Danny, is a younger version of the Dad. Even named after him."

"Which probably made it all the harder for Noah. The expectations, I mean."

"That's all fine and good, but I don't see how it helps us. We now know where Noah spent those extra minutes on his paper route, but Father Bill has no more an idea where Noah is now, nor do we."

"Find some place to pull over, Sera. I want to show you something."

Sera put her turn signal on and turned onto a narrow street, one of those in Santa Fe dotted with posh art galleries. Finding a parking spot, she stopped the car and waited.

Without saying a word, Father Fortis passed the brochure over to Sera. On the front was a photo of a simple adobe building. Above the photo were the words, *Be still, and know that I am God.*

On the inside pages, the building was identified as a retreat house affiliated with St. Mary of the Snows. Father Fortis recognized it as the place where Sister Anna was found stabbed four years before.

She looked up at Father Fortis. "Nick, you've got to be kidding. Noah can't be there."

"Why not?"

"Because you're at St. Mary's, and Chris is there, and Felipe is there, and the monks are there. There's no way Noah could be there and not be noticed."

"No, no, I agree. The boy didn't show up and knock on the front gate. But what if he found a way to the retreat house? Look on the back of the brochure, and you'll see a map to the place. The retreat house is close to a forest road and only two miles from a highway. It's possible that no one from the monastery has been out to the retreat house."

"Assuming it isn't being used by someone else," she said even as she recalled Pedro Morales' comment that Noah excelled in orienteering.

"Easy to find out. Why don't you call out there?"

The thought of Felipe and Noah Frost being within miles of one another stunned her. What would these two teenagers make of one another?

Just as Sera started to call St. Mary's, her phone rang.

"Sera, it's Dr. Bratton. I'm afraid I have bad news. Freddie experienced another psychotic episode this morning. Can you and your two friends come to the prison hospital immediately?"

CHAPTER THIRTY

"SHIT," FELIPE SAID. "THERE'S SOMEONE COMING. Quick, hide under the bed."

Noah ran from the kitchen into the bedroom and scooted under the bed.

After several minutes, Felipe heard a knock on the door. Felipe gave Noah another few seconds before walking slowly through the retreat house to answer it. He opened the door to two soldiers in full uniform, aviator glasses glistening in the late morning sun.

The soldier to the left stepped into the room. "Felipe Lacey, your father's attorney sent us to bring you back to Santa Fe."

"I don't understand."

"The lawyer needs you for a deposition and then to be on hand for the trial today."

Felipe noticed that the other soldier was chewing gum rapidly and looking back down the road. That was when Felipe noticed that the usual cloud of dust from an approaching vehicle wasn't to be seen.

"How'd you get here? You didn't take the main road from St. Mary's."

"We came in a back way, from the north," the lead soldier said, gesturing over his shoulder. "But the monastery knows all about this."

Looking in that direction, Felipe saw an Army truck, a cab with a canvas back, the type of vehicle he associated with troop carrying.

Thinking quickly, Felipe realized that this unexpected turn of events could work out to Noah's advantage. The two boys had spent the morning going over Noah's choices. Noah could either go back home, or he could continue to run. Felipe realized that if Noah got back to Santa Fe, he had the chance to do either. But for that to happen, Felipe had to draw the soldiers' attention away so Noah could hide in the back of the truck. He would try to stall as long as possible and hope that Noah understood his chance.

"My Dad's case isn't for another eight or nine days," Felipe said.

"The date of the trial was changed. Like I said, the trial is today."

"Huh. Nice to be kept informed," Felipe said.

"Son, I don't make the rules. I just drive. Got any things you want to bring with you?"

"Everything's back at the monastery."

The other soldier stepped forward and spoke for the first time. "Any toiletries or clothes you need you can get back in Santa Fe. Let's hit the road."

"You're going to have to give me a few minutes. I need to use the can before I leave, and the outhouse is out back. I won't be more than a couple of minutes, so I'll meet you out at the truck. By the way, am I riding up front or in back?"

"Up front," the lead soldier said.

As he walked to the outhouse, Felipe turned back. One of the soldiers was already climbing up into the cab, but the other was standing in front of the retreat house having a smoke. There was no way Noah could make his move as long as that soldier remained there.

"Hey," Freddie yelled to the soldier by the retreat house door, "would you find my canteen in the kitchen and fill it up over there at the well?"

The soldier starred at Felipe. "Why don't I just get you water from the kitchen?"

"The water from the well is colder. Comes up from way down," Felipe replied, surprised at how quickly his mind was working.

After five minutes in the outhouse, Felipe stepped outside and pretended to zip up his jeans. He looked over at the retreat house where someone besides Noah Frost would soon be staying.

He realized as he approached the truck that he'd miss the place. More than his room back at the monastery, the retreat house had become somehow his space, his and Noah Frost's. But he would miss the monastery as well. A place meant to be his punishment for assaulting the homeless man had become a place he was trusted—trusted first by the monks not to run away and then trusted by Noah Frost not to betray him.

He sat in the middle of the cab, flanked by the soldiers, neither of whom spoke as they took the road they came in on. As the truck bumped along the rutted road, he thought about the stowaway—the possible stowaway—in the back of the truck. Felipe thought it likely, no matter what decision Noah made, that they wouldn't see each other again. Noah's family was as much of a jail for Noah as any Felipe had known, and if Noah decided to go home, he would accept the equivalent of a life sentence where he'd be told what to think, believe, and feel and where his future was in the hands of his father. *Keep running, Noah,* Felipe thought. *Anything and anywhere would be better than that.*

But as soon as he thought that, he realized that he could be terribly wrong. Noah was a young fifteen-year-old, smart with a Bible and a compass, but not street smart. Noah could maybe hitch a ride to Phoenix or even Los Angeles, but Noah wouldn't survive forty-eight hours in either city. The crazy truth, Felipe realized, was that Noah had found his perfect place at St. Mary's retreat house.

A voice over an intercom in the truck interrupted his thoughts. "Have you taken delivery, over?"

The driver reached down and picked up a handheld mic. "Delivery picked up and secured. How about on your end?"

A voice crackled in response. "Everything on schedule. Further instructions later."

"What's this shit—'further instructions later?'" the soldier in the passenger seat said after the other soldier replaced the mic. "What're we supposed to do until then?"

As he said this, the truck slowed at an intersection with another unpaved road, one that looked more traveled. Directional signs were stacked on a pole, one pointing to the left for Santa Fe. The truck, however, turned right, away from the city.

In the same moment that Felipe opened his mouth to point out the mistake, he realized that the driver's Army uniform lacked a name patch over the left pocket. As if in slow motion, he swiveled and saw that the same patch was missing from the other soldier's uniform.

"Hey, what's going—"

The soldier in the passenger seat pulled a knife from a sheath. "Shut the fuck up, kid, or you won't live to see tomorrow."

As fear shot down his spine, Felipe thought, *What have I gotten Noah into?*

As soon as Brother Abram arrived at the retreat house a few minutes before noon, he felt something was amiss. Felipe made it a practice to come out and meet the jeep when it brought him lunch. But Felipe didn't appear this time.

It took him only a moment to search the retreat house and realize that Felipe was gone. Dejected, he sat outside on a log bench and shook his head. Contrary to what he believed and shared with Father Fortis and Christopher Worthy just the day before, Felipe had clearly run away.

Abram was so sure he saw in Felipe the first of the subtle changes that people often experienced after spending time at St. Mary's. They were the same changes he experienced himself on his first visit to the monastery. But the boy had fooled them all.

So stupid, Felipe. So stupid, he thought as he picked up a rock and threw it as far as he could. Brother Abram knew the community would continue to offer prayers for Felipe, but he feared that the boy, back in the city, would soon be back in lock-up. He said a short prayer, asking that God keep Felipe safe, wondering how much he believed the words he was thinking.

Chapter Thirty-One

Dr. Bratton's expression of concern said it all to Worthy as he was ushered into the psychiatrist's office. Father Fortis and Sera were already there, and Worthy could see that Sera had been crying.

"We never know in cases like this," Dr. Bratton began in a voice that sounded to Worthy like an apology. "But at breakfast time this morning, Freddie threw the tray at the wall of his cell and began banging his head on the floor. It was a repeat of how he behaved several weeks ago. We had to restrain and sedate him."

"Oh, God; oh, God," was all that Sera managed to say.

"We have a constant video feed from Freddie's cell. He was quiet throughout the night and was sitting calmly on his bed before breakfast. But something triggered his...his regression."

"What could have done that?" Father Fortis asked.

Dr. Bratton shook her head wearily. "Maybe a memory, a thought, or an association in his mind. With cases like Freddie's, the mind is so fragile."After a pause, she looked at the three of them and added, "We might have pushed too hard."

The room was quiet for a moment before Worthy said, "I don't buy it. Freddie wanted to get the truth out. He was ready."

"I'm not saying you're wrong, but I think it likely that Freddie, when the truth surfaced, reverted back to that horrible day in Afghanistan," Dr. Bratton answered in a tight voice.

Father Fortis looked at his friend. "You think it's more than that, Christopher?"

Worthy shrugged. "I'm not the doctor. So, I could be way off base."

"Or, maybe not," Sera replied.

Through the window, Worthy could see a view that was heartbreakingly beautiful, such a contrast to the greyness of the room. "In my line of work, when something unexpected happens, I start with the question 'who benefits from that?'"

"And the answer you come up with is what?" Father Fortis asked.

"Well, to state the obvious, I'm not saying Captain Mills is behind it, but the video will be all he needs to get the insanity verdict. And before you say I'm paranoid, Dr. Bratton, can we look at the video from breakfast?"

The psychiatrist sighed as she hit a few keys on her computer. "Are you sure you want to see this, Sera?"

Sera rose and with Worthy and Father Fortis came around behind the psychiatrist. "I think I need to."

After a few moments of blank screen, a picture emerged of Freddie sitting on his bed in his cell. He looked like he just awakened, but seemed calm until a soldier brought in a tray. With his back to the camera, the soldier put the tray down on a small table and unfolded the cutlery—what looked to Worthy like a plastic fork and spoon.

"No audio?" Worthy asked.

The psychiatrist shook her head. "Just visual."

As the soldier rose up from setting the food out, Freddie looked directly at the soldier but didn't say anything. When the soldier left the cell, Freddie stared at the tray of food. After a long moment, he began to sway back and forth on his bed as he brought his hands up to his head and grabbed tightly onto his hair. The next moment was an explosion of chaos, with Freddie grabbing the tray and slinging the food at the far wall. In an instant, Freddie dropped to his knees and began banging his head on the cement floor.

"I think we've seen enough," Dr. Bratton said, as Sera began sobbing.

"Keep it rolling," Worthy said.

"Are you sure?" the psychiatrist again addressed the question to Sera.

Sera glanced at Worthy and saw him nod. "Yes," she whispered.

Freddie's bizarre behavior continued on the tape, his head slamming repeatedly on the floor. They could all see blood appear on his forehead, first as a tiny blotch and then with each blow that blotch spreading. After what seemed minutes, the room was filled with soldiers who pulled Freddie from the floor and held him down on his bed until they could restrain his arms and legs.

"They sure took their time," Father Fortis commented after the video stopped.

"Exactly," Worthy said. "The tape will show that Freddie, without any doubt, looks completely insane, which is just what the defense needs for tomorrow. But what the tape doesn't show is what the soldier who brought in the tray said to Freddie."

"If the soldier said anything," Dr. Bratton said.

Sera wiped at her eyes. "Chris, I think we should let it go. We're the ones who said too much to Freddie. It's our fault, and my husband...my husband needs help."

Worthy turned toward her, his voice sharp and metallic. "Don't even think about giving up now, Sera. That's what they want us to do."

"But who is the 'they,' Christopher?" Father Fortis asked. "Do you really believe that Captain Mills did something like this to Freddie on purpose? I know Freddie's lawyer can be frustrating, but I've never doubted he thinks he's acting in the best interests of Freddie."

"I didn't say it's Mills," Worthy answered, still staring at Sera.

"Who, then?" Dr. Bratton asked.

"Let me get answers to a couple more questions before I explain who I think is behind this. Doctor, can you find out the identity of the soldier who brought in the tray?"

"That shouldn't be too hard," Dr. Bratton answered. "Do you want me to call him in?"

"Not yet. We just need to know who the soldier is."

After several minutes on her computer, Dr. Bratton pulled up military photos of two soldiers, one African-American, the other Caucasian. "Our guy was white, don't you agree?" she asked.

The photo remaining on the screen belonged to Cpl. Jay Conrad. Worthy leaned over Dr. Bratton's shoulder and studied the face. "Anyone recognize him?"

Father Fortis inhaled sharply. "He was one of the soldiers in the interrogation room whenever I met with Freddie."

"Huh. That means he heard everything that transpired," Dr. Bratton said.

"And he was the one who left the interrogation room the last time, right after Freddie began to answer your questions with the paper and pen," Worthy added. He turned to Dr. Bratton and said, "If you call to find out where this Conrad is now, I'm betting you're going to be surprised at the answer."

The psychiatrist picked up her phone and inquired of Cpl. Jay Conrad with someone on the other end.

"Okay, when was that?" Dr. Bratton asked the other party, nodding toward Worthy. "And can you tell me his off-base address?"

After Dr. Bratton told the other party not to let Cpl. Conrad know of her query, she hung up the phone. "He complained of feeling sick this morning. He's off the base."

"Let me guess," Worthy said. "Right after breakfast, right?"

The psychiatrist nodded.

"Oh, God, what have they done to Freddie?" Sera wailed.

Father Fortis put his arm around her. "We'll find out who did this, Sera. We'll find out." He looked at Worthy. "Well, who did this?"

"It's not Mills or anyone else who wants Freddie to be declared mentally incompetent tomorrow. If I'm right, it's the person who killed Burgess outside the bar."

"But what did this Conrad say to Freddie?" Sera asked.

"Only Freddie knows that, and he won't likely be able to answer that for some time—if ever," Dr. Bratton said.

Worthy shook his head. "Maybe not. Conrad has been working for someone throughout this whole process. And my list of possible perpetrators is getting shorter by the minute."

Noah struggled to make himself comfortable beneath the tarp in the back of the truck. But he was grateful for the chance Felipe gave him to get away from the retreat house.

So where am I going? he thought. Back at the retreat house, he heard what the soldiers said, that they were taking Felipe back to Santa Fe for something about his father's trial. That meant that the immediate answer to his question was that he was going back to Santa Fe. But from there, where would he go?

If he showed up at his home, he knew his father would be furious. His brother, Danny, also wouldn't spare him. But he knew below that anger would be what really mattered to his father—his embarrassment at his son's "prank." *I will be the prodigal son from the gospel story, except that this father won't give me ring and robe, won't kill the fatted calf.*

His running away, he knew, was hardest on his mother. She would welcome him back with open arms—tears too, but no accusations. If he could explain his actions to anyone, what he learned about himself by running away, it would be to her. But his mother had never been strong enough to push against his father, for his father was, in the end, Triple B—Bountiful Blessing Bible.

For Noah, the worst part of returning home would be not seeing Felipe again. How was it that Felipe, from a world that Noah was raised to fear, had yet protected him? Felipe made it clear that he wished for Noah a different future than returning home. But in their talks together, neither boy had come up with a plausible alternative.

There it was, the word "boy." If he were three years older, he'd legally be considered a man, old enough to chart his own future. But he was fifteen—in the eyes of his family and the law, just a boy.

He thought of Felipe and his future. From what he heard back at the retreat house, Felipe would return to the monastery after the hearing. Felipe, too, was considered a boy, a juvenile in the eyes of the law, someone whose future was in the hands of others.

He felt the truck slow down, but he knew they were still at least an hour away from Santa Fe. He peeked out from behind the tarp, and through the open flap at the back saw the directional signs. At the moment that he realized the truck was heading in the opposite direction from Santa Fe, he heard one of the soldiers shout over the whine of the engine, "Shut the fuck up, kid, or you won't live to see tomorrow."

His mind froze, and he began shaking as he drew the tarp over his head again. The truck driving away from Santa Fe and the threat could mean only one thing, that the soldiers didn't come to escort Felipe back to the city. A sudden urge to jump out the truck at his next chance, to make his way to some house or village and inform the police, nearly overpowered Noah. But as he looked out at the desert and the foothills, he realized it might take him hours to find help, hours that his new friend Felipe might not have. *No, I will not do that,* he thought.

Until that moment, Noah had battled pangs of guilt for running away. In his life, he was given little opportunity or permission to consider what he wanted, much less act on it. His father constantly reminded him, particularly the previous summer when he told his father about wanting a career close to nature, that for a Christian the issue wasn't one's career, but one's *vocation,* one's calling from God. In the weeks that followed, his father and brother tag-teamed on him, encouraging him to pray for God's guidance and especially to be open to a call to ministry.

Noah now saw that he ran away not simply because of the TV interview about the Bible contest but because he realized, in a rare moment of thinking for himself, that God would have a hard time showing him his vocation while his father and brother had already made that decision for him—and for God.

That was what made living with the pain he caused his mother in the last two weeks bearable, that he ran away in order to be with God alone, to listen for some clue to his vocation. As the truck rumbled along without any talking from the cab, Noah realized that the question of his vocation was, in fact, being answered in a way that he could never have imagined.

Was it coincidence or something more that Noah found the brochure about St. Mary's retreat house at the church on his paper route? Was it coincidence or something more that Felipe discovered him hiding in the retreat house and didn't turn him in? Was it coincidence or something more that in running away to be with God alone, he finally found a friend? And now, was it coincidence or something more that he was in a place, the back of a truck, where he might be able to help save his newfound friend's life?

He thought of his favorite Bible story, David and Goliath. David was a boy probably about his own age, and in seeing the giant, Goliath, David understood his vocation. *My vocation isn't something years down the road once I graduate from college, not at Bountiful Blessing, not even back at the retreat house. No, my vocation is right here and right now,* he thought.

Chapter Thirty-Two

As Sera sat in Dr. Bratton's office, she felt numb from her brain down to her heart and farther down to her legs. More than anything, she wanted to be with Freddie, to hold him and tell him what he was experiencing wasn't his fault, that someone was deliberately messing with his mind. But Freddie's lawyer, Captain Mills, wouldn't allow that. When the psychiatrist contacted Captain Mills and explained how Freddie's relapse was orchestrated by Cpl. Conrad and maybe others, Mills blamed the four of them for Freddie's setback, insisting that Cpl. Conrad had no role in Freddie's present condition. In the lawyer's opinion, the four of them were as delusional as Freddie.

The result of today's trial was no longer in doubt. Freddie might not be calm enough to attend, but the video of Freddie's outburst from that morning would be all the military court needed to send him away for the foreseeable future. Sera saw her future as her present agony endlessly played out, her showing up for visiting hours at the psych ward. The only uncertainty in her mind was whether she would be visiting alone or with Felipe.

Felipe. In the madness of the morning, Sera had almost forgotten about Felipe. He was at St. Mary's, safe for the time being. And, if Father Fortis was right, Felipe might not be too far away from Noah Frost.

In the psychiatrist's office, Worthy began pacing the room once Captain Mills had turned a deaf ear. *This is going to be a difficult morning for everyone, not just me,* Sera thought. She felt she would slip into total numbness or scream if she had to stay in Dr. Bratton's office one minute longer. *Good Lord, I'm turning into Freddie,* she thought.

"I need to do something," she said, standing up and looking at Worthy and Father Fortis. "Do either of you want to go with me out to St. Mary's? I want to find out about Noah, and I really need to see my son before the trial."

Worthy looked down at his watch. "Nick, why don't you do that? I'm going to stay here in town to check out a few things before trial begins."

That seemed to Sera an excuse, but she let it go. She could unburden herself freely to Father Fortis, which was just what she needed, this morning of all mornings.

As the two drove out of Santa Fe in the direction of Truchas, Sera shared the other part of her fears. "I've been a bad mother, Nick. I was so wounded by Felipe the last time we spoke and, to be honest, so relieved to know he's safe at the monastery, that I agreed to step back. My focus went completely to Freddie, but now? The day I need Felipe the most to look me in the eye and share my pain, I'm thinking he'll lash out at me for not caring. And he'll be right to do that."

Father Fortis turned toward her from the passenger seat. "There's a name for what you're doing to yourself, Sera. I can't recall what it is, but I know it isn't healthy. Felipe needed a complete change of environment, which is what you agreed to give him. Before you beat yourself up, let's wait to see how St. Mary's has affected him."

Sera thought about this for a moment. "You don't think he's hated every minute of being stuck out at the monastery?"

"The monastery isn't some sort of spiritual Alcatraz, Sera. When I saw him and spoke with him—granted, we haven't talked a lot—he seemed like he was okay with the place. Maybe not thrilled, but okay with it. And remember this: the community gave him a lot more freedom than he expected, and please don't discount the fact that they pray for him every day."

"Would they have told him they were praying for him? I mean, I can see Felipe feeling manipulated with the prayer thing."

"'The prayer thing?'Okay, I can see how prayer can seem a kind of 'thing,' and, to calm your fears, I doubt if anyone told Felipe he's been one of the community's prayer concerns. Prayer at a monastery is more like the air we breathe. Without prayer, a monastery wouldn't last much longer than a person without breath. But like breathing, we don't have to talk about prayer to know it's all around us every minute."

After a moment of silence, Sera said "You really love being a monk, don't you?"

Father Fortis nodded. "I do, Sera, though my abbot questions that."

"Because you work with Chris on cases?"

"What bothers him is not so much my working on cases but the fact that the detective business takes me away from my vocation and my community. I'm stretching one of the vows I took."

"Which one?"

"We take a vow of stability, a promise that we won't leave the monastery unless Christ, speaking though the abbot, moves us. I am not what you call a stable monk. But maybe you've figured out one of my secrets, Sera."

"You mean, why you insisted both times you've been out here that you and Chris stay at St. Mary's?"

Father Fortis smiled. "I guess that wasn't such a secret after all."

"The prayer thing again, right?"

"Yes, the prayer thing. I need to be in that atmosphere, especially during a homicide case."

"Do you think Chris feels that atmosphere?"

"If you're asking if I have some secret hope that by our staying at St. Mary's, Chris will find faith again, no, that's not why. Chris would sense that immediately, and our friendship would take a big hit. But Chris is more like a monk than he realizes. To use his gifts, he needs a quiet space where his thinking isn't interrupted with all the noise."

"Do you think that's why he didn't want to come with us today?"

"Yes, I do. Being with us would make it more difficult for him to accomplish what he's focused on," Father Fortis said.

"Even if we're all focused on the same thing?"

"I'm not sure we are, Sera. The last couple days, Christopher has been quieter than usual. With both of us. If I know my friend, he's trying to figure out how to get ahead of whoever is behind all this. He's trying to anticipate that person's next move."

"He doesn't have much time, Nick. None of us do."

"He knows that, Sera. But every time one of us—usually Christopher—figures out what this person is up to, Christopher gains a clearer sense of how that person's mind works. Remember how long it took us to figure out that Freddie's delusion was about the death of the Afghan boy? It took us weeks. Now think how quickly Christopher figured out about Conrad saying something at breakfast to throw Freddie into a tailspin. Minutes, Sera, minutes. Christopher is dialing in on the culprits."

"How does this help Freddie? The trial is in a couple of hours, and you saw what he's like."

Father Fortis nodded. "Yes, I know. But I believe Christopher is close to figuring out all kinds of things about this case, not just who killed Burgess."

"Like what?" Sera asked, but she felt hope again.

Father Fortis fingered his pectoral cross. "For some time, I've had a feeling that your family has experienced not just bad luck, but *too much* bad luck. It was something Christopher said that got me thinking about that. And, as a priest, I don't believe in luck, but I do know something about human misfortune. So either your family is living out a modern version of Job or..."Father Fortis left the unfinished sentence hanging in midair.

"Or what?"

Father Fortis didn't answer the question. "As soon as Christopher said we needed to take Freddie's delusion seriously, we began to work backwards on everything that's happened to you. Well, backwards at least to what happened to Freddie, Felipe, and you in the past three or four weeks. Start with today. Who needs Freddie to be declared incompetent to stand trial?"

"If Chris is right, whoever killed Burgess outside the bar," Sera said.

"Right. Now go back to Felipe being beaten up in detention."

"I thought that was because of me being a cop."

"In a way, I think that's true. But I think Felipe was targeted in order to, well..."

"To overwhelm me," Sera said, finishing the sentence.

"So that you'd be no good for Felipe, for Freddie, or for the case. Whoever is behind this knows that you're a good detective, and they did whatever they could so that you couldn't focus on figuring out what really happened to Freddie."

Sera took a halting breath. "They did a damn good job. And before that? Are you saying what happened at the bar was part of this plan?"

"Ah, that's the big question. I think it must be, but if I know Christopher, then neither of us believes that Burgess' death was part of the original plan."

"I keep thinking that Burgess, until that night, was the ringleader."

Father Fortis slapped his thigh. "Yes, yes, I think he was just that. But, for some reason that night, one of the other soldiers decided to take over that role."

Sera felt a tingling in her hands and feet. *It's like I'm waking up.*

"Did the killer do that to make sure Freddie would be charged with it?"

"Christopher sees it another way. He thinks one or all of them at the bar that night realized Freddie wasn't coming out of his fog anytime soon, that they were safe. That was probably the reason for the get-together—just to make sure they were all safe."

"So why the fight out in the parking lot?"

"That's the rest of Christopher's theory. He thinks that the original plan, if Freddie looked like he was coming back to reality, was for Burgess to take him outside and start a fight. And, I'm sorry to have to say this, but Christopher thinks Burgess wasn't too sure about Freddie and took him out to the parking lot to end it right there. He would claim that Freddie drew the knife on him and went berserk, and the rest of them would testify that Freddie was delusional in the bar."

"And one of them knifed the unconscious Burgess instead? Those bastards, those fucking bastards," she said banging the steering wheel with her fist.

"Sorry, Nick."

"No need to apologize. Even if I didn't say it out loud, what I was thinking was roughly the same."

After a moment, Sera asked, "But why kill Burgess?"

"I wish I knew the answer to that, my dear. I think Christopher is close to answering that question, and that's another reason he stayed in town. He's checking out something, maybe the last piece of the puzzle."

Sera pulled off the highway to the gravel road leading to St. Mary's and stopped. Through her tears she looked out at the foothills and the snow-capped mountains beyond. In that moment, something seemed to open within her and she took a long, deep breath. She felt the mountain air clear something, and that, somewhere below her surface doubts, she believed Nick.

Was it really possible that all the pain and sorrow her family had experienced was rooted in a twenty-second impulsive act in Afghanistan? And what did that mean for the future? Was it possible that the truth could begin to heal her family?

"I believe, help thou my unbelief," she whispered.

"Did I just hear you say what I think you said?" Father Fortis asked.

"It's something my grandmother taught me. She told me she repeated it every day when my grandfather was drinking heavily. That was before the Penitentes saved him from himself. If I didn't have hope, she told me I should at least ask God for hope."

Father Fortis sat in silence. Sera reached over and grabbed his meaty hand. "You've given me hope, Nick."

She felt Father Fortis' hand squeeze hers back. "Let's find this missing boy, Sera."

"And see my son," she said as she wiped her eyes.

†

It was a long shot, but Worthy saw no other route to take. He knocked on the door of the Burgess home, a Frank Lloyd Wright copy near the top of Museum Row. A tiny Latina answered the door. She took Worthy's business card and excused herself.

In a moment, a striking woman in her fifties, slim and tan in a white linen suit and a necklace of turquoise chunks, came to the door. "How can I help you, officer?" she said.

There was no warmth in the question, and Worthy suspected things wouldn't get warmer once he made his request.

"I'd like ten minutes of your time, Mrs. Burgess. I'm investigating your son's murder and would like to ask you a few questions."

Mrs. Burgess made no movement to let Worthy enter. "Are you working with the Army?"

Worthy thought about Burgess' mother being a lawyer and the likelihood of her cooperating if he told her the exact truth. Instead, he said, "Yes, I'm working with Lt. Col. Bratton on the case."

Opening the door, she said, "I'm not sure I remember all those Army names, but come in, please."

Worthy entered the house and followed Mrs. Burgess down a wide hallway to a large rectangular room that boasted two fireplaces in opposite corners. Native American rugs hung on the walls and a bronze statue of an Indian on a horse sat on a long coffee table made of reclaimed wood.

Mrs. Burgess motioned to a leather chair before she sat down on a matching sofa. A woven purse sat at her feet along with a Siamese cat. "Is there something last-minute, officer, about the case? We were informed that the trial would start this afternoon."

Worthy was grateful that Mrs. Burgess didn't question why a detective from Detroit would be involved in her son's case, but knew, now that he managed to face her directly, that his task became more difficult. He wondered if the mix of truth and fiction that he would present would achieve the needed outcome, but there was no turning back now.

"Mrs. Burgess, there are some last-minute developments, and that's why I'm in New Mexico assisting."

"Please explain." The detached tone in which she said these two simple words reminded Worthy of being on the witness stand.

"I'm working on behalf of the accused, Sgt. Frederick Contreras. We believe we can say with strong probability that your son was killed not by the accused but by someone else."

"Someone else? Certainly, you have some idea as to the identity of this person," Mrs. Burgess said, holding Worthy's gaze.

This is no grieving mother, Worthy thought. *This is a hard-shelled lawyer.*

"We believe one or more other members of your son's Army unit killed your son."

Worthy waited for Mrs. Burgess to demand some convincing evidence of the claim or to escort him to the door. Instead, she looked down at the rings on her hand and sat silently for a moment.

"I am aware, Lieutenant, that my son was not the easiest person to get along with. Ash was no angel. I guess you could say he was cursed with being an only son of indulgent and affluent parents. His social skills were sometimes... lacking. But for all his faults, our son didn't deserve to die that way."

Worthy was struck by Mrs. Burgess' final words, which contained the first hint of warmth. From it, Worthy deduced that this woman, this high-powered lawyer, had, since the death of her son, mentally put him on trial. She had searched her memories to determine his own part in his demise. "No, Mrs. Burgess, he didn't deserve this," he said.

Worthy waited for the question Mrs. Burgess had to utter before he could proceed.

Resting her hands on her knees, Mrs. Burgess asked, "Why would another of his fellow soldiers do that to Ash?"

Here, Worthy thought, would be where he would stretch truth so thin that any lawyer worth her fee should be able to see right through it. "We think there may have been blackmail involved."

Mrs. Burgess didn't look up, but asked, "Blackmail? But why?"

This is the truth part, Worthy thought, *or what I'm betting is the truth.* "Because of something that happened in Afghanistan during a firefight with the Taliban."

Mrs. Burgess closed her eyes as if not wanting to see something.

"And my son was...was caught up in this blackmail business?"

"That's what we're looking into."

"And what do you need from me?" she asked.

"Permission to see your son's bank statements after he returned from Afghanistan."

"And the confession by the accused?"

It was not a mother's question, but a thorough lawyer's question, Worthy noted, one that offered neither a yes or a no to his request.

And here is where truth bleeds again into fiction. "We have psychiatric testimony that the accused was delusional at the time of the confession. The admissibility of the confession will be challenged at trial."

"I see."

And Worthy understood that she did see. He waited for her decision.

From her purse, she drew out a pair of reading glasses, a cellphone, and a small notebook. The cat looked up at Mrs. Burgess and walked slowly from the room. Worthy waited while the woman found what she was looking for and punched in the numbers.

After asking for the bank president and waiting for a moment, Mrs. Burgess said, "Jerry, it's Camille. A police officer from Detroit will be stopping by shortly. His name is Lt. Worthy, and he has my permission to look at Ash's recent bank statements. No, I don't think we need to consult our lawyer on this, as I am my own lawyer, Jerry. Right, right. Thank you, Jerry. Give my love to Bitsy."

After she rang off, Camille rose from the sofa. "Will that do?"

The coldness of the phone conversation, its business tone, gave Worthy a slight shudder. He rose as well. "It's much appreciated, Mrs. Burgess."

At the door, the woman looked as if she wanted to ask another question.

And Worthy was sure that he knew what that question was: "Was my son the victim of blackmail or the blackmailer?"But at her core, Worthy realized, Camille Burgess was a lawyer, one who knew that sometimes it's better not to know the whole truth.

Chapter Thirty-Three

Sera and Father Fortis sat in Abbot Peter's office with Sera explaining their theory about the missing boy. "Noah Frost has been missing for nearly three weeks. We've recently discovered that on most of the days just prior to his running away, he sat quietly in the back of St. Jude's Catholic Church near his paper route. And we found this brochure in the narthex."

She handed the brochure over to Abbot Peter.

"You think he might be out at the retreat house?" he asked.

"It's the best lead we have so far," Sera replied.

The abbot studied the brochure for another moment before turning toward a two-way radio on a shelf below a window.

Punching a button, he asked, "Brother Abram, how far are you from my office?"

"About ten minutes out, Father."

"Okay, I have a police officer here along with Father Fortis. Is there any chance that a missing boy from Santa Fe is camping out at the retreat house?"

"No chance at all, Father."

"Ask him how he can be so certain," Sera said.

Brother Abram's voice boomed. "I heard the question. I know that for a fact because for the last couple of days, Felipe has worked both morning and afternoon at the house. If the boy is there, Felipe would know it and would... well, I think he would report it."

"You're saying my son is working at this same retreat house?"

"What?" came over the radio. "Your son? Is this Mrs. Lacey?"

"Lieutenant Lacey, in fact," Sera said.

"Sorry. The answer to your question is complicated," Brother Abram said.

"I don't understand," Sera said.

There was a long pause from the other end, leading Father Fortis to wonder if the connection had been cut. "Your son was at the retreat house, washing the floors and repainting the inside walls."

"I don't understand how that's complicated," Sera said.

Brother Abram again failed to answer directly. "Are you still there, Abram?" the abbot asked.

"Yeah, I'm here, Father. But there's bad news. I just came from the house and Felipe's gone. He ran away."

Sera looked like she was going to explode. "When?"

"Sometime this morning. I dropped him at eight, and when I came back with his lunch, I discovered he's gone."

Sera hands formed two fists. "Still think I should keep hope, Nick?"

"Sera," Father Fortis said. "Yes, I do. Now more than ever. I think Christopher would tell us we have to visit the retreat house."

"Why, Nick?"

"If for no other reason than to see where Felipe might be headed," Father Fortis replied. He didn't want to share Worthy's words that plagued his mind. "Who benefits from Felipe running away?" *Who benefits, indeed?* he thought.

Ten minutes later, Brother Abram arrived in a cloud of dust in front of St. Mary's administration building. With hardly a word from either, Father Fortis stepped into the back of the jeep and let Sera take the passenger seat. For once, he was grateful that the vehicle's noise prevented conversation. As they bounced along the rough road, Father Fortis had one question after another flood his mind. What prompted Felipe to run away? Why today? Would he find his way back to Santa Fe? How long before the police found him?

His thoughts turned to Noah Frost, the quiet son of a mega-preacher, the boy who sat in the back of a Catholic Church. More questions surfaced. If Noah wasn't at St. Mary's, then where is he? Father Fortis looked out at the unforgiving desert. Were Noah's bones out there somewhere?

They should call this "The Case of the Three Boys," he thought. Freddie's breakdown had followed the death of an Afghan boy, a boy he confused with Felipe. Sera's search for Noah Frost brought them to the very place where Felipe had been staying. Ibrahim, Noah, and Felipe—three boys, one dead, another possibly dead, and the third—yes, what about the third?

✝

AS WORTHY DROVE AWAY FROM THE Pacific National Bank, he felt he was closing in on the killer or killers. Reviewing Ash Burgess' transactions at the bank verified what Worthy suspected—Burgess received five anonymous transfers of $500 each at the beginning of the past two months.

Worthy admitted that the most obvious solution to the puzzle was that Burgess observed rather than participated in the slaughter of the Afghans in the interview room. That gave Burgess the leverage for blackmailing the others, not counting Sergeant Contreras, involved in the slaughter.

But Worthy was convinced that the obvious solution wasn't what happened. What wouldn't make sense to Worthy at first was beginning to do so. What first happened in that room was Burgess beginning the shooting, an impulsive act in response to the sound of the Taliban attack outside the room. Tragically, he targeted the Afghan chieftain, his son, and the rest of his entourage, assuming they were part of the assault.

What happened in the next second or two was Burgess' knee-jerk reaction causing the others in the room, besides Freddie, to begin firing. The scene must have looked like something from "Scarface."If Freddie in those brief seconds tried to do something to prevent the carnage, he failed.

Following that, Burgess took after the fleeing figure of Sergeant Contreras, aware that his sergeant was the only one who didn't join in the slaughter, and therefore the only one who could dispute any later version of the firefight. Perhaps Burgess intended to shoot his sergeant during the wider firefight, an easily explained outcome of close combat with the Taliban. But the Taliban surprised him by grabbing the fleeing figure of Sergeant Contreras and, ironically, saving his life.

The story, as Worthy understood it, changed once the unit was stateside when Burgess dreamt up something truly brazen. Burgess saw the very slaughter he initiated as an opportunity for blackmail. The very backwards logic of the blackmail scheme—Burgess benefitting from the tragic scene he created—became logical to Worthy when he kept in mind one key feature of the case. Burgess must have realized that the other members of the unit in the room had more to worry about, if the truth ever came out, than he did. Perhaps, Worthy imagined, Burgess thought that he could trade immunity for giving his version of the slaughter. More likely, however, Burgess knew he was the only member of the unit with a seasoned lawyer for a mother, someone who always gave him everything he asked for, and someone who would do anything to save her boy.

Worthy was impressed with the audacity of Burgess' scam. Burgess was rash and impulsive, the one who precipitated the unnecessary slaughter. But Burgess was also brash, willing to bluff with his cards and take his chances. As Camille Burgess admitted, Ash was no angel.

But Burgess overplayed his hand. His whole scheme would dissolve if Freddie Contreras' memories and sanity came back. As delusional as Freddie was that night at the Milky Way Bar, Burgess couldn't take any chances. But Freddie managed to defend himself in the parking lot and knock Burgess unconscious. And in the next few moments, someone else from the unit came out and saw an opportunity to end the monthly blackmail payments.

As Worthy drove through the gate of the Army base to share his findings with Captain Mills, he realized he should feel a lot better than he did. Yes, Mills would balk at opening an investigation based on Worthy's theory, but the lawyer would see that he was duty-bound to hold off on Freddie's trial.

The outcome could only be this: Freddie would be exonerated and transferred from prison to a hospital where his recovery could be jump-started again. *So why do I feel a ball of fear in my gut?*

Worthy thought back over the last twenty-four hours. Until yesterday, when Freddie did his best, limited as it was, to shed light on *both* the firefight in Afghanistan and the events at the Milky Way bar, Sera, Nick, and he lagged behind the perpetrators. First, it was Burgess who called the shots. Then, after his death, one of the other soldiers of the unit cleverly took over.

All that changed when Freddie began to scribble down what really happened, something Cpl. Conrad, the informant in the Army hospital, relayed immediately to Burgess' killer. Burgess' killer was no longer in control and was forced to react.

Yes, Worthy thought, we're closing in. The afternoon deadline would no longer hang over their heads. Sera, Nick, and I should be celebrating. *Then why am I dreading something?*

He thought back to the video of Cpl. Conrad entering Freddie's cell that morning. Yes, there was something here that they'd all overlooked. Once he admitted that, he realized what he was missing—the words Conrad said to Freddie that caused the meltdown.

Worthy pulled into a parking space, turned off the engine, and rolled down the windows. He felt a gust of clean New Mexican air blow into the car as he remembered Freddie's look of terror on the video right before he lost control and began tearing his cell apart.

The answer slowly dawned on Worthy, making his heart race and his face perspire. To cause such a reaction, Conrad must have said something about Felipe. He raked his hand through his hair and thought about Freddie's journey into and out of madness. Freddie first fell apart when he thought he was somehow responsible for Felipe's death.

Worthy was out of the car and running toward Captain Mills' office before the rest of the scene in Freddie's cell became clear. What Conrad told Freddie must have been something along the lines of this: "You testify and Felipe dies." Conrad, as one of the guards whenever Father Fortis and Dr. Bratton were with Freddie, must have heard Father Fortis explaining to Freddie about the monastery letting Felipe work alone in the retreat house. The killer knew Felipe's location and his vulnerability.

In Captain Mills' office, Worthy hurriedly spelled out his theory. Mills, however, looked uninterested, almost as if he might yawn. With greater force, Worthy ended by saying, "We have to make sure Felipe is safe."

"Too late, Lieutenant. I was just informed that Freddie's son ran away from St. Mary's this morning. So your theory just blew up."

Worthy leaned over and barely kept himself from grabbing the lapels of the lawyer. "Like hell it did," he said. "Don't you see? If they got to Felipe in juvenile detention, they could get to him at the monastery. Felipe didn't run away. He was abducted."

Chapter Thirty-Four

As the jeep crested a hill and approached the retreat house, Father Fortis recited all the prayers he knew for divine guidance and protection, holding up Sera, Freddie, and especially Felipe as he did so.

In a few seconds, the jeep ground to a half, but before they could exit the jeep and search the site, a call came though on the jeep's two-way radio.

"Go ahead, this is Brother Abram."

The three could hear Abbot Peter's voice on the other end. "I just got a call from Lieutenant Worthy. He needs to speak to Father Fortis."

Abram handed the mic to Father Fortis. "This is Nick, Christopher. I'm sure you've heard the bad news about Felipe."

"Listen, Nick. Have you searched the retreat house?"

"Not yet. We just got here."

"Okay. Sera, brace yourself. I am nearly positive that Felipe didn't run away but was taken. It's the killer's final attempt to silence Freddie."

"No, no, no. Oh, my God. Oh, my God," Sera said, slumping to the ground.

Worthy's voice was a shout from the radio. "Listen, Sera, and you, too, Nick. I know you're scared, Sera, but I'll tell you exactly what Nick told me in Venice last year when Allyson was abducted. He said what Allyson needed was for me to be a detective, the best I could be, and not a distraught parent. It's critical that you be that detective, now, Sera. Do you understand?"

After a pause, Sera replied in a shaky voice, "Yes, I understand."

"Good," Worthy said. "Start by looking for other vehicle tire tracks. They should be very recent, maybe only an hour or two old, and I doubt that the kidnappers bothered to conceal them. They're counting on us thinking Felipe ran away, so that's something about us that they don't know. Secondly, note especially the direction they arrived and left from. Brother Abram, are you listening?"

"Yes, I'm here."

"If...no, *once* you find the road they took, give me a call back. I have a plat map of the area with all the roads listed."

Sera nodded numbly. "As soon as we find the tire tracks, we'll follow."

"No, use the two-way radio to call back to the monastery, and they'll patch your call through to me. Cellphones won't have service out there. I have something I'm working on from this end that should link us directly with whoever took Felipe. Also, see if Felipe left anything in the retreat house to suggest he suspected something fishy."

Sera took a deep breath and wiped tears from her eyes. "Nick, you look in the retreat house for clues. Brother Abram and I will look for the tire tracks."

Father Fortis fought the urge to bolt into the house and rush his inspection. But he remembered how Worthy would insist on the opposite. He opened the door and stepped into a hallway. He looked for any evidence that the abductors used force when taking Felipe but found none.

In the chapel, he made the sign of the cross in front of the simple altar, offered a quick prayer, and studied the altar surface and the floor. Again, he found nothing more than evidence that the room was recently cleaned and repainted for the next guests.

In the kitchen, he saw the evidence that Felipe was having a snack when his abductors arrived. There were packets of cheese crackers scattered on the table as well as a jar of peanut butter. His first thought was to prevent Sera from entering the house. The reminders of Felipe's presence, these packets and glasses, might be more than she could take.

But then, his heart skipped a beat as he realized what he overlooked. There were two glasses with varying amounts of water. Why two? And as he studied the empty packets, he realized that they were in two distinct piles, opposite each other on the table. He looked carefully at the two chairs and saw that both were pulled away from the table. Was this evidence of one or more abductors or of something else?

He entered the bedroom and pulled back the blanket and sheet. Kneeling, he studied the surface of the bed. Yes, there were particles of sand in the low points of the mattress. *Someone slept here,* he realized.

Behind him, he heard the door to the retreat house swing open and Sera calling his name.

"I'm coming. I'll be right there."

He ran to the front door to block Sera's entrance and stepped outside. "Found anything?" he said.

Sera nodded. "We found the tire tracks. The tires are pretty far apart, side to side, and the lug tread designs suggest it's a truck."

"And the direction?"

"Brother Abram says they lead to a back way to several other forest roads. I still think we ought to follow them. Only God knows how much time we have."

Father Fortis nodded. *So true,* he thought, *only God knows.*

"I found some things inside that make me pause," he said.

The color of Sera's face turned ashen. "About Felipe?"

"No, nothing bad, my dear, but I think someone else was here beside Felipe. I don't mean whoever took Felipe, but someone else, someone who slept here."

"But Felipe sleeps back at St. Mary's." Sera paused, and then looked up sharply. "Noah Frost."

Father Fortis nodded. "And I think Felipe and Noah were in the kitchen having a snack when the abductors arrived."

"And Felipe never told Brother Abram," Sera said slowly. "It was their secret."

"I think they shared secrets, Sera."

"But where's Noah, then?"

Father Fortis put both hands on Sera's shoulders. "All I can assume is that the abductors took him as well. You did say the vehicle is a truck?"

Sera nodded, before scanning in all directions. "Or, he's still here and watching us right now." She paused for a moment before adding, "Okay, have Brother Abram call Chris. I'll look around. You're sure he's not hiding inside?"

"I'm sure."

In two long minutes, the call back to the monastery and then to Worthy came through. Father Fortis reported on what they discovered, first about Noah Frost and then about the tire tracks.

"I don't know if the Noah Frost business is good news or bad. No evidence of a struggle?" Worthy asked.

"None."

"Okay, that means that whoever picked up Felipe gave some excuse to bring him in. And if the abductor is working with Burgess' killer, I think we're looking for a military vehicle and at least one guy in uniform. Maybe even Conrad."

"That makes sense, Christopher."In the background, Father Fortis could see Sera studying the path leading to the outhouse. "I need to tell you that Sera is going to follow the tire tracks, no matter what you say."

"Yeah, I get that. Try to have her proceed carefully. And if you do come upon the vehicle, stay out of sight. If whoever is doing this sees you, he or they could take it out on Felipe."

"What will you be doing, Christopher?"

"I have a plan to catch whoever is behind this from this end. It'd take me too long to explain, so just wish me luck, Nick. We don't have much time."

"I've been doing something better than wishing. I've been praying. I don't believe God has brought us this close only to...well, only to fail."

"Keep that faith thing going, Nick," Worthy said and then signed off.

Father Fortis hardly had a moment to consider what Worthy just asked him.

†

Noah heard Felipe's voice from the cab. "I need to use the toilet again, and I need some water."

"Hold your horses, kid," one of the soldiers said. "We're coming to a place good for both."

Noah wondered if Felipe did in fact need to use a bathroom or if he was just angling for more time to think. Noah couldn't imagine what Felipe's options were, but he knew his new friend would do nothing to endanger him. *Yes*, he thought, *he is my friend*.

The truck turned off the road onto another road, one in even worse shape.

"Goddamn it, Jay, slow down," one of the soldiers said.

The driver did as he was commanded. After what seemed to Noah to be little more than a mile, the truck pulled to a stop.

Noah peeked out the back of the truck and saw a building with graffiti spray-painted on an outer wall and burn marks where someone tried to torch the building. It looked to Noah like the retreat house, and he remembered Felipe saying the house had once been a chapel of the Penitentes, a group Noah knew nothing about until Felipe told him about them.

The doors of the truck cab opened, and he heard the three exiting the vehicle. "There's a pump out back," the one named Jay said. "I'll keep an eye on the kid in the outhouse, and you go around back."Noah peeked out from under the tarp to see the two soldiers watching Felipe head toward the outhouse before one said in a low voice,"wait a minute."

Noah put his ear as close to the front of the truck's cab to hear what the two soldiers might say.

"I don't like this one bit," one said.

"Relax, Miguel, we're just delivering the kid." So one was Jay, the other Miguel.

"But the kid's going to be killed, right?"

"If we don't ask, then we don't know."

"And if we don't know, we can't be charged with abetting the crime—this crime, that is."

"Huh, I didn't know you knew the word 'abetting.' You're quite the lawyer all of a sudden."

"Hey, fuck you. You're just a latecomer, in this for the cash. I got blood on my hands from Kandahar; you don't. I saw Burgess smoke the kid, and I'm not going to be that kind of guy."

"I didn't know you were squeamish. Hell, I saw a boatload of Taliban stacked one body on top of another when I was over there. The Afghans torched them. Didn't bother me a bit," Jay boasted. "But this Burgess; you're saying he was the puppet master, right?"

"He *was* the puppet master, and now we got a new one," Miguel answered. "But after we deliver the kid, I'm taking off, getting as far away from here as I can. Down to Guatemala, where I got kin. If the puppet master ices the kid, I want no part of it. Now go fetch the water. I'm going to see what's holding up the kid."

Noah heard the two men's footsteps moving away from the truck. Noah's head spun with what he knew, that Felipe was going to be killed when the two delivered him to the "puppet master." That is, unless he did something.

He edged toward the opening in the canvas opening at the back of the truck. He looked around one side of the truck and then the other for either soldier. There was no one. He jumped down from the truck bed and ran to the side with the gas tank cover. Before he even thought out his plan completely, he opened the cover and reached down for a handful of sand. He dumped the sand in the gas tank and reached down for a second handful.

Replacing the gas cap, he heard one of the soldiers telling Felipe to hurry things up. Noah jumped back into the truck and scooted under the tarp again. He lay without moving and tried to calm his breathing while uttering a silent prayer.

Sensing Felipe was safe with the two soldiers, at least temporarily, Noah realized that all his action would accomplish was the truck would break down. That would give Felipe an extra hour or two, but had his action only postponed the inevitable?

He heard the three reenter the cab and the truck start up again. He had no idea if what he did would work, and for a few moments as the truck moved effortlessly back down the road, Noah remembered that the truck was the type used in Afghanistan and Iraq. Dejectedly, he thought that the truck could be equipped with some sort of filter to screen out the sand.

But fewer than five minutes later, to his joy, he heard the engine cough and then cough again. The truck shot forward but then slowed before repeating the jerky motion. Inside the cab, he heard the two soldiers cursing, using words he'd never heard before. But whatever they meant, they were music to his ears.

The truck stopped dead. The driver tried to restart it, but, again and again, the engine refused to return to life.

He heard both doors opening, and then the hood of the truck being raised.

"Know anything about these pieces of shit, Jay?" Miguel asked.

"Not enough to do anything out here. Not you, either?"

After a few moments, Noah heard the hood slam down. From the sudden silence he heard Miguel say, "Now what?"

"Don't panic, man. We got the radio. I'll just call in and let them know what happened."

Noah bit his lip. He'd forgotten about the radio.

Jay spoke over the radio mic. "You there?"

"Yeah, what's up?"

"The damn truck broke down. Engine just quit. You're going to have to come out and pick up the kid from here."

"You got a map?" the voice said over scratchy static.

"We got a map?" Jay said to Miguel.

Noah heard the glove compartment open. "Yeah, here's one."

"Good. Do you know where you are?"

Miguel answered. "Ah, no."

"Did you make it to the halfway place? The abandoned building?" the voice asked.

"Yeah, a couple of minutes ago."

"Okay. Did you stay on that same road?"

"Yeah, I did," Jay answered.

"Then I know where you are. I'll be out with another truck in about thirty minutes. Just sit tight. Is your passenger still doing okay?"

"So far, he is," Miguel said. "Hey, how are the two of us supposed to get back to town?"

"You can ride in my truck, stupid."

"But if you're going to do what I think you got in mind, I don't want to be in that truck. Know what I'm saying?" Miguel said.

"Suit yourself. Then you can walk back to town."

"Hey, shut the fuck up, Miguel," Jay said. "We can be dropped off in town before they do their thing. What I want to know is, when do I get my money?"

"Soon," the voice said. "Don't worry, I know where to find you."

The radio clicked off. "Now what? We just sit here?" Miguel asked.

"That's right, amigo."

"Don't call me 'amigo.'"

Jay laughed, and then the cab was silent.

Suddenly, Noah heard Felipe's voice speaking in Spanish.

"Speak English, kid, if you know what's good for you," Jay said.

"I was just telling Miguel that he owes me," Felipe said.

"He don't owe you shit," Jay said.

"What'd you mean, kid?" Miguel said.

"Look, I have a right to know what this is all about, going back all the way."

"Oh, you think this goes back aways?" Miguel asked. "It sure as hell does."

"So tell me," Felipe said.

Noah realized what Felipe was doing. If he was going to die, Felipe wanted Noah to be a witness to the truth. Noah would be the one witness who could name the killer.

"It was a huge cluster fuck, kid. One huge cluster fuck."

"Hey, Miguel, you don't have to say shit," Jay said.

"No, Jay, the kid is right. I owe him this. Anyway, as I was saying, it all goes back to Kandahar."

"You were in my Dad's unit?"

"Yeah, and I always liked your Dad. Never had a problem with him. But we were meeting with a warlord and his kin. Your Dad thought they were allies, so it wasn't really an interrogation. Then, while everyone was drinking tea and cokes, all hell broke loose outside in the camp. Mortars, rifle fire, all kinds of shit."

"What did my Dad do?"

"What could anyone do? Burgess, that fucking hothead, decides the whole meeting is a trap, so he empties rounds into the warlord and the rest of the Afghans in the room. Then the rest of us panic, I guess, because we start shooting the place up as well."

"Did my Dad do that, too?"

"No, kid. Your Dad tried to shelter the chieftain's kid—a kid about your age—but the kid took a head shot. Died right there. When the smoke cleared, we see your Dad running out of the room. Burgess yells, 'I'll get Sarge.'"

Miguel paused for a moment, as if he were visualizing the scene. "The fighting outside was dying down, and all I could think was, what would Burgess do to Sarge when he caught up with him?"

"Sounds like a real shit show," Jay said. "Ever think that Burgess was right, that the whole thing was a trap?"

"All I know is that before the meeting Sarge said the tribesmen we were meeting were bona fide okay. Burgess just reacted, the son of a bitch, and then we all did."

"Then, what happened?" Felipe asked in a lower voice.

"Five minutes later, Burgess returns, swearing up a storm. DeShan asks, 'Where's Sarge?' Burgess shakes his head. He said, 'He ran right out of camp, right toward the Taliban. The last I saw him, the Taliban have him.'"

"I knew it," Felipe said.

"Of course, you knew it. They must have told you your Dad was held by Taliban for two weeks," Jay said. "It's right there in the file."

"No one told me," Felipe said. "I just knew he came home sick, but I knew they weren't telling me everything."

"That's what saved our bacon," Miguel said. "Your Dad was so out of it he couldn't tell what happened over there."

"Shit," Jay said, "your Dad's not talking at all. It's like the Taliban tore out his voice box."

"So my Dad did kill Burgess at the bar?" Felipe asked in a quivering voice.

"No, kid. That was all Burgess' idea—the fucking reunion at the bar, I mean. We all needed to see for ourselves if your Dad was going to rat us out. The plan was, kid, that if we thought there was any chance your Dad would talk, then Burgess was going to take him outside, start a fight, and knife him. He'd then say your Dad went bananas and he had to kill him in self-defense. We'd all testify that your Dad was out of his fucking mind that night."

"Shit, man, this'd make a helluva movie," Jay said.

"It gets worse. Burgess was the puppet master. What I mean is, he'd already begun pulling a scam on the rest of us. He was one arrogant prick. I no sooner get home than he calls me. Tells me that he's decided to roll the dice. He says unless I pay him five hundred a month, he's gonna tell the Army his version of what happened in Kandahar."

"But he's the one who started the shooting," Jay said.

"No shit. But Burgess' mom is this big-time lawyer who knows all these lawyer tricks. He figured he'd get out of it and we'd be left holding the bag. But listen, kid, you need to know this. Your Dad was totally wasted, zonked out on some meds. He wasn't really there. So, all of us—everyone but Burgess—know this guy is no threat ever. I mean, he looked like he'd be writing with crayons for the rest of his life. No disrespect intended, son."

"So why did Burgess get in a fight with my Dad outside?"

"Who knows? But while the two of them were out there, DeShan and I compared notes. We realized Burgess hit all of us up for five big ones. I could have killed Burgess, but I didn't. I remember someone went to the bathroom, and the next thing I know, someone's yelling that there's a guy unconscious in the parking lot who looked like he been knifed. So, I go out, thinking I'm going to see your Dad on the ground."

"But it was Burgess," Felipe said. "God, I've been such a fool. I took it all out on my Mom."

"The next week, we all get a call to meet at another place—nothing public, this time. Now there's another puppet master. No more fat payments, this person says, and that's when I knew this was the one who knifed Burgess."

"It makes sense. No more blackmail," Jay observed, as if he approved of the puppet master's step.

"But then your Dad confessed to killing Burgess, and we weren't going to argue with that."

After a moment, Miguel added, "It all should have stopped there. We were out from under it, Burgess was dead, your Dad confessed. But the new puppet master wouldn't let it go."

"What do you mean?" Felipe said.

"Worried about your Mom, her being a righteous homicide detective. We were told we weren't safe unless your Mom was taken out of the picture."

"The puppet master wanted to ice the cop?" Jay asked.

Miguel shook his head. "We weren't going to go with that, the rest of us, I mean. So, the puppet master did what we thought would take your Mom over the edge. We got those guys in detention to...you know, to work you over."

"That's what brought me into the picture," Jay said. "I've been stationed at the hospital. I've been keeping an eye on your Dad until the trial, to make sure he wasn't going to wake up before he was sentenced."

None of the three said anything for a moment. Then Felipe said, "But I was the one who got myself in Juvi in the first place."

"Sorry to put it this way, but thanks for doing that," Miguel said.

"I gotta hand it to the puppet master," Jay said. "Whoever it is paid me good money to pass along what was happening. So when your Dad started to come around—"

"He did?" Felipe asked.

"Yep. Yesterday, he started to answer questions by writing. He was starting to remember Kandahar but wasn't clear on the fight at the bar. The puppet master left me a note last night. I was supposed to tell your dad that if he didn't take the fall for Burgess' death, then you'd be killed. We thought that would shut him up, but when I delivered the message this morning, he went bonkers. I reported being sick and, bingo, I pick up Miguel to come with me to nab you."

"How'd you know where I was?"

"'I heard the monk tell your Dad this morning about you working alone at that house back there."

Miguel lit a cigarette as the three sat in silence for a moment.

"So, what happens now?" Felipe said.

"Search me, but see that cloud of dust down the road?" Jay asked. "That's the puppet master, and you're just one more puppet."

But I'm not, Noah thought from the back of the truck. *But what can I do?*

Chapter Thirty-Five

As Worthy sat next to the others in the truck cab, he kept his eye on the stalled Army truck a quarter mile down the road.

"Is that them?" he asked.

The soldier next to him nodded slowly.

How he managed to be sitting in a truck full of Army military police in the back still astonished him. As soon as he realized that Felipe was abducted, he had Captain Mills order all members of Freddie's unit to the base for a supposed briefing about the trial. Luck held, and within the hour, three in the unit: Pvt. Durbin, Pvt. Gregory, and Cpl. Sanchez were sitting in a conference room, unaware of the true purpose of the meeting.

Captain Mills and Worthy entered the room together. Worthy noticed that when the three saw him, Durbin and Gregory instinctively shot a glance toward Sanchez.

"Any of you know where Cpl. Rosario and Cpl. Conrad are?" Captain Mills asked.

Gabby Sanchez immediately looked down, while Durbin and Gregory again both shot her a look.

"I take that as a no," Mills said. "I think most or all of you have met Lt. Worthy from the Detroit Police Department. I'm going to turn the meeting over to him. Lieutenant?"

Worthy sat and stared at the three of them. "We know everything," he said. "We know what happened in Kandahar, we know about Burgess' blackmail scheme, we know one of the unit, not Sgt. Contreras, killed him outside the bar, and we know about all the ways you tried to shut Sgt. Contreras up and make his family give up hope." He paused to let his words sink in. "We know everything," he repeated.

Now all three were looking down at their hands. His assumption that Gabby Sanchez was the ringleader would be confirmed in two ways. She would either answer for the others, or the others would jump at the chance to pin the blame on her.

"We don't know what you're talking about," Sanchez offered, holding Worthy's gaze.

"I figured you'd answer for them," Worthy said. "Okay, Durbin and Gregory, what I'm going to say next I'll say only once. This is a one-time offer. You'll have to stand trial for the slaughter in Kandahar. That's non-negotiable. If you come clean on your part in the bar incident and the subsequent attempts to harm both Sgt. Contreras and members of his family, Captain Mills will inform the court of your cooperation."

The room was deathly quiet for several moments. Worthy deliberately looked at his watch, as if to say that time was running out—which it was.

Finally, Pvt. Gregory blurted out, "Hey, I'm not going down for that. The only killing I did was in Afghanistan."

"Shut the fuck up," Durbin said.

Gabby Sanchez continued to stare at Worthy, not saying a word.

"I won't shut up. Goddamn it, I got a family. She did it. I had nothing to do with it," Gregory said.

Sanchez now turned her head slowly and stared at Gregory.

"What about you, Pvt. Durbin?" Captain Mills asked. "You willing to be charged as an accomplice in Burgess' death."

Durbin angled his chair so he couldn't see Sanchez's face. After a moment, he said almost in a whisper, "No. Like he said, she did it."

At that, the two privates were taken to another room, leaving Mills and Worthy with Gabby Sanchez. She slumped in her chair but said nothing.

"How will they contact you?" Worthy said.

"Sorry, who's that?" Sanchez replied with a smirk.

"Conrad and Rosario, the ones with Felipe."

Staring straight ahead, Sanchez said nothing.

"Cpl. Sanchez," Captain Mills said, "you have an opportunity to do one thing right. If you do, I promise to enter that into the record at trial."

"Meaning what?" she asked.

"I'll recommend that the court take the death penalty off the table," Mills said.

Sanchez sat in silence for several moments. "Goddamn Burgess," she said in a low voice. "Goddamn that arrogant son of a bitch. All he had to do was obey the chain of command and none of this would have happened. No bloodbath in Kandahar, no Sarge running out of the camp, no torture of

Sarge, no blackmail, no fight outside the bar, no need to kill the asshole, and none of the rest. All he had to do," she said, looking up at her interrogators as if wanting sympathy, "was wait for Sarge's signal in that room. But he didn't, and instead of getting married I'm facing a cell for the rest of my life because of..."She seemed to be trying to find the right word but settled for "because of him."

"You have an opportunity to improve your chances in court if you do the right thing now," Worthy said.

Sanchez closed her eyes for a moment. "I never had anything against Sarge," she said. "If he was willing to confess to my offing Burgess, I thought 'great.' He'd spend a tenner or two in a psych ward and then he'd be out, free as a bird."

"So do the right thing for Sgt. Contreras now and help us get his boy back," Mills said.

Sanchez looked up as if a thought had just come to mind. "If you offered the same deal to Burgess, you know what he'd do? He'd let the kid die."When she looked at him, Worthy saw a new look in her eyes. "But I'm not Burgess," she said.

Felipe watched as the other military truck stopped a hundred yards down the road.

"Time to go, kid," Miguel said. He opened the passenger door and exited it, pulling Felipe behind him. "I'm real sorry about this, kid, that it has to end this way."

Felipe heard the driver's door open and Jay get out. The three stood almost in a row and waited for movement from the other truck.

The passenger door of the other truck opened, and Felipe saw a soldier with cap bill pulled down over his eyes and a female soldier climb down. The two stood in front of their truck before the first soldier said something to the woman.

"We'll take him from here," the female soldier said. "Just bring the boy here."

Felipe heard Jay whisper hoarsely to Miguel, "You recognize that other guy?"

Miguel shook his head. "No, man, he's not one of ours."

"Something's not right," Jay said. "Here, give me your knife."

In that moment, the soldier hiding his eyes turned around and whistled. Immediately, one soldier after another jumped from the back of the truck, rifles raised. Miguel jumped to the side and, in that same moment, Felipe felt the knife blade on his neck.

"It's over, Conrad. There's no way out of here," the soldier said. He took off his cap, and Felipe recognized Lt. Worthy.

"I don't see it that way," Jay replied. "Looks to me like this kid is my ticket out. You either let us leave in that vehicle, or he dies right here."

Felipe saw every rifle barrel pointed directly at him. Other than that, there was deathly quiet.

"Where will you go from there?" Worthy asked. "You're only postponing—"

"Shut the fuck up. I'll decide what I'll do next."

"You're not a puppet master, Jay. You're not smart enough," Sanchez shouted.

Felipe felt more pressure from the knife edge on his neck. Out of his peripheral vision, he saw Miguel turn slightly sideways as if looking behind Jay. Slowly, he saw Miguel nod.

"Not smart enough, huh? I guess we'll see—"

In that moment, Felipe heard a thud behind him, and then the hand on his neck relaxed as Jay slumped to the ground. Felipe turned and saw Noah Frost, his small bare feet stirring a cloud of dust, holding two bulging socks as he stood over a barely conscious Jay Conrad.

"Shit, Noah, what do you have in there?" Felipe said, hardly conscious himself of the soldiers running toward them.

"Rocks and sand, the same thing I stuffed down the gas tank."

"That's it?" Felipe said in disbelief.

"David and Goliath, Felipe. It's all in the Bible."

Soldiers appeared out of nowhere, one handcuffing Conrad, another checking Felipe's neck and shining a light into his eyes while asking him if he knew his name and what day it was. He looked over and saw Noah standing confused as soldiers were slapping him on the back.

Noise of another vehicle temporarily obliterated all the words flying around, and then Felipe saw his mother running from a jeep, followed by Brother Abram and Father Fortis.

All Felipe managed to say as the two of them hugged and fell to the ground was, "It's all over, Mom."

Epilogue

April 22 Good Friday

It was the kind of morning in Santa Fe that made it difficult to believe that Afghanistan, Iraq, and Syria existed on the other side of the planet. The sky was cloudless, the same color of turquoise reflecting off Naomi Frost's small cross necklace.

The two mothers sat across from one another, drinking coffee at one of the tables set out in front of the bookstore. Naomi Frost had let her hair fall naturally on her shoulders, rather than securing it in the severe bun from over two weeks before.

"I feel so bad about how we treated you, when you came to our house," she said. "I had no idea that your son was in as much trouble as our own."

Sera shrugged. "How were you to know?"

"Yes, but still. After everything that was in the papers, about Felipe and your husband, I don't know how you managed to care about Noah at all."

"I wasn't sure where my head was most of the time. It never dawned on me that my family's drama was being orchestrated by someone else. It was Father Nick who told me to give up thinking of myself as another Job. I'll be honest with you. I did feel punished by God. My prayers seemed so pointless that after a while, I just gave them up."

Naomi Frost nodded, then looked up from her cup at Sera. "My prayers for Noah seemed to be lead weights, going nowhere." She paused a moment, as if deciding whether to share something or not. "I wish I could have gotten to know your friend. What he said in the paper, about the whole train of events starting with one thoughtless act in Afghanistan, about how so much of what we call evil is just so terribly sad. That's so incredibly wise. Is it pronounced Father For-tis?"

"Yeah, but he's still going to be around for a while. My husband, Freddie, and Nick have this...well, they have this special connection. Actually, it's a healing connection. And a week from Sunday is Father Nick's Easter, which strikes me as a good sign."

"And he's what they call a monk?"

"Yes, he's a Greek Orthodox monk from Ohio. That's why his Easter is on a different Sunday."

"I'm pretty sure I don't know anything about them. But if he's anything like Catholics, I've been kept pretty clear of them."She paused for a moment, seemingly deep in thought, before continuing. "It's just that being a monk, well, it's something Noah's talked to me about several times since he came home. Now that things have settled down a bit, he wants to go back to St. Mary's—legally, I mean, to stay for a few days."

"How's he doing—with his father, I mean?"

Naomi Frost's eyebrows shot up in a look of surprise. "He's different—Noah, that is. My husband will always be the way he is, God love him. But Noah isn't as timid as he was before. Before, he used to just listen to his brother and father and not say anything, although I knew he was hurting. Noah and I are a lot alike, I guess. But now, Noah's found his voice, I guess you'd say."

Sera reached across and held Naomi Frost's hand. "Noah saved my son's life."

"And your son saved mine," she replied, tears streaming down her face. "Do you mind me asking what will happen to Felipe?"

"No, not at all. He's under house detention while the courts reconsider his case. What he did to be arrested is serious. Being abducted doesn't make his assault on the homeless man just disappear."Now it was Sera who needed to collect herself for a moment. "But no matter what, I have my son back. Felipe's back. The two of us visit Freddie every day in the hospital, and for those forty-five minutes we're a family again. And most evenings, the two of us spend a lot of the time just talking. My family has a long way to go, but I believe, with Father Nick's help, we're going to make it. Of course, Nick would correct me on that. He'd say 'with God's help.'"

"I suppose I shouldn't be surprised," Naomi Frost said, "but this week, while my husband was writing his Easter sermon for Sunday, I found myself thinking of your family. I realized how it wasn't just your husband who almost died, but your whole family. And yet, you didn't die."She paused for a moment, before adding, "I wish I could tell the judge that Felipe's suffered enough."

"From your mouth to God's ears," Sera said.

Naomi laughed. "I've never heard that. I like it. 'From your mouth to God's ears.'I guess that makes what I said a prayer."

Sera wiped her own tears. "I'd like to ask you something."

"By all means, go ahead."

"I'd like Felipe and Noah to stay friends."

"I was thinking the same thing. And, given what our sons have been through, I hope we can be friends as well."

Sera smiled. "Despite what your husband might say?"

Naomi Frost sat up straighter in her chair and looked down the street leading to Santa Fe's cathedral. "Noah's changed, and that's changing me. I will always respect my husband, because that's what Scripture teaches, but I now realize that Noah wouldn't have run away if I hadn't been so quiet, so submissive—if I'd been another adult in our family."

Worthy knocked on Sera's office door and entered when he heard her voice. He looked around and saw the same photo of Felipe in his Little League uniform on her desk that he'd seen four years before.

"Just thought I'd drop by and say goodbye. My flight leaves this morning."

Sera rose from behind her desk and came around to face Worthy. "It's like déjà vu," she said. "You did the same thing last time, stopping by here to say goodbye. I thought I'd never see you again. Not Nick, either."

Worthy tried to find a way to keep the goodbye light. "Yeah, I was thinking the same thing as I drove into town. Maybe we shouldn't say goodbye, but 'see you later.'"

Sera stepped toward him and, putting her arms around his neck, hugged him tightly. "I keep having this terrible thought," she said, not letting him go. "I'm going to wake up and realize you and Nick never came to help. Freddie would forever be labeled a killer. And Felipe, well, he'd be lost."

Worthy slowly extricated himself and looked into Sera's tearful face. "Nick would say there was never a chance of that. Everything has worked out as it was supposed to, with Nick staying to be with Freddie, and Felipe coming home."

Sera nodded but had to look away while she collected herself. "You gave me my family back, Chris. Everything just overwhelmed me, but you put the pieces together."

"If all this had been dumped on me," Worthy said, "I would never have done as well as you."

Sera slowly nodded. "I still can't get over that all this happened to Freddie... to us because of an impulsive act by one arrogant rich kid. A decision that took less than a second led to all this misery."After another pause, she said, "I like to believe Nick's right—that all this was supposed to work out as it did. I suppose that means I still believe in God."

Worthy knew that four years before, he'd have bristled at that language. But that was four years ago. "Something or somebody has me hanging around people like you and Nick...staying in monasteries, for God's sake. I don't have Nick's faith, but...I'll tell you something I haven't even told him."

With a tissue, Sera wiped at her eyes. "What's that, Chris?"

"It won't make any sense, so try not to laugh. Anyway, God left me four years ago. All at once; no warning; boom, God was gone. When Susan and then Allyson walked out of my life, God did too. Now, I've got Allyson back, which is great, but that's all I've got back. What I'm trying to say is, when I see all you've been through, and when I'm with Nick...I don't know." He paused and shook his head.

Sera waited in silence, as if she knew he had to finish this on his own.

"Here's the best I can do to explain what I'm getting at: it means something to me—I'm not sure what—that Nick and you believe in God."

Sera offered a weak smile. "So, now that I'm praying again, you won't mind if someone besides Nick prays for you?"

Worthy laughed. "No, I guess I just gave you permission to do that. But only you two, okay?"

Sera laughed in return, though the laugh ended in a quiet sob. "It'll be our secret, Chris."

✝

DEAR ALLYSON,

I'm sure through the resources of the FBI you know the case I've been working on is finally over. The last time I wrote I said I didn't know whether we were near the end, at the halfway point, or just beginning of the case. It was like a pool that had no bottom.

As Nick is fond of saying, what or who lurks at the bottom of so many homicides is not some evil mastermind, but a normal person who took a bad turn and, instead of admitting the mistake, continues down that dark path. The same is sure true in this case. We didn't find some Moriarty-type figure, but rather a tight unit of soldiers who were doing honorable work in Afghanistan until one of them made a split-second decision, a terribly wrong one. There was nothing premeditated in this act. It was just that, a horrible mistake. But what followed was a premeditated campaign to destroy a soldier and his family.

What I'm trying to say is that maybe I'm getting to the age when it's not good for me to just move on right away to another case. My Dad would laugh to hear me admit this, but I need to sort out what I learned from the last four weeks. So, I hope you don't mind being a sounding board for my middle-aged ramblings, but here goes.

The biggest lesson I learned is that we wouldn't have solved this case if everything had been left up to me. Please don't think I'm being falsely modest, and, yes, if you read the newspaper accounts from out here, you might think I did solve this on my own.

Going back to that image of the pool, I do best when I'm allowed to leave others up at the surface while I dive down to try to find that bottom. Yes, in this case as in others, I'm the one down there in the murky darkness, but these past weeks in New Mexico reminded me again of the importance of those on the surface, the ones eager to hear what I stirred up from below and eager to help me make sense of it.

That's what Nick did for me on this case. Okay, I'm often given credit for being the one who gathers the evidence, but Nick is the sifter, the one who turns over what I've dug up to make sense of it.

I know I've been accused back in Detroit of moving too slowly in cases, but the truth is, I proceed slowly until I find the evidence that I sense matters. Then I switch into another gear and am too often in a rush. That's when I can become a liability to my own case. Nick, whose abbot thinks he talks too much and too rapidly, sifts the evidence with a care and patience I don't have.

But Nick contributed something else in this case. I suppose he's always done this other thing, but I didn't really notice it until this case. If Nick remains at the surface, he doesn't just wait for me to come up with my bag of evidence. Nick was like in a boat with Sera Lacey, and Sera was one wounded person, close to giving up.

So many times in the last days of the case, I realized that the ups and the more numerous downs Sera was experiencing were issues I'd be no good at dealing with. In fact, she was far stronger than I would have been in her shoes. But by the end, her hope was as brittle as a dry piece of balsa wood, and I knew, if I had any chance of finding the evidence to clear her husband, I could spare none of my energy for her.

But Nick? Nick not only worked with me on sifting through the evidence, discarding the worthless while identifying the valuable, but he (okay, I'll use my Dad's term) "ministered" to Sera, as much as to Freddie, through the whole ordeal. He gave her hope when she was almost in as bad shape as her husband and son. Of course, if I were to point this out to Nick, he'd be totally confused by it. He would say he did little to nothing.

I know that Freddie right now would be locked up on some psych ward in a military prison if Nick hadn't been with me on this case. Nick's abbot is a bit of a prick, in my opinion. He keeps badgering Nick, telling him he has to choose between being a detective and a monk. I know this question bothers Nick more than he'll ever admit.

As I write this, I know you could say that I have no room to talk. When

I was on a case, I wasn't really there as a dad for you and your sister, and I wasn't much of a husband. You accused me in the past of bringing presents home after I closed a case. You were right—these were guilt offerings. I know that the complaints made about me by partners on cases in the past—Worthy's a loner—are too many to be false. And, as I wrote above, at times I had to turn off my friendship with Sera on this case to have a chance of clearing her husband. I am a man of parts.

Because of this, maybe it's up to me to tell Nick that I know him better than he does. Through this case, I finally see how widely Nick's abbot has missed the mark with him. Nick can't be split into parts—this part detective, this part monk, this part priestly confessor. No, Nick's vocation is that he is, without knowing it, always all three.

Nick is what I hope to be some day—a whole person.

Love,

Dad

DAVID CARLSON WAS BORN IN THE western suburbs of Chicago and grew up in parsonages in various cities of Illinois. His grade school years were spent in Springfield, Illinois, where the numerous Abraham Lincoln sites initiated his lifelong love of history. His childhood hope was to play professional baseball, a dream that died ignominiously one day in high school.

He attended Wheaton College (Illinois) where he majored in political science and planned on going to law school. Not sure how to respond to the Vietnam War, he decided to attend seminary for a year to weigh his options. To his surprise, he fell in love with theological thinking—especially theological questioning—and his career plan shifted to college teaching in religious studies. He earned a doctorate at University of Aberdeen, Scotland, where he learned that research is a process of digging and then digging deeper. He believes the same process of digging and digging deeper has helped him in his nonfiction and mystery writing.

Franklin College, a traditional liberal arts college in central Indiana, has been his home for the past forty-one years. David has been particularly attracted to the topics of faith development, Catholic-Orthodox relations, and Muslim-Christian dialogue. In the last thirteen years, however, religious terrorism has become his area of specialty. In 2007, he conducted interviews across the country in monasteries and convents about monastic responses to 9/11 and religious terrorism. The book based on that experience, *Peace*

Be with You: Monastic Wisdom for a Terror-Filled World, was published in 2011 by Thomas Nelson and was selected as one of the Best Books of 2011 in the area of Spiritual Living by Library Journal. He has subsequently written a second book on religious terrorism, *Countering Religious Extremism: The Healing Power of Spiritual Friendships* (New City Press, 2017).

Much of his time in the last three years has been spent giving talks as well as being interviewed on radio and TV about ISIS. Nevertheless, he is still able to spend summers in Wisconsin where he enjoys sailing, fishing, kayaking, and restoring an old log cabin.

His wife, Kathy, is a retired English professor, an award-winning artist, and an excellent editor. Their two sons took parental advice to follow their passions. The older, Leif, is a photographer, and the younger, Marten, is a filmmaker.

For more information, please visit: www.davidccarlson.org.

CPSIA information can be obtained
at www.ICGtesting.com
Printed in the USA
LVHW041514261121
704539LV00026B/3875

9 781941 890714